W9-BGG-453

"We owe each other.

"You risked your life to save me," Luke said, his gaze holding hers. "I know what it must have cost you to watch that horse trailer disappearing, and still you turned around and came back for me."

"I had to be certain you weren't hurt."

"I would have been dead." He reached up to brush the hair from her forehead. "Those men would have killed me."

Dawn felt as if she'd stepped next to a blazing fire. From the touch of his hand on her cheek warmth spread throughout her body. Luke was a striking man whose controlled power was compelling. All too compelling. Dawn needed to step back from it.

"I still haven't figured out why someone sent us that videotape of Private Stock. Have you?" She shifted slightly, out of his reach. The loss of his touch was like a sudden chill.

"Nope. I'm still stuck with the same conclusion. Someone wants us to chase this filly. And another someone wants to kill us for it."

ABOUT THE AUTHOR

Riding and owning horses have always been important parts of life for Caroline Burnes. Currently she owns two horses and tries to ride daily. Horses were the focus of Caroline's first two Intrigues—#86 A Deadly Breed and #100 Measure of Deceit—of which Phantom Filly is a spin-off, featuring as its heroine Dawn Markey, who appeared as the horse trainer in both previous books.

Books by Caroline Burnes

HARLEQUIN INTRIGUE
86–A DEADLY BREED
100–MEASURE OF DECEIT

Don't miss any of our special offers. Write to us at the following address for information on our newest releases.

Harlequin Reader Service
901 Fuhrmann Blvd., P.O. Box 1397, Buffalo, NY 14240
Canadian address: P.O. Box 603,
Fort Erie, Ont. L2A 5X3

Phantom Filly

Caroline Burnes

Harlequin Books

TORONTO • NEW YORK • LONDON
AMSTERDAM • PARIS • SYDNEY • HAMBURG
STOCKHOLM • ATHENS • TOKYO • MILAN

For Jennifer Haines
and Miranda Pruett,
two young ladies
who share my love of horses

Harlequin Intrigue edition published June 1989

ISBN 0-373-22115-0

Copyright © 1989 Carolyn Haines. All rights reserved.
Except for use in any review, the reproduction or utilization of
this work in whole or in part in any form by any electronic,
mechanical or other means, now known or hereafter invented,
including xerography, photocopying and recording, or in any
information storage or retrieval system, is forbidden without
the permission of the publisher, Harlequin Enterprises Limited,
225 Duncan Mill Road, Don Mills, Ontario, Canada M3B 3K9, or
Harlequin Books, P.O. Box 958, North Sydney, Australia 2060.

All the characters in this book have no existence outside the
imagination of the author and have no relation whatsoever to
anyone bearing the same name or names. They are not even
distantly inspired by any individual known or unknown to the
author, and all incidents are pure invention.

® are Trademarks registered in the United States Patent and
Trademark Office and in other countries.

Printed in U.S.A.

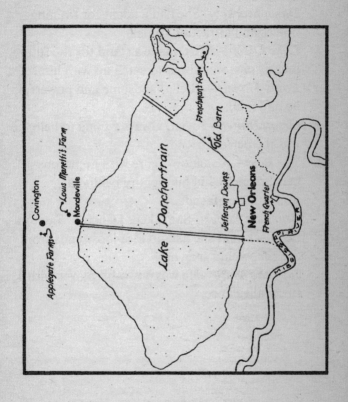

CAST OF CHARACTERS

Dawn Markey—She had a talent for training horses and attracting trouble.

Luke O'Neil—He'd made a stand for the future, but his past was about to catch up with him.

Louis Manetti—Rich, handsome and powerful, he had it all.

Orson Rinter—Jovial, always willing to help, he was the perfect friend.

The Boss—A shadow figure with numerous henchmen, he hid his identity behind a sophisticated facade.

Ann Tate Roper—She'd kept Dancing Water in the black, but she had no idea loose ends from the past would snag her.

Jack the Knife—He was a two-bit player with a fuzzy allegiance.

Chapter One

Rain slashed viciously against the large window. From the old rocker across the den, Dawn Markey watched the pecan trees yield and bend to the superior force of the storm. Several brittle limbs broke with sickening snaps.

The afternoon sky was heavy and gray, giving the illusion of a winter evening. The only color in the scene was offered by the bright green leaves of late March that littered the wet ground.

Slipping wet boots from her feet, Dawn picked up the television set's remote control, then put it down again. The gesture was smooth and confident.

Long, dark hair clung damply to her face, but she ignored it as she picked up a legal pad and checked the list she'd made that morning. All of the horses at Dancing Water Ranch were safely stalled against the lightning that popped on the western horizon. Fresh hay had been distributed. There was nothing she could do except wait for the worst of the storm to pass. In the southern part of Mississippi, thunderstorms were a common occurrence, and luckily didn't last too long. With fifteen foals that needed handling, two dozen mares to train and Easy Dancer waiting for some attention, it was hard for her to sit around. March was an incredibly busy month on the breeding farm, and Dawn was solely responsible; the owner, Ann Tate Roper, was off on an extended honeymoon.

A loud knock was followed by a blast of rain-soaked wind. A short, white-haired man stepped inside and slammed the door. Water ran down his lined face, but his blue eyes were clear and undisturbed.

"If this keeps up, I'm going to have to get a few of the men and dig a trench down the west boundary. The lower pasture is almost a shallow lake." Freddie Weston shook himself like a dog, sending a shower of raindrops to the floor.

"Look in the yellow pages. See if there's a listing for Noah," Dawn replied. She cast a quick, assessing look at the old man. He was recovering from a brush with death, but his color was good. In fact, he seemed to be thriving on the bad weather and the problems that came with it. "How about some coffee, Freddie?"

Nodding, he withdrew a handful of envelopes from beneath his yellow rain slicker. "The mailman came, despite the flood. And Orson Rinter from Applegate telephoned. Wanted to know if we'd had any trouble. I guess the storm hit pretty hard over in Covington." He sorted through the envelopes, while Dawn headed for the kitchen.

"Well, well . . ." Freddie mumbled.

"What is it?"

He held up a thickly padded envelope. A bold hand had scrawled Ann Tate's name and address with a brief message. "Open Immediately! Urgent!"

The kitchen door swung behind Dawn as she balanced a steaming mug, sugar and cream. She handed Freddie the coffee and took the parcel, hefting it to judge the contents. "Videotape of some sort, I'd say."

"What could be so important about a videotape?" Freddie's face was alive with curiosity.

"Maybe Ann belongs to some movie club."

"A movie with an expiration date?"

"You've got a point." Dawn's brown eyes were round and serious. She and Freddie were old friends. He'd taught her to ride, had helped her take over the job of trainer at Dancing Water. She read concern all over his face. There was something foreboding about the handwritten message.

"There's no return address? I don't have my glasses."

"None." Dawn flipped over the package. The postmark was Florida, but the name of the town was too smeared to read. "Should we open it?"

"Well, we're in charge," Freddie responded, standing up to think better. "It does say urgent."

Their gazes met and held. Dawn ripped the seal and slid the black videocassette onto the top of the desk. There was no mark or label.

She switched on the television set and inserted the tape into the VCR. The blank screen fluttered, then a long view of a racetrack came on. It was a wide shot that revealed neat but empty grounds.

"I hope this isn't a scheme to sell Ann an interest in a racehorse," Dawn said, settling on the edge of a chair.

The tape showed white fences and an oval track. Nothing remarkable caught her attention.

"So, we see a clean racetrack during the off-season," Freddie commented dryly. "So?"

A man's hand holding a stopwatch came into view, close up and clear. Then the camera panned to a tall, mahogany-bay horse stepping into the starting gate. There was an air of furtiveness about the man who led the horse, and the jockey wore goggles with a hat pulled low, as if he sought to remain anonymous.

"What is this?" Freddie leaned forward.

Before Dawn could respond, the bay horse burst from the gate. In one great stride she was stretching down the track, giving her heart and soul to the run.

"Sweet Bessie!" Freddie whispered aloud. He reached one hand out, as if to touch the horse on the screen.

Dawn sat motionless in her chair, her hand on the television controls rigid. Her eyes were riveted on the filly tearing around the track. On the backstretch the camera lost the horse for a few seconds, then she rounded the corner, lean, elegant and fast.

As she went under the wire at the mile and a quarter mark, the hand holding the stopwatch reappeared. The time was a record breaker for a track of this length—Derby length. In a matter of seconds, the screen fuzzed and grew black again. The tape was over.

The only sound in the room was the static from the television set. Dawn's hand still gripped the controls. Freddie continued to sit on the sofa. Each avoided the other's gaze.

A gust of small limbs and leaves spattered against the den window. They both looked up, but neither spoke. At last Dawn turned off the television and stood. "There's no need to look at the tape again, is there?"

"No." Freddie's voice was surprisingly calm.

"How old is she?"

"Three. A big three-year-old."

"That would mean she was bred the spring after Speed Dancer was stolen. There's no doubt she's his, is there?" Dawn turned to Freddie at last. Moisture had collected in the corners of her eyes, and she hurriedly brushed it away. "I never believed he was dead, but I guess I never thought I'd hear a word about him again. She looks exactly like him. If she were a stud, I'd swear it was him! I've seen thousands of bay horses, but none that moved the way he did, none that ran with such an attitude of confidence."

"She's the spitting image of him," Freddie replied slowly. He put a hand on Dawn's shoulder. "That stallion meant a lot to you, girl. I know this is hard."

"Yes, but..." She walked to the VCR and rewound the tape. "It's also very calculated. Someone is trying to manipulate Ann with this tape." Hitting the Eject button, she held up the cassette. "Who sent this? And why? Someone wants Ann to know that a daughter to Speed Dancer is alive and undeniably ready for a winning season on the track. But what track? Where? This is obviously someone who knows the story of Cybil Matheson losing her mind." Dawn clenched one fist. "Someone who wants to dig up the old horror of Cybil murdering Ann's husband and stealing Speed Dancer. A friend wouldn't send an anonymous tape." She turned to Freddie with a sudden question. "If not a friend, who? Is it possible Cybil had an accomplice when she planned the theft of Speed Dancer? Maybe someone was using her, because of her mental illness."

A million questions, none with answers, seemed to batter Dawn like the storm that was smashing at the house.

"With Cybil under medical care, we probably will never know what made her turn on Ann like that." Freddie's face had lost much of its healthy color. "Even I find it hard to think about, so let's look at practical reality instead. Without proper registration papers, that filly can't run in any decent race. That's why the jockey acted so strange, hiding his face. I mean, she can run around the track against a stopwatch till... Well, it doesn't mean anything. She can't run on a legitimate track without registration papers."

"That's the point I was going to make," Dawn commented.

Freddie grew angrier as he continued. "Cybil Matheson stole that stallion and hid him somewhere. Since she can't tell us where, we've been left without so much as a first lead to follow for all these years."

"Now we've got a bay filly on an empty track, who runs like a hot wind down a desert interstate," Dawn continued. "The question is, who sent the tape, and what do they want?

Why now?'' She turned to Freddie, excitement in her dark eyes. "Maybe they want registration papers on the filly?"

"Ann didn't breed the mare. She can't give papers. She wouldn't do anything illegal.'' Freddie sat down on the sofa and sipped his coffee, which had grown cold. He didn't notice. "I've never seen a filly cover the ground like that.'' He shook his head in amazement. "That's the fastest time I've seen clocked. The filly is—"

"Speed Dancer's daughter,'' Dawn broke in. "And we're going to find her."

Freddie shook off his daze and looked at Dancing Water Ranch's trainer. Her face was set in an expression of intense determination. In the line of her jaw, the high cheekbones and the deep, brown eyes, Freddie saw her grandmother, a Choctaw princess.

Dawn slid the tape back into the machine and punched the Play button. "Now sit down and pay attention,'' she said quickly.

"I don't need to see the tape again,'' Freddie answered.

"Oh, yes, you do. It's the only clue we have. The postmark was Florida, and maybe by looking at the track we can find out where in Florida. You know the tracks pretty well. You traveled enough of them with Ann's father.'' She gave him an affectionate look. "From what I hear, you and Mr. Tate dropped a few greenbacks at betting windows all over the nation."

Lighted by pleasant memories, Freddie's face softened. "We did that, and we won some money, too. Okay, let's look at it again."

They were silent as the video started. Several seconds passed before Freddie signaled to stop the tape. "See that?'' He pointed at the spectator stands. "The seating is small, private club on top, not that large of a capacity."

Dawn eagerly followed his words, taking in each detail he mentioned. At his motion she ran the tape forward a few more frames, then stopped again when he held up his hand.

"Of course, we have no way of knowing how old the tape is, but it was warm, wherever it was shot."

"The jockey's sweating," she pointed out.

"And the guy leading the horse is in short sleeves. I think we'd be safe in assuming this is a Florida track, but there must be several hundred of them. I can tell you it isn't Hialeah. In fact, it could easily be a private track, Dawn. There's a lot of money in Florida, and plenty of those breeding farms could have a private track for the king of sports."

Dawn felt a sickening drop in her expectations. Freddie was right. There could be a million places like the one on the tape. A million. She forwarded the tape. The man's large, neatly manicured hand flashed by, stopwatch at the ready.

In the next sequence the filly broke from the gate and Dawn was once again swept away in the breathtaking speed, the power of the animal's body surging forward. They lost the horse in the backstretch, and then picked her up again as she rounded the corner. As she broke under the wire, Dawn froze the tape. Rapidly she rewound.

"What gives?" Freddie asked.

"Wait." She started it over, then stopped once more. "There are two flags. Maybe one is special, like the flag of that track."

Freddie stood up and rushed to her chair, grabbing her shoulder with his hand. "You're right! You're right!"

Dawn jumped up to clasp Freddie in a giant hug. "Can you watch the farm this afternoon?"

"Sure. Where are you going?"

"To the library. I may be able to find some information on racing flags, or city flags or whatever it takes to pinpoint this. Just let me sketch this down quickly." She found a pad and pencil and made a small drawing. Black and gold were the colors of the top flag. The combination was striking, but an erratic breeze made it impossible for Dawn to see the insignia clearly. The other, though, was simple and clearly visible—a red horse striding across a white background.

"Dawn?" There was an edge of worry in Freddie's voice.

"Yeah?"

"That top flag isn't a track flag."

"What if it isn't?"

Freddie put a hand on her shoulder. "This could be part of a setup. For Ann, or for you, if you take Ann's place."

THE TABLES in the dining club were filled. Dawn adjusted her hat with one hand as she scanned the crowded room. In the other she clutched an envelope with photos of the mysterious filly. A photographer in Biloxi had made fairly decent enlargements from the video. They were grainy and blurred, but a real horseman could see that the filly was top quality.

She gave her name to the maître d' and followed him to a table. It was the last race of the season, and the Tampa Horse Track was jammed. Women in bright dresses and hats decorated the long tables like exotic floral arrangements. The murmur and bustle of a busy restaurant filled the air with the pleasant sounds of conversation, cutlery rattling and jovial toast proposals.

As Dawn settled at a small table near the window at the far end of the room, she brushed the skirt of her jade silk dress. The matching hat dipped on one side, spilling a slight, mysterious shadow onto her face.

She eagerly turned her attention to the track. Although the perspective was different, it was the same raceway that the videotape had shown—the fencing, design, even the patterns of the shrubs and flowers. Her stomach clenched nervously and she took a deep breath.

Already the horses for the first race were taking their traditional walk before the stands. She eyed them critically, then picked the number four horse to win. Only tremendous self-restraint kept her from going to the betting window and making a small wager. She was there to look for Speed Dancer's daughter, but the excitement of the opening race was exhilarating.

She scanned the crowd. People laughed and talked, pulling out racing forms and pencils as they calculated the odds on their favorites.

"Always bet on names with four consonants," a woman at the next table advised her friend.

Dawn smiled to herself. Betting theories were as numerous as flies in a stable.

Earlier that morning, dressed in faded jeans, paddock boots and a T-shirt, she'd hung around the stables, pretending to look for work as a hot walker.

Her overtures had been met with firm refusals. No one wanted a stranger around their horses on the last day of racing. Still, the act of looking had given her an opportunity to visit every stall on the racetrack premises. The mahogany-bay filly was not there. Dawn had even risked asking a few questions about a big filly that could run fast. No one even acted as if they knew what she was talking about.

So far, a dead end.

She tried not to think about it that way. The trip to Tampa had been made on impulse, without approval from Ann Tate. Dawn hadn't had time to track Ann down, and besides, it wouldn't have mattered, even if Ann had tried to dissuade her. Years before, when Speed Dancer had been a green horse with a world of potential, he'd hung his leg in a fence. No one had thought he'd live. No one except Dawn. She'd moved a cot into the barn and stayed with him day and night for weeks. Her strong will had joined with the stallion's, and somehow he'd survived.

During his recuperation a strong bond had been forged between the two. While Ann preferred Easy Dancer, Dawn's affections had never wavered from Speed Dancer. The two women had often debated the merits of the two stallions, who were full brothers. When Speed Dancer was stolen, Ann had been buried in a host of personal problems. Dawn had borne the brunt of the loss in silence. But she'd never given up hope that one day she'd have a chance to find him. And now that day had come.

She and Freddie had discovered that the Tampa track was the one shown in the video. And since it was the last race of the season in Tampa, Dawn knew she had to be there or lose the trail of the filly completely.

"Would you care for a drink before lunch?" The waitress stood at her elbow, tired but polite.

"A martini," Dawn answered automatically. "Looks like you've had a busy day."

"Busy enough to suit me. Last day of the season, and some folks think the better horses have moved on to bigger tracks." The waitress put a hand on the back of an empty chair and rested for a moment. "But I don't see it that way. I hear the owners and trainers talk, and a few are holding out till later in the season. Look at the number four horse. He's nice."

"Do you follow the horses?" Dawn had noticed the waitress's quick assessment as the horses were led to the gate.

"When there's time. Juniper Jumps is my pick this race. I know his owner, and he's a fine man."

"A fine man doesn't make a fast horse," Dawn said, chuckling.

"No, but it makes a sound horse." The waitress grinned. "A sound horse runs with heart. They can pop them up with drugs, but it won't give them heart." She shook her head wisely and rested her empty tray on one hip as she surveyed the room and found all of her tables content.

On an impulse, Dawn picked up the large manila envelope. Sliding out the photos, she looked at the woman. "I'm looking for a particular horse. Maybe you've seen her. Or heard about her." She tried to hand the waitress the photos, but the woman stepped back.

"I don't make it my business to know anything about horses around here. I just look at them and pick my favorite." She glanced around the room and started to walk away.

"Please," Dawn spoke in a low tone that commanded attention. "I'm not here to start trouble. I'm here to look for a horse that's been a big part of my life."

The waitress turned back and gave Dawn a slow look that took in her regal posture, the smoldering fire of determination in her brown eyes. Her dark hair was bundled into a French twist beneath her hat, giving her a sophisticated look.

"What horse? Make it quick, I've got seven tables to watch."

Dawn handed her the pictures. The woman's chin jerked in acknowledgment as she looked twice from the pictures to Dawn. "Funny how some horses get your attention, the way they carry themselves, like this one. Your friend already asked me about this horse. I'm telling you the same as I told him. I've never seen her on this track. 'Course, that doesn't mean she hasn't run, it means I've never seen her. But you can bet if a filly that big came tearing around the dirt, someone would be talking about her. A lot. So I'd say she isn't here. Hasn't been here. Stoli martini on the rocks, right?"

"Right," Dawn mumbled, still trying to decipher what the waitress meant. What friend? Before she could ask, the waitress was gone.

Dawn's gaze roved over the room once again. The horses broke from the gate and the room came alive with people standing and urging their favorites on. For three minutes a current welded together the people in the room as they watched the beautiful Thoroughbreds run. Then, amid groans and laughter, the race was over.

Threading her way through the tables, the waitress returned with Dawn's drink. She deliberately avoided eye contact.

"I'm really not trying to start trouble," Dawn said softly. "This horse I'm looking for could lead me to another horse, one that I've got to find. I didn't really understand what you said before, about my friend showing you pictures already. I came here alone."

The waitress gave her an exasperated look. "Sure. Then you'd better tell your friend to start asking about a different horse, because he's been working the bar area. Benny, the bartender, said he told him the same thing. He's looking for a bay horse, and he doesn't want to cause trouble."

The room was suddenly too small, too crowded. "Where is this man?"

Something in Dawn's face made the waitress relent. "He was sitting in the west section. He seemed like a nice enough man. Are you okay?"

"Of course." Dawn fumbled with her purse. "This man. He asked about a bay filly?"

"Benny said he was asking about a horse that sounds just like the one in your pictures. Of course, there must be several dozen bay fillies on the track at any given time. Are you ready to order?" She held up her tray, all business.

"I've changed my mind. I won't be having lunch, after all." Dawn dropped a ten onto the table and stood. The horses for the second race were parading in front of the stands. She gathered her purse and photos and walked out of the room.

The new information was hard to absorb. Someone else was looking for the filly. The skin on her neck tightened at the thought. That someone could have a legitimate reason for looking for the horse, or he could have ulterior motives. Dawn decided the safest route would be to find the man before he found out about her.

The betting windows were crowded, and spectators milled in large and small clusters all over the track. Dawn kept her hat pulled down as far as possible and assumed a position near the wall. She had no idea how to go about finding the man who was looking for the filly. She was at an impasse, and needed some time to figure out what her next step should be.

LUKE O'NEIL lowered the racing form long enough to survey the woman in the green silk dress. She was obviously looking for someone. She'd also been at the stables earlier in the day, dressed in jeans and pretending to look for work. Several of the grooms had commented on her and her questions about a big, bay filly.

He glanced at the racing form again, then chanced another look. She was an attractive woman, self-possessed and athletic with a lean build. She held herself with dignity and grace, and he found his eyes lingering on her slender neck, the perfectly balanced body that started with squared shoulders and tapered to a very small waist. She had the figure of a young girl, but she was every inch a woman in the way she carried herself.

In other circumstances, he might have found it amusing that he and a strange woman were looking for the same horse. But nothing about the bay filly was amusing. The mysterious videotape showing the filly breaking a track record had turned his life upside down. Though racing wasn't his game, horses were, and he'd known from the moment he saw the video that he had to find the filly and find out her history. Now he discovered that a slender, dark-haired woman was playing the same game. The question he had to ask was whether she'd sent him the tape, and if so, why.

He saw her shift, her gaze traveling uncertainly around the room. Was she waiting to meet someone? An accomplice? Luke ducked behind the racing form again. He'd wait, all day if necessary. When he'd left the chilly spring in Kentucky and headed for Florida, he'd made up his mind that he wouldn't go home until he had some answers.

THE SENSATION of eyes watching her made Dawn shift uncomfortably. She was standing around like a nitwit. What did she think, that the owner of the filly would walk up and introduce himself? The truth of the matter was that she had hopped a plane to Tampa on an emotional impulse. Instead of a plan, she had only a feeling. She sighed deeply. Her grandmother would be disappointed with her. She'd assumed that one of the grooms would have seen the filly and would volunteer helpful information. She thought of Freddie's reservations about her trip, all apparently valid. He'd warned her that a lot of track workers didn't take well to women, wouldn't appreciate questions from a female. The fact that women jockeys raced every day didn't cut any ice with some men.

Action was required. She gripped her envelope tighter and headed for the bar. Perhaps Benny would prove helpful.

Leaning against the bar, Dawn didn't waste any time. She drew her photos from the envelope and tossed them onto the bar. "Who else was asking about this horse?"

The bartender, a man in his late thirties, sauntered over to her. He took his time looking at the photos. "Who says anyone else was asking for the horse?"

"A waitress." Dawn felt like gritting her teeth, but kept her face calm.

"Seems I recall someone else asking about a brown horse." The bartender grinned. "Is it a stolen animal? Is there a reward?"

"Perhaps." Dawn kept her face impassive.

"It was a tall man, gray suit, Irish name. McNeil, something like that. Now how about my reward?" He grinned.

"How about a specific name?" Dawn replied coolly.

"Luke O'Neil." A tanned, masculine hand reached over her shoulder and picked up the photographs.

Dawn turned to confront the owner of the hand and the voice. She had to lift her eyes considerably to find clear, blue eyes that regarded her with a bold intensity. His tanned face was framed by sandy-brown hair, highlighted in broad streaks by the sun. Before she could protest, one hand clutched her pictures and the other her arm.

Chapter Two

"Now that you know my name, what's yours?" Luke's calm voice belied his angry grip on her arm.

"Ms. Markey." Dawn threw her name at him as she grabbed for the photographs, but the man was faster. Holding them out of reach with his left hand, he tightened his grip on her arm so hard that she thought the bone would snap.

"I believe we have something to discuss. Alone." Luke felt the anger that had been growing for two days spread like wildfire. The woman was cool, abrasively cool.

She started to protest, but the fingers digging into her arm stopped her short. She had no choice but to follow him as he led her down the stairs, through the exit and out into the Florida heat.

"You're breaking my arm," she whispered through clenched teeth.

His grip relaxed, but only a fraction. He seemed intent on his destination, and where that was, Dawn hadn't a clue. They left the racetrack and started through the parking lot. Her tight skirt made it difficult to keep up with his long-legged stride. Gusts of wind kept snatching at her hat, further impeding her progress. When she didn't walk fast enough, he half carried her. As they neared the outskirts of the parking lot, a security guard eyed them suspiciously.

Dawn started to call out, but Luke forestalled her, twisting her arm painfully.

"My wife just dropped our money for the house note on the first race," Luke said to the guard. "I think it's time I took her home."

The guard shrugged and turned away.

Dawn felt a cold dread touch her stomach. Like a vision from a nightmare, the idea that she might be in real danger came to her. She dared a look at the man who had taken her captive, and what she saw didn't calm her fears. His lean jaw twitched with an emotion that could only be called fury. His gaze was dead ahead, never swerving to the right or left. He still held her photographs in his left hand, along with another manila folder.

"Who are you?" She found she was short of breath.

"Luke O'Neil. I told you."

He didn't bother to look at her; he just kept walking.

"Why are you doing this?"

That question stopped him. He swung around to confront her, eyes sparkling with anger. "That's the very question you're going to answer for me. I don't have time for guessing games, and I don't like riddles. Just as soon as we're completely alone, I intend to get some answers out of you. However I have to." He added the last with a renewed grip on her arm. Before she could respond, they were walking out of the parking lot and toward a stand of willow trees.

Dawn's arm was throbbing, and with the unremitting pain, her own temper ignited.

"You jerk." She rounded on him suddenly and struck him full in the face with her purse. "You're hurting my arm!"

The blow momentarily stunned him, but not enough to make him let her go. When she drew back for another blow, he dropped the pictures and used both hands to restrain her.

A sudden gust of wind picked up the photos, blowing them across the grass. Watching her only clues to the filly tumble toward the woods, Dawn was momentarily distracted. "The pictures," she said, struggling to break free. "Get them. They're blowing away!"

"So?" He held her.

"I have to have those picture to find that filly!" Dawn felt ready to explode. She was helpless against his strength, and without those photos she'd have no way to identify the horse.

"Where is that horse?" He almost shook her.

She gave him a scathing look. "If I knew that, would I be here now?"

The pictures drifted farther and farther away, and she twisted with anger. "I'm going to press charges against you for kidnapping, assault and anything else I can think of. You're a lunatic."

The woman in his hands was unbelievably strong for her size. She was as wiry as a jockey and twice as mean as a tethered panther. But she hadn't been able to hide the panic at the idea of her pictures disappearing. Something about that gave Luke pause.

"What is that filly to you?" he asked, slightly relaxing his grip.

"Let me get my pictures, and I'll tell you." Dawn was panting. She chanced a look into his eyes. "You have my word on it. I'll tell you everything, but I have to get those pictures back. It's the only clue I have."

The steady quality of her gaze, the true desperation in her eyes, made him drop his hands to his side. Together they hurried through the grass, recapturing the photos. When they had them all together, he handed them to her.

"I don't know who you are, Luke O'Neil, but I can tell you that you are in a whole lot of trouble." Dawn forced herself to look him squarely in the eye. "If you know anything about that filly, you'd better tell me now. Before I call the police."

"I'm looking for the horse."

They stood only a couple of feet apart, each assessing the other.

"I'm looking for her, too," Dawn said.

"Why?" The one word was a challenge.

"Someone sent a video to the farm where I work. I believe this horse may be a clue to another one that we've been looking for."

"Someone mailed you a video?" His brow furrowed.

"That's right, and you?"

"The same. I got this anonymous package in the mail and was able to trace it to this track."

"Have you seen the filly?" Dawn couldn't restrain herself any longer. "Did you find her?"

Looking into the sudden hope that filled Dawn's brown eyes, Luke O'Neil felt the last of his anger slip away. What he saw in the woman he faced was someone who cared about a horse. It wasn't money and it wasn't glory. It was genuine affection and concern. "You care about this horse, don't you?"

When the hard anger disappeared from Luke O'Neil's eyes, Dawn saw something entirely different. In the clear blue there was compassion and determination. She knew she could tell him the truth, and he would understand.

"I'm looking for another horse, a part of my past," she said, never breaking their gaze. "I think this filly's an offspring of that horse. It's something of a personal quest, you could say."

Something changed in his expression. It was minor, a tightening of a muscle or a weariness that entered his gaze. Dawn saw it, but continued, anyway.

"The horse I'm looking for is Speed Dancer, a bay stallion that would be eight years old. That filly is the image of him. If I can find her, then I might be able to find her sire."

"This Speed Dancer. Did you sell him, and now you want to buy him back?"

Dawn shook her head. "He was stolen. He belongs to my boss, Ann Tate Roper. She has a farm over near Ocean Springs, Mississippi, called Dancing Water. I'm her trainer."

Luke wiped his forehead with the back of his hand. The heat was bearing down on them, making their clothes stick. "Let's head back. We need to find a place where we can sit down and talk," he suggested. "I'm looking for the filly, too. That video has created a lot of questions that I need answered."

The grass gave way to asphalt and they walked slowly back toward the track. The guard gave them a curious look.

"My wife, she's got two hundred in her purse and we think maybe we can win back the money we lost," Luke said as they passed.

The guard shrugged his shoulders, shook his head and turned away. "A fool and his money are soon parted," he said, loudly enough for Luke and Dawn to hear.

When they were out of earshot, she looked up at Luke. He was deep in thought, his bottom lip slightly tucked as he concentrated. His blond hair, worn slightly longer than the current style, was neatly layered in a blend of highlights, and his skin was bronzed by long hours in the sun. Tiny wrinkles near his eyes indicated that he could laugh as well as glower. He walked with the easy confidence of a man who worked outdoors, while the gray linen suit indicated he was perfectly at ease in the corporate world.

Realizing that he was the subject of an intense study, Luke pulled back from his thoughts. He'd been trying to decide how much to tell this woman who walked beside him. Dawn

Markey. He looked down at her, arrested once again by her regal posture and by the pride in her eyes.

"When did you get your tape?" He needed to buy a little time. "Day before yesterday. And you?"

"The same." They passed through the turnstile and walked up the steps. The blast of the air conditioner was sweet relief. The jade silk dress, once so beautiful, was clinging to Dawn in several places. She felt hot, sticky and ready to change.

Luke led her back toward the third-floor dining area. "How about a drink?" he asked.

"Only if you promise not to bruise my other arm."

Luke laughed, and to her delight she saw that the lines around his eyes fell into a pattern of humor. They were indeed laugh lines.

"How about some lunch? And I promise, no force-feeding."

To Dawn's amazement she found she was hungry. She nodded and together they went to the restaurant. The fourth race was in progress. Most of the spectators had already eaten and were engrossed in watching the horses arrive at the track.

A waitress took their orders and in only a few moments, Dawn eagerly picked up the glass of tea. The cool, sweet liquid immediately made her feel better.

A grin pulled at the corners of Luke's mouth. Dawn's attack on the tea was somehow very pleasing. She was so open in her enjoyment, the quenching of her thirst. He drank his own tea and smiled to himself.

"Why did someone send you a tape?"

Dawn's question brought him back to the puzzle that had driven him nearly insane for two days. "I don't know, exactly," he answered. "I don't even know what I'm doing here. There are a million and one things I need to be doing at home." He shook his head as if disgusted with himself.

"Anyway, I did a little legwork and figured the tape was made at this track. Since it was the weekend for the last race of the season, I felt like I had to hustle down here and ask a few questions, or the opportunity would be gone."

"Amazing," Dawn said. She was leaning across the table, eyes wide, golden sparks alive in their depths. "That is exactly my own reasoning."

"You got the tape, figured out the track business, and came to look for her, too?"

"I never gave up hope of finding Speed Dancer." Dawn grew animated as she talked. "I could never believe he was dead, but each year that passed, it got harder to believe that he might still be alive. We have a full brother to him, Easy Dancer, that we're using as a stud. He's a wonderful horse."

"Then why the hunt for Speed Dancer?" Luke kept the question carefully controlled.

"Ann doesn't even know I'm here," Dawn confessed. "I came on my own, hoping that I might find some answers. That horse was very special to me. There wasn't anything he wouldn't try for me. Ann prefers Easy, but I always thought Speed Dancer was the better stud, or would have been."

"Then your boss didn't breed him to get that bay filly that just beat the world record time on a mile and a quarter track?"

"No, my boss didn't breed him at all. He was really still a baby when he was stolen. I saw the potential in him, but he hadn't proven himself yet."

Watching her brown eyes, he couldn't help but believe her. She'd come to Tampa to search for a horse everyone else had given up as dead. A horse that she cared about.

"Luke?"

Hesitation touched her voice and broke into his reverie. "I'm sorry," he apologized. "Any idea why someone sent that video to you? There's someone out there who knows about the past, someone who's toying with us." The frustration and anger he'd felt for the past two days reentered his voice.

Dawn's shoulders lifted in an eloquent shrug. "I've gone over it again and again. Whoever sent that tape knew Ann would recognize the filly as an offspring of Speed Dancer. So we can safely assume they'd know that Ann would likely begin hunting for the filly, right?"

Luke nodded, watching Dawn's expressive hands. Every movement was so confident, so controlled. He was willing to bet, a lot, that she was an excellent rider.

"So whoever sent the tape doesn't own the filly, or they wouldn't want me looking for her. Or would they?" She shook her head. "If they can prove Speed Dancer's the father, maybe they're hoping Ann would give them registration papers."

"I've been wondering about that myself," Luke admitted. "There's been not one peep of publicity about the filly. As fast as she is, she'd be all over the national news, if those sportswriters had any idea about her."

"Maybe the owners plan to spring her as a field horse in the Derby!"

"No." Luke shook his head.

"Why not? That would be the story of the century. An unknown, and a filly at that, beats the biggest names in racing! The filly would be an international sensation!" She almost stood up in excitement. Sitting was one of her weak points.

Luke reached a hand across the table and captured hers. "Sit," he commanded with a grin, "unless you're going to place a bet." He glanced toward the window as the horses broke from the gate.

Caught in the spell, Dawn watched the race. A large, chestnut stallion took the lead and put his heart into the race. He was three lengths ahead of a black horse, and the rest of the field was six lengths behind them.

"Two-horse race," Luke commented. He was leaning forward in his seat, his hands clenched.

"The black," Dawn said, her hands gripping the table. "See the way his hind legs power him forward. He'll win over the distance."

The horses came around the final turn, the chestnut still in the lead. It wasn't until the homestretch that the black made his move. With a surge of power he drove forward, winning by half a length.

"Good call." Luke was watching Dawn more than he was watching the race. Her face was alive, her skin fairly vibrating with tension. "You know your horses."

"It's my business."

"You ride as well as train?" He recalled her taut body as she'd struggled against him. She was fit, no doubt a superior rider.

"What do you think?" She flashed him a grin. "I couldn't live without it. That's my reward at the end of a long day. Do you ride?"

"Here and there." Luke looked up, just as the waitress delivered their lunch. "What would you do if you found Speed Dancer?"

Dawn looked up. Her eyes were wide with surprised thought. "I've often dreamed about that," she answered, a fierce determination taking over the soft planes of her face. "I'd take him straight home, back where he belongs. Nobody could stop me."

"I see," Luke said, dropping his gaze to his food. "You are very adamant."

There was a strange quality to his words and Dawn watched him for several seconds. It was as if he were testing her, seeking some reaction. "Why does someone want you to hunt the filly?" she countered.

"I'm not certain." The strange tension had returned to his eyes when he looked at her. Worry touched the corners of his mouth. "I make it a habit to mind my own business. When the video first came, I thought I should just ignore it. I couldn't. When I figured out it was the Tampa track, then I felt certain someone wanted me here, that I'd find the reason once I arrived."

"And you thought I knew?"

"Right. Several of the grooms told me about you. It was easy to figure you were looking for the same horse."

Dawn's interest in food completely disappeared. "Did they tell you anything? They acted as if I had the plague."

"Not much." His eyes returned to his food and he pushed salad around on his plate.

"They didn't tell you anything?" she pressed.

"She didn't run in any of the regular races here." Luke kept his eyes focused on his food.

"Does that mean she wasn't here?" Dawn's temper notched up slightly. Luke O'Neil wasn't shooting straight with her, and he wasn't very good at hiding it.

"She was here, but no one will talk about it."

Excitement tingled over her. "How did you find that tid-bit?"

"Ben Franklin can be mighty persuasive, but he wasn't good enough to get any real solid detail."

"You bribed them!" Dawn felt a rush of heat at her own stupidity. She'd never even thought of offering money.

Luke signaled the waitress in a ploy to gain more time. He was hedging, and Dawn Markey had picked up on it. For a flash he saw the miles of white fences around his Kentucky farm. Fences he'd just painted. Pastures he'd just bought the supplies to fertilize. The truth could destroy the one thing he'd built his future on.

"Luke?" Dawn touched his hand, unexpectedly aware of the warmth and roughness of his skin. Whatever the suit said about his corporate skills, his body said outdoors. She withdrew her hand immediately. "I asked you how you found out she'd been at this track?"

"One of the jockeys saw her. She was trailered in on an off day, early in the morning. If you'll recall, the shadows in the video were long because the sun was on the horizon. They ran her and someone had a camera right down there—" he pointed to the spectator stands that were some distance from the track "—and the film was made. That's why the quality of the video is so poor. And if you'll recall, the camera lost the horse on the backstretch. I'm positive the people running the horse had no idea someone was taping them."

As he described the scene, Dawn saw a replay of the video in her mind. She'd watched the darn thing at least a million times.

"What's the next step?" She forced her mind to the immediate problem.

"Wait for someone to contact us, I suppose." Even as he said it, the idea made him uneasy. That meant someone was orchestrating their movements. Someone had drawn two complete strangers to the Florida coast, and neither knew why. Worry made him straighten his back and glance from side to side.

"Something wrong?"

"Nope, just seeing what I could see." He didn't want to frighten Dawn.

"You think we're being watched, don't you?" An army of goose bumps attacked the tender skin at the nape of her neck.

"Just paranoia, I'm sure." But even as he denied it, he felt as if someone watched them closely. "You have to admit, we've been manipulated fairly well."

"I can see why someone would send Ann a tape. Her connection to the filly is clear. But I'm still confused about you. You said you weren't involved in racing?'' She left the question hanging.

''I don't race, but I like horses.'' Luke lifted his napkin to his mouth. ''If you'll excuse me, I'll be back in a moment.''

Before she could press her question, Luke stood up and left the table. She followed his progress through the room until he disappeared near the men's room.

Once he was gone, Dawn forced herself to sit back and assess the day's bizarre events. Were there other people at the track who'd received a video of the bay filly running? The feeling of being observed made her shiver involuntarily. It was possible. Ann and Luke had been targeted, why not someone else? Another concern involved Luke's real interest in the filly. If not racing, what?

The questions came at her from all directions. She sipped her tea and tried to concentrate on the horses for the sixth race. The last race had gone by and she hadn't even noticed.

''Ms. Markey?'' The young man was dressed in the uniform of a race employee. He was holding a bouquet of incredible flowers.

''Yes.''

''These are for you.''

Taken aback, she fumbled in her purse for a tip. ''Who sent them?''

''He didn't leave his name. He simply signed the note and asked me to deliver them to you.''

The only man Dawn knew in Tampa was Luke O'Neil, but why in the world would he send flowers to her when he went to the men's room? She took the large bouquet of Rubrum lilies and picked up the note. The flowers were such an extravagant gesture, one designed to make her feel very feminine. Luke O'Neil was a handsome man, a compelling

man. She slit the envelope and took out the card it en-
closed.

"Go home or die! Quit snooping!"

The words were boldly written in black ink.

Dawn's exclamation of surprise was drowned by the noise
of the crowd as the horses broke for the sixth race. Cheers
and curses were a ringing cacophony as she held the flowers
to her chest and the note in her hand. For one blinding moment she felt both deaf and paralyzed, as if a thick, cotton
quilt had been wrapped over all her senses. Slowly the room
came back into focus, the noises grew distinct, and she felt
the dew of the flowers seeping through her dress to her skin.

Dropping the flowers onto the table, she found cash in her
purse to cover the bill. Luke O'Neil was gone. She was sure
of that much. He'd pumped her for all of her facts and then
pulled a sly maneuver. But he hadn't counted on her fierce
determination, or the slow burn of anger that now fueled
her. He couldn't scare her away with flowers and threatening notes. She stalked out of the restaurant and to her car.
At least she knew the filly had been seen, and money was
one way of getting the information she wanted. It hadn't
been a wasted encounter.

Her eyes were lowered against the glare of the sun as she
walked across the hot parking lot. By design, she avoided
the guard at the west end. She had to walk the long way
around, and the heat was uncomfortable. In a patch of loose
gravel, one of her high heels turned and she almost fell.

As she leaned on the fender of a car to check her heel, she
heard the sound of tires spraying rocks. The low brim of her
hat blocked her view, and she had to turn completely to see
the yellow Buick coming straight at her.

Acting purely on instinct, she hit the ground and rolled
beside a parked car. She could feel the hot wind from the
speeding tires of the car as it passed with only a few inches
to spare.

Chapter Three

Luke was still breathing hard when he returned to the dining room. There was no sign of Dawn, and a riot of flowers covered the tabletop, thrown carelessly onto the dirty plates. What was going on? He'd been gone longer than he expected, but he thought Dawn would still be waiting for him. Unless she was part of the setup.

He picked up several of the delicate lilies and found the money Dawn had left. He called the waitress over. "What happened to the woman who was sitting here?" he asked.

"Some delivery boy brought the flowers, she threw them on the table and took off." The waitress was clearly intrigued.

"Did she say anything?"

"No, but she looked plenty mad."

Luke felt a strange dread growing in his stomach. When he'd first seen the small man watching him so intently, he'd felt the flutter of apprehension that warned of a trap. He had to investigate. He'd left the table, walked toward the men's room and then followed the small man out to the paddocks. The man acted guilty, glancing over his shoulder and increasing his pace whenever Luke drew near. Just when Luke thought he had him cornered at the end of the saddling racks, he darted into the jockeys' room and completely disappeared.

Luke's initial feeling that he'd been taken on a wild-goose chase was confirmed.

"What about the flowers?" the waitress asked, eyeing them with open curiosity. "Want me to look for something to put them in?"

"Throw them away."

He hurried out of the restaurant and down to the paddock area. Walking through the spectators' seats, he sought a striking lady in a jade silk dress. All efforts met with failure. Dawn was nowhere on the track.

Disappointment and concern tightened his jaw as he left the track and went to his own car. The next step was to call the airport to make sure she didn't have a flight booked out. As he searched for Dawn, he'd come to one serious conclusion. He had to find her, to stay linked with her. All of his intuitions warned him that danger surrounded both Dawn and himself. They were being watched. Carefully watched. He'd been deliberately lured from the table so that Dawn was left alone. Someone knew them well enough to successfully manipulate them, and that in itself smacked of danger.

Luke made another pass through the spectators' seats, unable to shake the sensation that an unfriendly gaze bored directly into his spine.

From a seat in the press box the small man watched Luke's search of the racetrack grounds. He smiled with satisfaction, then picked up a telephone and made a call.

"O'Neil showed. The girl's name is Dawn Markey. I did like you said and threw a scare into her. Right. Like rubber on asphalt, Boss. If she don't take the hint, I know what to do." He hung up.

DAWN STEPPED out of the dress and let it fall to the floor. It was beyond repair. A hole had been torn in the skirt, one sleeve virtually ripped out and smudges, grime and dirt were everywhere. It was a mirror image of her own battered body.

Her knees had quit bleeding. At last. But not before a small trickle of blood had oozed down into her shoe. She wasn't hurt seriously, but her roll on the pavement had certainly cost her some skin.

She locked the hotel room door, threw the dead bolt and the chain and turned on the shower. At least she hadn't told Luke O'Neil where she was staying. It would take him a while to call all the hotels and find where she was registered. If he even bothered. He was probably sure she was boarding a plane now to run home.

Well, he was wrong!

She gritted her teeth as the first blast of hot water stung her tender skin. She washed the cuts and scrapes, stepped out of the water and gingerly toweled dry. With the blood gone, it wasn't as bad as it first looked, but she could still win a prize for most scuffed female.

Even though it wasn't even six o'clock, she slipped into a nightgown and sat in a comfortable chair. She had to think, to sort through what had happened.

After ten minutes without a coherent thought, she picked up the phone and called Freddie. She tried to downplay the danger of the day's events, but told him about Luke O'Neil. Freddie was a veteran. He had connections who knew everyone who had ever breathed the word horse. Luke had gotten the drop on her once, but it wouldn't happen again.

"Ask around about this guy, would you?" She could hear disapproval in Freddie's long silence.

"Come home," he urged her. "Catch the next flight. The women around Dancing Water are always trying to get themselves killed over a horse. Now you come home, and we'll call Miss Ann and hire someone to do this." Freddie was practically jumping through the telephone.

"No."

"Dawn Markey, I'm telling you to come home!"

"Freddie Weston, you can't order me," Dawn replied. She stood up and almost jerked the telephone off the stand.

"You're coming home!" Freddie's voice was ragged. "Or I'm comin' to get you!"

A fleeting smile touched Dawn's face. It was the first tension breaker she'd had all day. The talk with Freddie was familiar ground. They argued about everything, in a vocal, aggressive manner. And she had to admit that after a day of abuse, it was nice to know someone cared.

"Freddie," she said, her voice pleading, "don't fuss with me. I need your help."

The soft request took the steam out of Freddie. "Are you hurt, girl?"

"No, Freddie, but I can't quit now. I should never have left the track. When I lost O'Neil, I lost my clue."

"What are you going to do?"

That was the question. "I'm going to stay a few more days. Go back to the track tomorrow. A lot of folks will be there, maybe someone will have seen the horse. Or Luke."

"Be careful, Dawn. The ranch is running smooth, but we miss you."

"Has Ann called?"

"Not yet, but when she does, I'll make her understand."

"Thanks."

She replaced the receiver and returned to her chair. So she had a plan for tomorrow, but what about the rest of the evening? Her body was already getting stiff and sore. She eyed the bed thoughtfully. It wouldn't be a bad idea, and then she could get an early start the next morning.

Slipping beneath the covers, she felt slightly odd. It had been years since she'd gone to bed before dark. Long years. But the events of the day had taken a heavy toll, and soon she was sound asleep.

At first she thought it was someone in the room next door. She stirred, rolled over and burrowed deeper into the pillow.

The tiny metallic click disturbed her again.

She'd left the heavy draperies slightly open, and a sliver of moonlight crossed the bed and struck the door. Otherwise, the hotel room was dark, cool and empty. Dawn sat up, sleepily looking for the source of the noise. The room was perfectly still.

Snuggling back beneath the sheets, she sighed. It must have been a dream. Her eyes were closing when she heard it again, the slight bump of metal against metal.

More fully awake, she looked at the door. As she watched, the dead bolt turned slowly counterclockwise. Her heart pulsed with a force that threatened to choke her. Clawing out of the covers, she swung her feet to the floor. She watched in horror as the doorknob slowly turned. The lock had already been picked.

The door opened to the length of the chain, then slowly closed again. Dawn rushed to the wall beside the door and dropped to her knees. Whoever was coming in, she had only one defense. That was to escape when they entered.

The door was hurled open with a force so sudden that Dawn almost screamed. In a blinding flash a big, dark figure stepped into the one shaft of moonlight. A silver arc whizzed through the room and implanted itself in the bed, and the figure turned and ran.

Dawn huddled against the wall, her breath rasping in her ears, legs so weak that they jelled beneath her. She didn't have to go to the bed and look. She knew what she'd find. A knife, stuck shaft deep in the mattress, where only a moment before she'd been sleeping.

THE FIRST RAYS of the sun crept through the open window and illuminated the hotel room. Dawn sat, feet curled under her, in a chair where she had a good view of the window and the door. As the room lightened, she turned to stare again at the knife protruding from the mattress. Since the attack she'd debated calling the police. At last she'd given up the idea. Her gut instinct told her that to do so might endanger the filly's life. Someone very dangerous was after that horse. It only stood to reason that someone ruthless enough to try and kill a person would certainly kill a horse. With just a little more time, she might be able to turn up a clue, find the horse and get back to Dancing Water Ranch, safe and sound.

As soon as she'd quit shaking, she'd called the desk clerk. There were no messages. The clerk didn't remember if anyone had called, asking if she was registered.

Well, the clerk might have a bad memory, but Dawn didn't. Information could be bought. She'd learned that trick from a very resourceful man. At the thought of Luke O'Neil she stiffened. If he wanted her dead, why hadn't he simply broken her neck when he had her in the woods near the racetrack? The guard! He'd seen them leaving together.

The soft denim of her jeans brushed against her raw knees as she stood and picked up her single bag. She'd thought about leaving the hotel earlier, but there was really no other place for her to go. And in the daylight she had a better chance of making sure she wasn't being tailed.

She went to the bed and took a T-shirt from her case. With great care she removed the knife, wrapped it in the shirt and put it into the bag.

The threatening note in the flowers had been one thing, but the attack last night had been no threat. Dawn rubbed her cold hands together as she looked around the room one last time. Luke O'Neil was a physically powerful man, of a very similar build to the man who'd broken into her room last night. The intruder had worn a mask of some sort. She couldn't positively identify him as Luke. But she couldn't rule him out as a suspect. In fact, since she'd first laid eyes on him, she'd been nearly run down, threatened and attacked with a knife. All in all, he was company she couldn't afford to keep—or lose.

Instead of stopping in the hotel restaurant, she threw her bag into the trunk of the rental car and went out to the racetrack. Trailers and vans were everywhere, as horses with bright leg wraps and blankets were loaded for trips to other tracks. Their destinations could be anywhere from California to New York. She had a fleeting moment of pleasure when she thought that in the next year, thanks to the work of her friends, some of the elegant animals would be heading to the new horse track in Biloxi, Mississippi.

That pleasant memory was quickly dispelled as she saw the lanky figure of Luke O'Neil walk around a horse trailer. Luke stopped one of the grooms and talked, making gestures with his hands. Acting on instinct, Dawn ducked beside the truck where she stood.

Peeping over the fender, she watched as Luke and the man walked slowly to the stable area. About a hundred yards away a half-ton truck rumbled toward Luke and the groom. As Ann watched, the truck picked up speed at an amazing rate, until it was going far too fast to be safe in an area where high-strung horses were tethered.

It took a moment for Dawn to realize that the truck was heading directly for Luke and the groom.

"Luke!" She stood and yelled, waving her hands at the men.

Spinning on his heel, Luke turned to her, just in time to catch sight of the truck bearing down on him. Leaping sideways, he pushed the groom to safety and fell on top of him. The truck careened through the loading grounds as horses reared and plunged, some breaking stout ropes as they struggled to free themselves.

The entire grounds broke into pandemonium as grooms set off in hot pursuit of the horses and several hot-blooded trainers took out on foot after the rampaging truck, waving fists and yelling curses at the driver.

Dawn didn't wait to think. She ran across the grounds to Luke and the still prostrate groom. Luke was bending over the man, talking quietly.

"Is he hurt?" Dawn was breathless as she skidded to a stop.

"Not as bad as he would have been if that truck had hit us. I'm afraid he broke my fall and wrenched his back."

"It's nothing, really," the groom insisted. "It just knocked the wind out of me." To prove his words he sat up, shaking his head and rubbing his back. In another few moments he was on his feet. "I'd like to get my hands on that driver," he muttered as he walked off.

In the melee of horses, men, equipment and trucks, Dawn and Luke were suddenly alone. Her suspicions returned and she lowered her gaze to the ground.

"Thanks for the warning." He spoke with an edge of anger.

"Yeah, well, thanks for yours!" She looked up, brown eyes fired with her own fury. "The flowers were a nice touch, but all in all, the knife was more effective, and less costly." She whirled and stalked away.

"Dawn!"

The word was an order, one she could easily ignore. She was ten feet away when she felt his hand on her arm, gripping in the same place he'd held her the day before.

"Let me go," she warned him as she stopped without turning around.

His hand dropped. "What are you talking about? What flowers? What knife?"

Without looking at him she knew his clear, blue gaze would be troubled, confused. She swung around. Perplexity was in the line of his mouth, the hesitant way he held his hands.

"Surely you saw the flowers, if you even bothered to return to the table?" She wasn't ready to believe him. Not by a long shot. But just a few moments before, he'd been a target as surely as herself. Hadn't he?

"I did return to the table, and I saw those flowers. What I didn't see was you. No trace. No message. *Nada*. Care to explain?" He lifted his eyebrows a fraction.

"Oh, it's just a little peculiarity I have. When someone threatens my life with a floral note, I tend to want to walk around. It's hard to sit still when your life is being threatened." She pulled the note from the pocket of her jeans and handed it to him.

"That sort of looks like the same handwriting that addressed the videotape package to me," he said at last.

Dawn looked at the card again. Damn! He was right! It was the same, sloping backhand *G*. The small, pointed *s*'s.

"What knife?" he pressed.

She told him quickly about the car nearly hitting her and the knife attack in her hotel room.

As soon as she finished, he took her elbow and started walking back toward her rental car. "Where are we going?" she asked, amazed at his quick action. "Do you have a plan?"

"I do," he agreed. His blue eyes never looked at her as he put her into the passenger seat and walked around to get behind the wheel. She handed him the keys automatically, stunned by his ability to take control.

"Well, where are we going?"

"To the airport, where you are going to board the next flight home."

"Wait a minute!" She reached across and swiftly shut off the ignition, pocketing the key. "Where do you get off, thinking you can haul me around like some baggage? I'm not going home until I find out something about that filly."

Luke kept his hands on the steering wheel as he slowly relaxed. Chancing a look at her he took in the stony profile, the rapid rise and fall of her chest beneath the aqua cotton shirt. She was plenty mad. He realized he'd just made a terrible miscalculation. Dawn Markey was not a lady to order around.

The silence in the car grew thicker and thicker. Dawn felt her own anger seep away, but she couldn't look at Luke. The very idea that he had even attempted to treat her like an inconvenient six-year-old refueled her anger.

"I owe you an apology, Dawn." His words were calm, sincere. The touch of his hand on her jaw was very gentle as he brought her face around to his. "I guess I'm used to handling my younger sister. She has a knack for getting herself in trouble, and over the years I've found it simpler to step in, take charge and bundle her off to safety."

His grin was her undoing. She smiled back. "I'm not your little sister."

"I'll keep that in mind in the future," he said, his gaze lingering for a moment on her face before he turned away. "So I guess along with an apology, I have a question. What are you going to do? You can't hang around here as the target for new threats and attacks."

"And you aren't a target?" she asked, cocking her head. "It seems a big truck came very close to making road butter out of you. If I hadn't called out . . ."

"Well put," he said, grinning wider. "How about some breakfast?"

Dawn turned to look at the horses. "I haven't had a chance to ask any questions," she said, a note of reluctance creeping into her voice. "It's as if that filly never existed in the flesh."

"She was here, but she left two days ago," Luke answered. "The groom I was talking to, when the truck tried to hit me, said he thought she went to an Arkansas track."

"He saw her?" Dawn leaned forward in the seat. "When? Where? Who owns her? Will they race her? Did he know where she came from?"

"Whoa!" Luke put a restraining hand on her knee, removing it quickly when she flinched.

"Pavement scrape," she explained. "But what about the horse?"

"I don't know much, but I'll share over some breakfast. We'll drive down to this coffee shop across from the stables. It's as good a place as any to start listening."

With breakfast platters and steaming cups of coffee before them, Luke buttered a biscuit and told Dawn the few facts he'd unearthed. The groom, Gary Smith, had helped load the big, bay mare. She'd appeared one night in an empty stall and left the next morning at ten. Track gossip had it that she ran once, just after dawn, in a blistering workout, but Smith himself hadn't seen it. She was a phantom filly that left behind a ghostly trail of rumors.

"What about stall records?" Dawn asked. "Surely someone had to sign and pay for the stall, even if it was just for one night."

"I checked. The stall was registered in the name Mr. D's Private Stock."

"Some sense of humor," she said bitterly. "That sounds more like some cheap bottle of wine than a horse. Smith thinks the horse was headed for Arkansas?"

"The track there is highly competitive, but I called and there was no such horse listed as residing in the track stables." Luke sipped his coffee slowly. "Of course, there are a million stables the horse could be at."

"This is impossible." Dawn sighed wearily. "The only thing that makes me consider keeping on is that we must be worrying someone, or else why would they try and hurt us?"

"That's a good question, but one with a troubling answer. I'm afraid we may be caught in the middle of some type of war. And my past experience has taught me that it's always the innocent who suffer when the powers start to fight."

Not even the hot cup of coffee in her hands could stop the chill that touched her at his words. "A war?"

"Someone wants us to be here, and someone else wants us gone, even dead. That's two clear-cut, diverse interests. It appears to me that you, me and the filly are pawns in this game. I don't have to tell you that we humans are expendable, and maybe the filly, too."

"It would make sense that the person who has the horse doesn't want us to find her." Dawn dumped another teaspoonful of sugar into her coffee. "Any ideas what we can do?"

"I need to go back to Kentucky." He picked up his spoon. "I've got horses to ride, riders to train and hours of physical labor to put in before summer." A slow smile moved from his mouth to his eyes. "But I think, instead, I'm going to Arkansas."

"I had exactly that same thought." Dawn grinned.

"You two looking for a big, bay filly?" The man who walked up to their table was of medium height, balding and sweaty. His worn jeans and cotton shirt defined no occupation. Dawn could see only that he worked outdoors. His skin was dark and leathery from the sun.

"Who wants to know?" Luke gave Dawn an apologetic look for the cliché.

The man thrust out a note to Luke. When he didn't take it, the man dropped it onto the tabletop. "Some man gave me a twenty to give this to you. So consider it delivered." He walked out of the coffee shop, climbed into a red pickup and blasted away, leaving a trail of dust.

When Luke didn't touch the note, Dawn picked it up and slit the envelope with her thumbnail. The letter was one page, handwritten in a bold, sloping script.

"Try the Oakdale Stables. The filly wants to be found."

She handed the note to Luke. As their gazes met, they both stood and walked out of the restaurant. They stopped only long enough to pick up Luke's luggage at his hotel, then drove to the Tampa airport.

Chapter Four

Oakdale Stables was listed in the Hot Springs phone directory, and Dawn placed the call while Luke rented a car. On the fifth ring, the telephone was answered by a gruff male voice.

"Are you boarding a big, bay filly by the name of Private Stock?" she asked.

"What are you, an insurance investigator?" There was challenge in the man's voice.

Too late, Dawn realized her mistake. The man on the phone was suspicious, all defenses on the alert.

"Of course not, how silly of you," she answered with her best drawl. "I'm an agent and I'm looking for a mount for an upper-level dressage competitor. This particular horse was mentioned, and if she's there and for sale, I'd like to take a look at her." Sweat dripped down her back. It was the best and least threatening excuse she could think of on the spur of the moment.

"Dressage?" The man's tone was scornful. "We don't have any useless show horses here. None of our horses are for sale. And we don't need any people stopping by, so forget it."

Dawn removed the phone from her ear just in time to avoid the loud click that signaled the man had hung up on her.

"I'm afraid I blew it," she said, returning to Luke. "I did everything wrong. I as much as told them I was hunting the horse, and he hung up."

Luke picked up the keys to the car, turning to face Dawn. For the first time he saw her despair. Her face was tense with worry. She'd stood up to a lot of physical and emotional battering, and he could plainly see she needed reassurance. He draped an arm across her shoulders and gave her a hug. "Not to worry. Somehow I never expected to walk into the stables and find the filly standing in a stall." He started to pick up the luggage, then paused. "There is something that's bothering me, though."

"What?" She stepped closer, watching the tension in his face.

"Be cool, but to your left, behind that column, there's a man who was on the plane with us. If I'm not mistaken, he was in the airport in Tampa and booked this flight after we did. Now he's acting like a lost soul. I get the feeling he's waiting for us to make our move."

To get a good look, Dawn bent to her shoe, working the laces for a moment and examining the airport area that Luke had indicated. The man was standing behind a column, pretending to read a monitor. He was short, wiry, and definitely looked stealthy.

"I think he's the man I followed at the track yesterday— the one who gave me the slip." Luke offered his hand and helped her rise.

"Why would he be following us?" A tingle rushed over Dawn's skin. The image of the knife whizzing through the air was as real as it had been the night before.

"Good question. I feel like a mouse, caught between two hungry cats. Somehow I get the idea that we're in trouble." He felt a surge of protectiveness toward the woman who had entered so unwittingly into such a deadly game. His hand touched the small of her back in a gentle, protective gesture.

"I know exactly what you mean. Why don't we get the car and head out toward the stables? Maybe we'll find out for certain if we're being tailed." Luke's hand was the perfect comfort. He was an attractive man; she'd known that from the first moment she saw him, but he was more. He was capable of giving those important gestures of reassurance. He was the best partner she could ever have wished for in hunting the phantom filly.

"Good thinking." Luke hefted both suitcases and they left the airport.

Though she kept a sharp eye on the road behind them, there was no sign of another car or of the short, wiry man. Twenty miles from the airport she finally relaxed.

"Thanks for the encouragement back at the airport, Luke. I was feeling pretty low." She gave him a crooked grin from her side of the car. "Momentary loss of faith."

"You're a remarkable woman, Dawn." Luke kept his eyes on the road. There was more he could add, but not at that moment.

Oakdale Stables was down a red dirt road bordered by unpainted houses and barking dogs. Dawn reserved her comments, but with each mile her heart sank. Surely this wasn't the environment for one of the fastest horses in the world. The only other conclusion was that she and Luke had been led on a wild-goose chase over a large portion of the South. She thought of the airline tickets on her credit card and groaned.

"Don't give up hope." Luke took his gaze off the rutted road for long enough to give her a smile of encouragement. "She may be hidden. Think of that."

"Why drag her all the way to Arkansas to hide her in the backwoods?" Dawn grumped. "It doesn't make sense."

"Nothing about this whole episode makes any sense," he reminded her.

They rounded a curve and came on a mailbox, rusted and askew, that bore the name of the stables. Instead of stopping, Luke kept driving. Dawn strained to get a glimpse down the driveway, but the foliage was thick and overgrown.

"This looks like it," she said with a sigh.

"We'll go down the road and turn around, then we'll come back. I think I'm going to get out and do a little reconnoitering. Will you turn around and drive back, giving me about twenty minutes? Plan on picking me up—" he pointed at a dense thicket of huckleberries and small brush "—there."

More than anything Dawn wanted to go with him, but she realized the wisdom of his plan. Two people were twice as likely to get spotted, and someone had to stay with the car.

"Sure," she said. "Good luck."

When he stopped and got out, she slid across the seat and behind the wheel. "Twenty minutes," she said, checking her watch. A terrible thought struck her. "What if you aren't here?"

"Wait another twenty minutes and then get the marines." He grinned, a devil-may-care grin of excitement and confidence. "But I'll be there." Then he was gone, disappearing almost magically into the woods.

Luke followed a track parallel to the driveway, but deep enough in the woods so he wasn't an obvious target for anyone who might be scanning the area. As a young boy he and his brothers had spent hours playing games, hiding and hunting each other, honing the guerrilla skills that had made the American Indians such formidable adversaries. But as he stepped through the dry underbrush, he realized that he wasn't involved in a game this time. He was trespassing. He was deliberately moving onto someone else's property with the intention of spying. It was a novel act, one that he as a landowner could thoroughly disapprove of. He also knew that if he caught someone lurking around his own stables, he'd slug first and ask questions later.

A long, unkempt shed came into view and he crouched lower to the ground, pausing for a moment to establish some landmarks in his mind. As he watched, a heavyset man came out of one door, a metal bucket in one hand. He seemed to be whistling under his breath as he walked down the length of the building and dumped the bucket of feed into a stall. A low whinny greeted his action, but he didn't respond.

Estimating the length of the building, Luke guessed five stalls and a feed room. The pastures were obviously behind the barn. There was no way to tell how many horses might be housed there, or how many people worked at the stables. Judging by the appearance, Luke didn't count on a full staff.

He waited until the man disappeared, then edged closer to the barn. With each step his anticipation grew. The stall was dark, and he couldn't see the horse until he was right at the door. A questioning whinny let him know the horse had seen him and sensed his approach.

Luke threw open the door of the stall, allowing light to enter. The bay filly from the videotape continued to eat. She watched him, but showed no fear.

"Easy, girl," he whispered. He walked to her, running his hand down her neck, feeling the length of her shoulder and the depth of her chest. She was a perfect example of horse-flesh, the epitome of centuries of breeding.

She was even more spectacular than her father.

The mare snorted and jerked up her head. Before Luke could turn around, something hard struck him across the back of his head. The last thing he remembered was falling slowly into the shavings on the floor of the stall.

THE PLUME of red dust was a trail Dawn couldn't ignore. She checked her watch again. It had been twenty-five minutes since Luke disappeared into the woods by the side of the road. Twenty-five of the longest minutes of her life. With careful planning, she'd driven down the red dirt road for fifteen minutes at a very slow pace. Then with another five for a speedier return, she was back at the clump of huckleberries exactly on time. But no Luke.

She'd continued her drive, her nerves growing tauter with each passing minute. When she returned to the designated pickup point, she was just in time to see the dust stirred by a horse trailer that was disappearing down the road at breakneck speed.

Her foot squeezed on the accelerator and she took off in pursuit of the disappearing trailer. As she sped away, her eyes nervously searched the roadside for Luke. Where could he be?

The answer to that question was—anywhere!

He could be in the horse trailer, making an escape with the filly. He could be back at the stables, injured in some way. Or he could still be hiding in the woods, watching, and unable to come out.

She chased the horse trailer for five miles, then gradually began to drop back. She couldn't go off and leave Luke behind, even if it meant losing the trailer. There was a chance the horse wasn't Private Stock. Judging by the speed the trailer was going, it might even be empty. She felt her heart sink as she applied the brake and turned. If the filly was being taken away, she would lose the trail. But she couldn't leave without knowing that Luke was safe.

If pressed, she'd admit that she didn't know much about him. But whenever she thought about his willingness to reassure her, the way he tried to look out for her, she would feel his hand at her back. However it had come about, they were partners. They had agreed to hunt the filly together, and she couldn't run off and leave Luke. At the thought of him, injured, she stepped harder on the gas pedal. If there'd been more time to be honest with herself, she knew she'd have had to admit that it wasn't only loyalty that made her so worried about Luke O'Neil. There were other feelings, emotions she didn't choose to pull out and explore.

Returning to Oakdale Stables, Dawn cruised down the driveway at a steady pace. She concocted a quick story, in case she was stopped. She decided to pretend she was an agent, just as she'd said on the phone. She'd simply brazen her way around the property, talking nonstop about her quest for the perfect dressage horse. They could throw her out, but at least she'd get a chance to scout around for Luke. She was really worried about him.

The driveway, shaded by large oaks, was pretty, but it didn't hide the sagging, dangerous fencing or the run-down condition of the pastures. Whoever ran Oakdale did a very poor job of it.

There was a small house, then several hundred yards behind it, almost hidden by oak trees, was a long, narrow barn that looked more like a shed. Instead of parking, she backed down the driveway to a secluded turnaround point. Some sixth sense warned her to use every precaution. The very stillness of the stables made her abandon her plans to try and bluff her way in. The attempted hit and run, the knife in her bed—someone knew who she was, and that someone might just call her bluff. She parked and got out, standing for a moment in anticipation of a challenge. Backing off a few steps, she was relieved to see the car was well hidden. Anyone coming down the driveway wouldn't see it, unless they knew to look there.

Darting from cover to cover, she approached the house. The continuing quiet made her uneasy. If Private Stock had been at this barn, it was a sure bet that the trailer disappearing down the dirt road had contained her. With a sinking feeling, Dawn edged past the house. The place was too quiet. The pounding of her heart told her that Luke was in serious trouble. If he weren't, he would have met her at the road. Glancing over her shoulder, she slipped toward the barn.

The first door opened onto a feed room, a small enclosure that contained several bales of hay, some sweet feed, ropes, empty sacks and odds and ends. There was no sign of a disturbance, no indication that Luke had been there. She closed the door and moved on.

The first stall was empty, but the shavings were dirty, as if a horse had recently been there.

Something rattled at the end of the barn, and Dawn pressed herself into the stall. Somewhere nearby was the sound of horse's hooves. Though she strained her ears, she couldn't tell which direction they came from. There was another sound, too, an eerie, muffled sound. Pressed against the rough wood of the stall, she could feel her heart beating.

"He had to have someone with him." The man's voice was clipped, very different from the Arkansas accents she'd heard at the airport. Much harsher than the Mississippi drawl her ear was used to. And the accent was laid on a foundation of ruthlessness.

"I checked the road. No cars were parked there."

The second voice was slower. Just as ruthless sounding, but not as quick. Dawn could tell this was a man who took orders, instead of giving them. Where was Luke?

The soft moan came again from somewhere down the barn. The acoustics were so poor that she couldn't be certain if there was another row of stalls behind her, or if the barn was a single line.

"When he comes to, find out what he knows and then get rid of him."

"But the boss said not to stir things up any more. He said if we started losing people again that the feds might get too curious. He said..."

"Don't tell me what *he* said, dummy. I heard him. I also know that he expects me to keep things running smooth. This yokel from the bluegrass and his girlfriend with the nose are gettin' in the way. That means they disappear. Got it?"

"Yeah!" The second man acquiesced without further struggle. "I'll find out what he knows and then get rid of him."

"Good boy, Ricky." The man's tone was derogatory. "Then call New Orleans and tell Manetti the filly's on the way."

"Anything else?" There was a tinge of bitter sarcasm in the question.

"Yeah! Do a good job and I'll see that you get a gold star on your chart for the day." The man laughed, and before Dawn could completely catch her breath, he walked by the stall door. In the bright sunlight he was only a tall, dark shadow with no distinguishing features. Then he was gone.

"Good boy, Ricky!" The voice sneered just down the barn from her. "One day, he'll get his. The boss is gonna find out what he's skimmin' off the top. Then he'll be sorry." There was a pause. "Hey!" Dawn heard the sound of a thud and a low, painful moan. "Still nappin' like a baby. Well, I'll be back."

Dawn cowered in the stall, hoping that the darkness hid her completely from any searching eyes. She was so afraid that she could hardly pull air into her lungs. If she wasn't mistaken, she'd just heard one man order another to kill Luke.

The second man passed, going slowly enough for her to discern longish black hair, a beaked nose and a portly, out of shape body. Only her eyes moved as she followed the man's progress until he was out of sight. Creeping forward in a crouch, she made it to the door and looked out. The yard was empty, but how long would it be before someone noticed the car in the copse of woods? It wasn't exactly camouflaged.

Fighting the fear that threatened to immobilize her, she crept out of the stall and down the length of the barn. At the very end another moan stopped her. She slid into the darkness, her eyes adjusting quickly. Against the far wall was a human body. A long, muscular man stirred slightly and moaned again.

"Luke!" Her breath rushed out as she stumbled over to him. A quick survey showed her his tied hands and feet. Her skillful fingers worked the knots in a matter of moments. She checked his head and found an enormous lump where he'd clearly been struck. There was dried blood on his shirt, and his face had been hit several times. Her hands searched his arms and legs, but found no broken bones.

"Concussion," she murmured to herself. "Maybe, maybe not, but there's no time to wait around. Luke!" She bent to his face. Her fingers gently stroked his cheek. She had to get him out of that place. She'd been able to suppress her feelings earlier, but looking at him, injured and helpless, she realized that a strong tie had been formed between them. She cared what happened to Luke, and not just as a partner in the search for a horse. What she had to do was summon all of her clearheadedness and figure a way out for them. Luke didn't need her emotions now, he needed her common sense. "Luke, we've got to get out of here," she whispered, forcing her voice to be firm but calm. "Luke, you've got to wake up. Come on, Luke."

He heard her calling as if from a long distance away. Somehow he struggled from beneath the hundreds of blankets that pressed him down, down, down. He fought to answer her, because he could hear something urgent, frightened in her voice. He also heard a deeper, stronger emotion. She was calling him back to her.

"Thank goodness." She smiled as his eyelids opened. "We've got to get out of here. These guys have plans for you tonight, and it isn't the kind of invitation you want to accept." She put one of his arms around her shoulders and started to pull him to his feet.

Luke shook his head to clear his vision and rose. Every muscle in his body hurt. "I found the filly," he said, his voice still thick. "She's here."

Dawn helped him to the stall door, giving the yard a quick look. "We can sneak into the woods and then cut down to the car. I sort of hid it down the driveway."

"I found the filly." Luke was persistent. "We just can't walk off and leave her."

"We'll come back. With the law. Luke, those men will kill us if they catch us here. Believe it."

Her tone was not to be argued with, and as he came more to his senses, he recalled the vicious blow to his head, then needless slugs he'd been given when he was tied up and helpless. The guys at Oakdale weren't exactly the type of playmates he liked. If Dawn hadn't come back for him, he'd have been dead in a matter of hours. He looked at her, feeling the tension that crept through her body. She was frightened, and for good reason, but that hadn't kept her from coming back for him. She was steadfast. He'd known it earlier, had been drawn to that quality. Now she'd saved his life.

"I know you're shaky, but we've got to get out of here," she said as she moved away from him. "I feel like any moment they'll be back to finish you off."

Peeking around the door again, Dawn drew back. The second man, Ricky, was entering the feed room. If they tried to run south to the car, he'd have a perfect view of them.

Hiding in the stall was no alternative. Without a weapon, they couldn't wait for him to come and kill them.

"Let's run to the woods in back of the barn," she suggested quickly. "We can make a bigger circle back to the car. It's the only way."

Nodding, Luke checked the yard, then gave the signal to run. Together they scooted around the end of the barn, slipped through the barbed wire fence that marked the limits of a mangy-looking pasture, and cut across open ground to the woods.

Stepping into the shadows provided by the trees, Dawn at last took a breath. Her lungs were on fire, as if she'd been forced under water for half an hour. Luke leaned against a tree, his face gray. A new trickle of blood had started by his eye, where he'd been hit.

"We've got to get you to a doctor," Dawn said, her hand automatically reaching up to check the wound. "You could stand a stitch or two, or you're going to have a nasty scar."

"Great," he said. "Let's worry about surviving first, scars later." He grinned.

A sudden crash in the woods next to them made Dawn jump. Luke turned, his hands up for a fight.

A pair of large, brown eyes confronted them, then a brown nose pushed through the trees.

"It's a horse," Luke said, relief making him light-headed. "I almost slugged a horse."

Dawn couldn't take her eyes off the horse. The broad, intelligent forehead was marked by a white design shaped exactly like the Russian hammer and sickle. The black mane was long and uncombed, and the hide was dirty, unbrushed and bleached from long hours in the sun.

"Luke?" Even to herself she sounded fuzzy. "Do you remember a match race seven years ago between a filly and a stallion?"

"Not really. I'm not much of a racing fan," he said. He was watching her, seeing the sharp focus of her eyes on the strange horse. He looked at the animal again. The mare had an excellent conformation, good shoulders, a good chest, wise and intelligent eyes.

"It was a grudge race between the owners, just before the Derby. The mare was rated to win. It was a big stakes race, the two horses, a little excitement to whet the appetite for the Triple Crown run." Dawn talked softly, nonstop, as if she were reciting a lesson in school.

"I'm getting a vague memory," Luke said. "There was a tragedy. Something awful happened, didn't it?"

"Keep thinking."

"I will—" he touched her shoulder "—but maybe we should do some of this thinking a little farther down the road."

"No." Dawn walked up to the mare and stroked her velvety muzzle. "The mare was Russian Roulette. A big, athletic filly. Coming down the homestretch she broke her leg and had to be destroyed."

"That's right." Luke motioned toward the barn. "Any minute now they're going to find me gone. Then all hell is going to break loose. I appreciate your history of racing, but another time, Dawn."

"Luke—" Dawn grabbed his elbow "—this horse is Russian Roulette. And if I'm not mistaken, she's Private Stock's mother."

It took a few seconds for the full impact of her words to hit Luke. Then he reached out and touched the mare, as if he wanted to make sure she was real.

"She was destroyed. I remember the owners collected about ten million in insurance." He probed deeper for the memory. "It was a nightmare. She fell on the track. They sent out the medics and tried to set her leg, but coming out of the anesthesia she struggled, and they had to destroy her.''

"So everyone thought.'' Dawn bent to examine the mare's leg. There were several scars on the right front—exactly the type of scars that might result from surgery to reset a bone.

"Is it her?''

"I'm positive. Apparently the leg healed, and the rumor that she was destroyed was a lie. They killed another horse, collected the insurance, and they've been breeding her to produce racing babies.'' Dawn's voice hardened. "A stolen stallion, a mare who's supposed to be dead! This is a real racket!''

"And the men who would concoct such a scheme would surely kill either of us without a second thought. Let's get moving.'' Luke physically propelled her toward the woods. "We don't have time to waste, Dawn. They will kill us!''

As they ducked through the trees, the mare followed them. Dawn cast a look over her shoulder and saw her ribs, the poor condition of her coat. She fought back tears.

"That horse was the top of the line, Luke. She was something, and look how they treat her! They don't even feed her when she isn't pregnant!''

"We'll worry about this later. We'll rescue her, just as soon as we get to the authorities.''

They came to a gate and Luke jumped over, not bothering with the lock. Turning back, he offered her his hand.

Dawn stopped. The mare nuzzled her back, whispering a soft whinny against her neck.

"Come on!'' Luke urged her.

"I can't!'' Dawn turned from the horse to him. Her brown eyes were large and anxious. "Luke, I can't walk off and leave this horse. Look at her. They may move her before we can get help. We'd never find her then.''

"You have to leave her!" Luke reached out, encouraging her with his hands. "Dawn, there's nothing we can do right now. We'll get the police and come back."

"No." She shook her head slowly. "I can't." She put a hand into her pocket and drew out the key to the car. Handing it to him, she squeezed his hand. "Go and get help."

"What are you going to do? Wait around and try and talk them out of killing you?"

"Nope." She worked the latch on the gate, pushed it open, then grabbed the mare's mane and swung up on her back with the grace of a dancer. "I'm going to ride her through the woods. I don't think there's any way they'll ever be able to follow me."

"And do what?"

"Wait for you to get a horse trailer and pick me up on the road. Remember that bridge about twenty miles from here? It went over a little creek. We'll hide down in that gully until I hear you whistling. Something nice. Say, 'Run for the Roses.'"

"You're a crazy woman." Luke finally allowed a smile to touch his face. "They could kill you, you know."

"They will kill this horse, and you know it. If they can't move her quick enough, they'll kill her."

He nodded. "Give me three hours."

"We should be there by then," she agreed, "barring any fences we can't get through."

"I don't think there's a fence made that could contain you." He patted her leg. "You'd risk your life for that horse."

"Isn't that what we're both doing here, anyway?"

The question was left unanswered as a shout came from the woods behind them.

"They've found out you're gone," Dawn whispered, eyes widening.

"Get going!" He slapped her leg this time and stepped aside as the mare obediently trotted through the gate. Luke took an extra moment to refasten it, hoping that the men wouldn't think to look for the mare for a long, long time.

"Check the road!" The man's voice echoed eerily through the woods. "Don't hesitate to shoot him, or the woman."

Luke remembered that voice, the voice of the man who'd taken such pleasure in hitting him. He started through the woods at a run, intending to make it to the car before one of them found it. It was his only hope, and Dawn's only chance.

Chapter Five

The metallic bronze color of the car was hard to see among the trees. Luke spotted it, then worked his way in a circle around it to make certain a trap hadn't been set. At last he ran toward it, swung in behind the wheel and cranked the engine. Dawn had wisely parked so that he didn't have to turn around, and he didn't waste a second looking over his shoulder. The road was rutted, but he kept his foot firmly on the gas pedal as he lurched forward.

His worst fears were realized when he saw Ricky standing in the road. A deadly-looking, black pistol was pointed at the car. Luke never wavered. He hit the accelerator as hard as he could and aimed straight ahead.

When the windshield shattered, he instinctively ducked to the left, pressing his face against the cool window. He gripped the wheel and kept going. Through the cracks and lines of the shattered glass he saw Ricky, the gun leveled for another shot.

A front tire struck a deep hole and the car rocked, then jerked to the left. The second shot penetrated the car somewhere at the front.

Luke was almost at the road. Another few yards and he would have to maneuver a hard left. Ricky still stood in front of him, ready to shoot again.

Pressing himself against the door, Luke sought a clear field of vision through the broken glass. In the corner of one eye he saw the other man crashing through the woods, angling so that he could cut Luke off. Luke slumped behind the wheel and pressed harder on the accelerator. Now he saw Ricky's face in the shattered glass as if in a nightmare, heard his surprised cry as the car rushed at him. There was no choice. Luke knew if he stopped or slowed, they'd kill him. He couldn't afford to use the brake.

At the last moment, Ricky flung himself out of the car's path. Luke watched as the stout-bodied man reeled into an embankment. He struck with such force that the gun was knocked from his hand. Trying to regain his balance, Ricky stumbled backward and rolled into the ditch.

Calling on every ounce of power he had, Luke turned the wheel and sent the car into a treacherous slide in the loose sand. All control was gone as he felt the car buck and jump across the ruts. The bank on the far side of the road seemed to rush at him, and he braced for the impact. In a final, desperate move he jerked the wheel to the right. The car came out of the rutted track sideways, its nose pointed toward the highway.

Another gunshot blasted the back passenger window. Luke ducked as low as he could behind the dash and drove for his life.

A final round of gunshots followed him, and just before the rear window rained down into the back seat, he saw Ricky and the other man, both standing in the road, weapons spitting bullets.

Any elation he felt in escaping was quickly overshadowed by worry about Dawn. Luke scanned the woods, knowing that she was deep within them. She was a savvy lady with plenty of smarts about woods and directions, but the men pursuing them were completely ruthless.

He quickly examined the gauges in the car. Somehow the bullets had missed everything vital. Or at least it looked that way for the moment. Luke headed for town, time ticking away in his head as he turned onto the asphalt and drove as fast as he could.

SHE HADN'T FIGURED on the mosquitoes. The villainous insects hummed about her, latching onto unguarded flesh with pinching bites. The resulting itch made her slap at her arms and face.

The mare grazed placidly on the side of the stream. Though the grass was wild, it was clearly still better than anything she'd had to eat for a long time. Dawn felt a wave of anger touch her as she thought about the men who'd neglected to care for the animal. She wanted ten minutes alone with them before the police carted them off. Ten minutes.

"Roulette!" She whistled softly and the mare lifted her head. She whinnied, then returned to the grass. Dawn kicked off her shoes and edged down to the sandy-bottomed creek. Looking around, she felt completely safe. There was no path leading to this small, secluded pool, which meant it wasn't a popular swimming hole. The creek made a sharp bend, and in the curve of the bank the water ran slowly and looked inviting.

"What the heck," she mumbled as she slipped out of her jeans and shirt and walked into the water. The first touch was icy cold, and then she fell forward, letting the water completely cover her.

When she came up, water running from her thick, black hair into her eyes, she wiped it away and looked at the horse. Roulette was watching her with a wide, knowing look. Then the horse approached the water and gracefully waded in. She stopped at knee level and drank.

"We'll get you out of this mess. I promise." Dawn reimmersed herself, swimming the length of the pool several times before returning to the bank. An old tree root provided a perfect seat as she allowed the sun to dry her. It was only March, actually too cool for swimming, she realized, as a chill touched her. The ripple of gooseflesh had also coincided with thoughts of Luke. Had he made it? She couldn't even allow herself to think that he hadn't. He was smart, strong. He had made it, and he would be waiting for her at the bridge. She calculated she was about five miles upstream.

Her body was dry, though her hair was still wet and heavy as she pulled her clothes back on. She noticed the cuts, scrapes and bruises. It looked as if she'd been used for the puck in a hockey game. Those guys had a lot to answer for. In her mind she'd already connected her near brushes with death with the men who'd beaten Luke and mistreated Roulette. And they still had Private Stock! But not for long, she silently vowed as she buttoned her shirt. She'd never rest until she found both the filly, and Speed Dancer. She felt a rush of anxiety. There was no telling what they'd done with the stallion.

She called softly and the mare came to her. Dawn noticed the slight limp as she walked. It would be undetectable to an untrained eye, but it was there. Roulette had ended her budding career in a tragedy on the track. Dawn bent to examine the old wound again. Had someone deliberately weakened her leg? That disgusting thought made her reach up to stroke the mare's neck. "They'll wish they'd never heard of you," she whispered as her fingers worked to untangle the mane. "They'll wish they'd never heard of either of us."

Since the trees grew thickly, Dawn walked, letting the mare follow her. She could clearly hear the sound of traffic on the bridge, and knew she wasn't too far from the road. She checked her watch. According to Luke's time schedule, she had about half an hour to kill. She wondered where he'd found a trailer to rent. When she could see the bridge through a thicket of trees, she stopped and waited.

She spent the time working on Roulette's tangled mane and tail. She found a sharp stick and cleaned the horse's feet, examining each hoof for cuts, bruises or disease.

Whenever a car passed, she looked up, watching the flash of metal as it crossed the bridge. She was watching when a white truck and trailer began to slow.

"That's our ride, girl." She grabbed Roulette's halter and began to guide her up the steep bank. She'd never been so glad to see anyone in her life. She needed a dose of Luke's humor, a dollop of his warm reassurance. She needed to see him, safe and sound. She hustled the mare up the last few feet.

"You made it!" Luke was out of the truck and at her side. His hug was spontaneous, hungry, as he pressed her against his chest for a long moment. "I've been worried to death." His hands on her shoulders were lightly caressing, as if he couldn't get enough of the feel of her. "The whole time I was gone, I was afraid they'd caught you, that maybe they'd hurt you." He brushed her damp hair from her cheek and then brushed a kiss onto her forehead. "Thank goodness you're safe."

"I've had a bad moment about you, too," she admitted. She started to say more, but held back. They needed time to sort through things, before any more feelings were verbalized. "Nice rig." She nodded to the truck and trailer. "Rental?"

Luke glanced at the mare. "Not exactly. Let's get her loaded and on the road. I've been thinking where we could take her, and I have a friend in Arizona. They'd never think to look for her there." He didn't add that he also hoped to leave Dawn in the relative safety of a distant state.

"Arizona!" Dawn said the word as if she'd never heard it before. "I was thinking of taking her back to Dancing Water."

"And put your friend's farm in jeopardy? They know us, Dawn. The ranch where you work, or mine, would be the first places they looked." A shadow covered his face for a moment. "And believe me, I have plenty to worry about without that."

Dawn watched him closely for a moment. There was something, an edge in his voice that made her pause. For no apparent reason he'd closed himself up to her. "There's something I have to tell you. I think they're taking the filly to New Orleans. I heard the tall, thin guy tell Ricky to call Manetti and tell him she was on the way."

"New Orleans." Luke repeated the words thoughtfully. "If that's the case, we shouldn't be heading in the opposite direction."

"My thoughts exactly. I know some farms around New Orleans, very secluded places. My friends would take Roulette and keep their mouths shut."

"Okay," he assented. "That's where we'll go. You have to tell these people how dangerous it is to accept Roulette. Those men will be hunting for her." He hated to give up on putting Dawn in a safe place, but he knew her well enough now to realize that she'd probably never accept that plan, anyway.

"I know," Dawn agreed. "Don't I know."

She unlocked the trailer door, checked the interior and found a small serving of sweet feed and a flake of alicia Bermuda hay already in the feeding compartment.

"The horse looked hungry," Luke explained sheepishly. "I didn't get much feed. I doubt she'd had grain in a while."

"You really are something." She touched his cheek softly. "Sitting on the tree root at an old creek, I wondered for just a moment if you'd really come back for us. You could have kept going, unburdened by me and a stolen horse.''

"When I was in trouble, you came back for me." He captured her hand and pressed the palm against his cheek. "You risked your life for me."

Standing beside the still country road with the murmur of the creek beside them, Dawn felt eternity shift. She held Luke's gaze. There was nothing shadowed in his eyes as he looked at her. He drew her like no other man. There were layers and layers to Luke O'Neil, and she wanted to unwrap them slowly, to find the core of him. "I have to be very careful," she said, unaware that she'd spoken aloud until she saw him smile.

"You and me both," he said, squeezing her hand before he realized it.

Before anything else could be said, she led the mare to the trailer. Roulette stepped in as if she knew she was being rescued.

"At least she loads," Luke remarked.

"Just watch me," Dawn answered as she fastened the trailer door and then ran around to the passenger side and jumped into the truck. "I load, too, and I'm ready to leave this state behind."

They didn't stop for the first fifty miles, then Dawn insisted that they buy medical supplies and burgers. At a sign that indicated a lake and rest area, she urged Luke to pull off the highway.

"I want to clean that cut on your cheek," she told him. "We should have had it stitched, and the last thing we need is an infection."

In a shady grove of trees they pulled over. Dawn made quick work of his cuts and scrapes, applying peroxide, antibiotics and bandages with cool skill. "It's going to scar," she told him as she put a butterfly closure on his cheek. "It'll add a little character.'' She grinned as she picked up the medicine and put it back into the cab of the truck.

"We need to stop at a telephone.'' Luke scanned the grove of trees, obviously ill at ease.

"I don't think we're being followed,'' Dawn teased him. "It'll take them some time to check all the trailer rentals.''

"It won't do them any good.''

She looked up from her hamburger and saw the false innocence in his eyes. "What are you saying?''

"I didn't rent the trailer. We're going to have to stay off the interstate.''

"You stole the truck and trailer?'' She almost choked.

"Think about it, Dawn. I left the rental car and took the truck. If I'd had to explain bullet holes in the car and all the other damage, I'd still be filling out forms at the airport. Besides, they'd never have rented me anything else. I'd probably be in jail. The simplest thing to do was take the truck and trailer. We'll leave it as soon as we can, safe and sound.'' He gave her a level look. "Besides, you've already stolen a horse. That's a hanging offense.''

Dawn sipped her Coke slowly, all the time watching him. "I never know what to expect from you. Truck thief?'' Slowly she shook her head.

"You were counting on me to come back for you,'' he reminded her with perfect logic. "Besides, my insurance company will pay in full for an inconvenience. And the rental car took a few bullets.'' He didn't give her time to comment. "My insurance will cover that, too. Just keep thinking, 'Where would I be now if Luke had gotten stuck dealing with a rental agency about a shot-up car?' ''

That was a good question, one Dawn didn't want to contemplate. "Thanks, Luke.'' She touched his shoulder and her hand lingered on the solid muscle. "I owe you a lot.''

The warmth of her fingers on his skin was tantalizing. He reached up and covered her hand with his own, aware of the contrasts—the softness of her skin, and the calluses. She was like that, tough as nails one minute and soft and vulnerable the next.

"We owe each other," he said, his gaze holding hers. "You risked your life to save me. I know what it must have cost you to watch that horse trailer disappearing, and still you turned around and came back for me."

"I had to be certain you weren't hurt."

"I would have been dead." His other hand reached up to brush the hair from her forehead. A long, unruly lock had dropped across one eye. "Those men would have killed me."

Dawn felt as if she'd stepped up to a blazing fire. From the touch of his hand on her cheek warmth spread throughout her body. She was drawn to him, to his kindness and integrity. He was a striking man, whose controlled power was compelling. Sensations he'd aroused near the creek returned, intensified. She needed to step back from the flames.

"I still haven't figured out why someone sent us that videotape of Private Stock. Have you?" She shifted slightly and he withdrew his hand. The loss of his touch was like a sudden chill.

He shook his head. "Nope. I'm still stuck with the same conclusion. Someone wants us to chase this filly. And another someone wants to kill us for it. I can only assume it's two separate factions."

"Meaning?"

"That's as far as I've gotten." His face took on a rueful look. "Even as a kid I hated crossword puzzles, treasure hunts, clues hidden around. I've always had too much to do to play games." The feelings he had for Dawn weren't part of any game, though; they were serious. But he had to wait until he had been completely honest with her.

"You grew up around horses, didn't you?"

He nodded. "At least I grew up near horses. I wanted to ride more than anything, but my folks didn't have the resources to give me a horse."

"But you do ride?" She dropped her gaze to his legs, the lean muscles. She'd also watched him with Roulette. He knew what he was doing with a horse.

"Yes, I do now. As a kid I cleaned a lot of stalls. The only horses I got to ride were the ones no one else wanted."

"Stable brat?" she guessed. One of the kids who worked at a large stable and rode before sunrise or after dark. Horse-crazy kids who sacrificed everything to ride.

"Stable brat with a dream." He laughed, but it wasn't the soft, mellow laughter she'd grown to enjoy.

"And?"

"I almost made it, but the horse I trained . . . had some difficulty." The pause was four heartbeats. "Blue Jack won the trials that year, then he went lame."

"That's too bad."

"That's life." He smiled, and all of the tension was gone. "It was a long time ago. I don't know how I got off into those dregs of personal history."

"I asked." She gathered up the litter and put it into a trash can by a tree. "Do you still jump?"

"Whenever I can. Mostly I train." He didn't mind talking about the past, but the present was slightly uncomfortable. There were things Dawn didn't know. Things he wasn't yet prepared to tell her. He closed the subject by walking around the truck and getting in. "Let's hit the road. It's going to be a good ten-hour drive."

"I'll spell you in a few hours."

The engine roared to life and Dawn couldn't suppress her grin. "You did a bang-up job on stealing a truck. This one runs like it's brand-new."

"Only fifteen thousand miles," he answered, laughing at her startled expression. "Well, the jail term is just as long for an old truck as a new one."

"Good point." She settled down in the seat, watching the countryside flash by the window. Dusk was settling over the rolling hills with all the mauve hues of spring. When she stopped to think of everything that had happened, she couldn't believe it had been only a single day since they'd left Tampa, two days since she'd left the peace and security of Dancing Water Ranch.

In that short time, the man beside her had become a trusted friend. She smiled to herself as she thought of them, two strangers driving down a back road, in a stolen truck and trailer, with a stolen horse that was supposed to be dead.

In all her twenty-nine years, she'd never been involved in any felonious behavior. Now she was a regular Ma Barker. Her partner in crime was an unexpected plus, too! Her smile grew warmer as she leaned against the window and shut her eyes. She didn't have to look at Luke to see his lean jaw, the depth of his blue eyes or the windblown hair that gave him a rakish look.

In the fading pink tones of the twilight, Luke couldn't resist gazing at her. At rest, her features gave her the guileless air of a sleeping child. He was captivated by the high cheekbones that created cool hollows on her face. Her dark lashes were thick as they fanned across her smooth skin. At rest, her mouth was soft, generous. He had to admit he was charmed by her smile. She was such an odd mixture of regal dignity and hellion, of determined will and capricious imp. When he'd told her the truck was stolen, she hadn't batted an eye. He could almost see the wheels of her mind spinning. The primary goal was to save the horse. The method was a matter of expedience. He smiled to himself as he watched the center line of the road slide beneath the wheels.

At Lake Village he woke her for food and let her take over the driving. They were near the Mississippi line.

"We'll make Covington before daybreak," Dawn said, stifling a yawn. They were at a small diner and she sipped the fresh coffee. "I can't wait to stop somewhere, take a hot bath and find a clean bed."

"Ditto." Luke cast several looks around the café. The place was empty. It was late, and the location was off the interstate route. It seemed safe to stop.

"How about some apple pie?" Luke asked the short-order cook.

"Fresh made," the man responded. "Be right with you." He paused as a pair of headlights shone through the windows. "Another customer."

Dawn waited for the car to stop. It took a moment for the siren on top to register, for the portly man in a black uniform to become real to her. She felt her spine jerk involuntarily.

"Stay calm," Luke whispered.

"Easy for you to say." She touched his hand, her fingers gliding over his rigid knuckles.

He loosened his grip and picked up a fork. "Are you going back to your ranch after we deliver Roulette?"

Dawn had considered the question, but had come up with no suitable answer. "I should. But I can't just abandon Private Stock. Especially not after seeing how they've treated Roulette. Luke, her accident may have been deliberate. Some people have been known to fracture a horse's leg. In the stress of the race, it snaps."

Only the tightening of his jaw gave away the anger he felt. He knew the dirty tricks in the horse world. It wasn't just racing, it was jumping, walking horses, western pleasure, timed events. Every aspect of the industry had criminals who stopped at nothing. Private Stock wasn't his horse or his problem, but he knew he was as involved as Dawn. Once he'd seen the filly run, had seen her heart and spirit, he could never leave her to a fate that might involve abuse.

Dawn watched the play of anger that touched his eyes and lips. She knew what he was thinking, felt what he felt. She reached across the table and touched his hand again. "We can't give up, can we?" The words were a bond.

"I suppose not." His gaze connected with hers and he felt the force of her will. They were so much alike. "We're headed for a rough time. I don't suppose those Manetti people are going to be any nicer than Ricky and his friend at Oakdale."

"No, I don't think they will. So we need to make a plan."

"You don't have to say it, but a better plan than my last one."

She chuckled softly. "That one nearly got you killed, and it scarred that handsome face." She stopped, her mouth open slightly. A flush touched her olive skin.

"I can take a few scars. It's your pretty hide I'm concerned about." He picked up her hand and squeezed it, the pressure sure and steady. They were staring at each other when the easy voice interrupted them.

"What kind of horse you hauling?"

Dawn broke away from Luke's absorbing gaze to face the state trooper. He stood at their table, a cup of coffee in one hand.

"Jumper," Dawn said quickly. "There's a big show in Atlanta."

"I thought maybe you were coming off the Hot Springs track. I see a lot of horses moving around during this season."

"I'm sorry to disappoint you. Racing isn't my sport." Luke picked up the check and stood, signaling Dawn with an eyebrow.

"Folks say there's a lot of money in racing." The trooper sipped his coffee.

"I've heard that," Luke agreed. "But that only applies to the winners. I've heard it can be very expensive."

"King of sports, right?" The patrolman laughed. "I've lost a few bets, I'll tell you. My wife and I always enjoyed the track. We haven't been in a while."

"We'd better get on our way." Luke went to the register and paid the check.

"Me, too. Maybe I'll come out and have a look at the jumper. I don't think I've ever seen one of those."

"They're not much different from any other horse," Luke said smoothly. "They like to go over fences, and they have the nerve to do it. Looking at one, though, I don't think you could tell what kind of horse it was."

"You'd be surprised what I can tell. My grandfather raised walking horses. He taught me to look at a horse, see the way they're put together. No matter what anyone says, there aren't two alike."

Dawn threw Luke a worried glance. She knew they had to do something quickly. It was just their luck to tie up with someone who might actually recognize Roulette.

Luke hesitated at the door of the café, Dawn at his side. The trooper was with them like glue. "Sweetheart, did you find a newspaper?"

For a moment Dawn didn't understand. "No, I didn't."

"But you were just saying how much you wanted one. There must be one here somewhere." He took her hand and squeezed it with a suddenness that made her spine straighten.

"Yes, that's right." Dawn smiled at the patrolman. "Where could I buy a daily newspaper? Sometimes we get so wrapped up in the horse business, we forget to keep up with what's happening in the rest of the world."

"Not much happening here," the trooper said. "There's a news rack just at the corner there." He pointed around the side of the building.

"It's a little dark around there." Dawn had just the right amount of worry in her voice.

"I'll be glad to walk with you." The officer gave Luke a curious look.

"You're too kind." Dawn lightly touched the trooper's arm as she led him away. "When my mother was a young girl, she ran away from home. This sheriff in Natchez found her and decided to give her the lesson of her life. . . ." Dawn talked a mile a minute.

Luke slipped away from them and walked rapidly to the truck. He could only hope that Dawn could distract the patrolman into forgetting about horses. He watched her walk, head turning up to the cop constantly. The smile spread over his face. Dawn was a very effective distraction.

He hurried into the cab and pulled the trailer around to the side of the building. Leaving the motor running, he got out and circled back to the patrol car. His luck held. The door was unlocked. With a quick motion he reached in and flipped on the siren. Before the first whoop was out, he was back in the truck.

Dawn and the patrolman came running, but the officer didn't stop at the horse trailer. He continued around the café. Luke threw open the passenger door and Dawn hurled herself into the seat, just as he started rolling away.

Chapter Six

There was no sign of blue lights in the rearview mirror, but Dawn didn't begin to feel relaxed at the wheel until they were well inside Louisiana. The trooper had been a friendly guy. Too friendly. She looked across the seat at Luke. He was awake but silent.

At Tallulah, Louisiana they picked up the interstate to Vicksburg and headed due south for Baton Rouge. Crossing the Mississippi River, Dawn slowed.

"My grandmother grew up on this river," she said. "Her home was farther south, but the Mississippi was very much a part of her life."

"Your family still there?" Luke shifted so that he could see her easier.

"No. My mother died when I was born, and my grandmother died twelve years ago." She lifted her right shoulder in an eloquent shrug. "That's the maternal side. My father remarried, and they live in Ohio." She smiled a slightly crooked smile. "He's a psychologist. I disappointed him a lot when I decided to make my career in the world of horses instead of academics."

"Everybody has to choose for themselves."

"I can see you aren't a parent," she said with a laugh. "That type of logic has no effect on daddies, or grandmothers. Grandma wanted me to become a lawyer, to fight for the land that was once her people's.''

"No interest?"

"Sure, an interest. But I realize that you can't go backward in time. You can't return to the 1800s and make right what happened then. Can you see the current landowners voluntarily giving land back to the Choctaws?"

Luke heard the underlying note of anger in her voice. "No. I think you're right. There would be no way to wrest back the land."

"I never wanted the courtroom, the suits, the tricks. I like the outdoors. Especially when you have a horse that works for you. That one horse that knows what you want and gives it to you before you even think to ask. You know what I mean?"

Luke knew. He knew exactly what she meant, and he knew which horse she referred to. His voice grew cool. "Isn't that as much a fancy as Indian reparation?"

The sudden shift in his tone confused her. In the darkness of the cab, she couldn't see his expression. "No. I don't think that's a fancy at all. In fact, if you ever knew Speed Dancer, you'd see. He was that kind of horse. At least for me. That's why he's so important to me."

"I'm sorry, Dawn." Luke didn't elaborate. Instead he slumped deeper into his seat and pretended to sleep.

Dawn pulled the trailer into Covington at 4:00 a.m. She was beat, exhausted and ready to stretch her legs. She'd traveled to Applegate Farms by sheer instinct. As she pulled into the driveway, a pack of dogs rushed out, barking loudly. Lights came on in the house and barn, and she saw her friend Orson Rinter pull on his second shoe as he came down the steps.

"Dawn!" He was shocked when he recognized her as she got out of the cab. "What's going on?"

"I need a big favor, Orson. A really big favor." She made the introductions with Luke, then quickly explained their plight. She skipped the details involving Speed Dancer. There'd be time to explain later, and Orson was such a good friend that he wouldn't insist on knowing everything.

"Russian Roulette." Orson whistled. "Alive! How'd you find her?"

"That's another long story. Will you keep her?"

"Does a cat have claws! Of course. But don't blame me if she gets in with my stallion. I'd like to see that filly Private Stock, too. She'd certainly be welcome in my stallion's paddock."

Dawn knew he was teasing her. Orson Rinter was not the kind of man who would pull any funny business. He'd been in the horse business for years, barely hanging on. There were many times when Dawn wondered how he made it. Still, he struggled along, producing quality horses and maintaining a reputation for being a good neighbor.

"Once you see Roulette, you'll think she needs some food, rest and light exercise, Orson. The last thing she needs is another foal." As she spoke, she backed the mare out of the trailer.

"You're right," Orson said grimly. "To the barn for a light feeding. A bath tomorrow and a romp in a pasture."

Impulsively Dawn hugged him and kissed his cheek. "You're the greatest." She turned to Luke. "I told you we could count on Orson."

"Keep the mare out of sight as much as possible," Luke said softly. "And if anyone asks about us, try to evade the question. I won't ask you to lie outright, but any time you can wrangle for us will give us a better chance of finding Private Stock."

"There are a million ways to answer a question," Orson said, hooking his fingers into his belt. "I prefer the obtuse. I'm afraid I have a very backward nature."

"What Orson is trying to tell you is that he's an artist when it comes to spreading bull." Dawn hugged her friend again. "We've got to get out of here and dump this trailer."

"What are you going to do?"

Dawn looked at Luke. When he didn't say anything, she answered. "We haven't really decided, but my first idea is to drive the truck and trailer into the French Quarter and leave it somewhere that will attract the cops. They'll get it back to Hot Springs, and we certainly haven't hurt it. Then Luke and I will be on foot. That may be an asset. If we need a car..."

"There's always my talented hands." Luke held out both hands and the three of them laughed.

"You have a real talent," Orson said, slapping Luke on the shoulder, "and excellent taste in women."

"I'm already up to my waist," Dawn groaned. "Let's go before we drown."

"Do you have any idea where to look?" Orson took the lead rope from Dawn's hand and gently stroked Roulette's neck.

"We have a name. Manetti. Mean anything to you?"

"Big breeder, lots of gambling and horses. Owns his own farm." Orson's forehead wrinkled and he failed to meet Dawn's gaze. "He's got money, and like most men with money, he's got a reputation for ruthlessness. Don't fool around with him, Dawn. Read the New Orleans newspaper. Every so often a body floats up in the Mississippi River."

"We'll be careful," Dawn promised as she gave Roulette one last pat. "Take care of this mare for me. I hate to leave her, but we'd better go."

Luke drove as they turned around and headed for the Crescent City. The miles clicked away in silence as they continued through the flatlands of Louisiana.

"They call New Orleans the town that care forgot," Dawn said softly as they sped into the darkness. She'd give a lot to be able to forget her cares, to be headed for New Orleans for a leisurely trip with the man beside her. "Whoever said that wasn't looking for horse thieves," she added dryly.

"I've heard it called the city of romance." Luke's gaze lingered on her, almost a touch.

"It is a romantic city. The streets seemed designed for adventure and love. Romance, history, so many things." She looked out the window. "Maybe on another trip there'll be time to explore the other aspects of New Orleans. This time all we have is a dangerous man's name and a dream of finding that filly."

"That's enough, Dawn. We also have each other, a partnership. When all of this is over, we'll have some time. Time together," he promised.

"Luke, why are you doing this? The filly doesn't mean that much to you, does she?"

"Let's just say that finding the answers to this means a lot to me." He took a deep breath. "And making things right for you, that's important to me, too."

Across the dark seat of the truck, Dawn reached out and touched his arm. "Why? Two days ago you didn't even know me."

"Two days ago I would have been willing to bet my bank account that I wouldn't be in New Orleans with a stolen vehicle and a crazy woman from Mississippi. Two days ago there were a lot of things I didn't know." He wanted to pull her to his side, but he didn't. "In two days, I've learned a lot about you, and about myself."

Dawn pulled her legs under her so that she could turn and face him. "If you could go back and undo it all, pick up the day the video arrived and just not get it in the mail, would you?"

Luke laughed, a rich sound that made her warm and happy. "I should say yes. That's the sensible answer. But I can't. This isn't my life. I'm not the kind of man to go running around the country, but I'm doing it. And I wouldn't change it. Because I wouldn't have met you."

"I wouldn't change it either, even though we're both lucky to be alive. Luke, I think maybe we've both lost our minds."

"There's a good chance of that. Now what do I do, once I get off this bridge?"

Dawn saw the first glimmer of the lengthy span that crossed Lake Pontchartrain. "Don't get in a rush, it's a real long bridge."

Luke was ready to abandon the trailer on the busy interstate before they finally arrived in the French Quarter. "Good grief, it's 5:00 a.m. This place is wide-awake and the traffic is frantic."

"New Orleans seldom sleeps. Sunday mornings, just a little." Dawn skillfully directed him through the streets until she signaled to a parking space on Esplanade. "This is the west boundary of the Quarter. This is a pretty good place to leave the truck." She patted the dash. "Let's find a place to sleep. I'm exhausted."

Luke lifted their suitcases from the back of the truck and was rewarded with an exclamation of wonder.

"You got our clothes!" Dawn did a mini-war dance on the sidewalk. "A clean shirt, clean socks! My toothbrush!" She circled Luke, leaping and jumping.

"I thought you were tired."

"A moment's exuberance," she said, slowing down to catch her breath. "Lead on."

He pointed across the street to a beveled glass door. There was a discreet sign, John Morrow's House.

Before Dawn could say a word, he had led her across the street and had talked the reluctant clerk into giving them a private suite. "Don't dare argue," he warned her as he took the heavy, brass key and opened the privacy fence that surrounded the apartment. "It's close, we're here and it's done."

Looking around at the lush plants, the private pool and the two-storied suite that they had rented, Dawn couldn't think of a single argument. When she stepped inside and saw the antiques, the rich and elegant decor, she sighed.

"We could have gotten a couple of rooms out by the track."

"We could have," he said, "but that might not have been to our best advantage."

"What are you talking about? We'll have to find a bus or something to go back and forth to the track. It's a matter of expedience."

"Think about it, Dawn. We have to find a man called Manetti, and then make him tell us where he's hiding a valuable horse. We already know this man may be involved in a major insurance scam with Roulette. What are we going to do, walk up to him and ask him politely to incriminate himself? We need a cover. We need to look affluent, wealthy, the kind of people who might put up big money on a running horse, even if her papers are forged."

"What are we going to do?" Dawn felt apprehension all the way to the soles of her feet.

"We're going to con them, just like they conned others."

"Somehow I don't like the sound of this." She dropped her suitcase by the sofa and slowly sank into the soft cushions. "Unfortunately, I'm too tired to do anything to stop you. I'm going to have a hot bath. You can make all the plans you want."

The bathroom was another surprise. Floor-to-ceiling bottle glass gave plenty of light to the tropical plants. The sunken Jacuzzi was large enough for two, a fact Dawn noticed as she stepped into it. The warm water soothed the

tension from her tired body as she sank lower and lower. But
instead of succumbing to the temptation to sleep, her
thoughts turned to Luke. A lazy smile drifted across her
face. Her first impression of him had been of a man to be
reckoned with. That hadn't changed. But as she'd gotten to
know him better, she had grown aware of a gentler side.
When he'd stolen the truck and trailer, he'd taken the time
to steal feed and hay for Roulette, as well. That was the action of a compassionate man, a man who loved horses.

A knock on the door brought her out of her reverie.

"Did you drown?" The boldly asked question was un-
dercut with humor.

"You should know never to harass a lady in her bath,"
she shot back, sinking so low that her chin rested on the
water. One shapely leg rose, and she turned on the faucet
with her foot. A stream of hot water jetted into the nearly
full tub.

"Ten minutes, Miss Amphibian. Then I'm coming in to
take my turn."

Dawn cast a glance at the door and saw that the latch remained unturned. She wasn't worried. He would never,
never do such a thing. Or would he?

Ten minutes later she stepped out of the tub and began
drying herself off. One thing she'd learned about Luke
O'Neil was never to underestimate what he might and might
not do. She pulled on clean clothes and sauntered out of the
bath. Luke was nowhere to be found. She searched the two
bedrooms, then the kitchen and the pool area. Returning to
the den, she finally saw him, sacked out on the sofa. He was
so sound asleep that she didn't have the heart to wake him.
Instead she found a blanket in the bedroom and covered
him.

SUNLIGHT WAS COMING IN through the louvered blinds,
casting soft shadows in the sheers that floated on a light

breeze. Dawn stretched beneath the cool sheets and snuggled deeper. It was still daylight. She'd been asleep only ten minutes, it seemed.

"Hey, sleepyhead, how about some coffee?"

The deep, masculine voice pulled her from the last remnants of sleep. She sat up, then pulled the sheet higher as she saw Luke standing at the foot of the beautiful, old brass bed.

"Coffee?" he repeated, holding the cup toward her.

She nodded, sitting up, her gaze never leaving his face. She saw his swift glance take in her shape beneath the sheet. It made her intensely aware of her nude state. As her fingers wrapped around the mug, their hands met. The touch was electric. Never relinquishing the cup, he slowly sat down on the edge of the bed, giving her time to balance the cup before he released it. In a spontaneous move he picked up a strand of her hair. The fine, black curl had fallen over her shoulder as she slept.

"One of the first things I noticed about you was your hair. You had it all tucked up in a bun under that hat, and I wondered what it would look like, down like this."

He let his fingers brush through it, ordering the disarray on her pillow. "It's lovely hair." He picked up another strand and let it fall through his fingers, black silk against the bronzed silk of her skin.

She cleared her throat to answer, but could think of no reply. Instead, she sipped the coffee. "This is wonderful, strong and full of chicory." She wanted him to touch her, but she was hesitant. They were so new to each other. Time had been compressed for them, hurrying them forward in their search and in their feelings. She found a shaky smile for him. "My grandmother used to say that chicory was good for men."

"So that's what it is," he said, laughing. "This stuff is strong enough to take the enamel off your teeth."

"Traditional New Orleans coffee. It's delicious with hot milk and *beignets*." She looked for the clock. "What time is it?"

"Early evening. I'm sorry to wake you, but we need to plan. I woke up about three and waited. We need to be at the track tonight."

She threw a hand over her forehead in a mock-dramatic gesture. "Gambling tonight! I just don't know—I feel faint!"

While her eyes were still closed, he removed the coffee cup, bent down and brushed his lips across hers. He'd wanted to kiss her for a long time, but he'd been able to hold himself in check so far. Now, still a little sleepy and all tucked beneath the covers, she was irresistible. Her lips were as soft as he'd anticipated. The scent of her skin was sleepy and mingled with the clean smell of soap. He wanted to kiss her deeply, to draw her out of the warmth of the bed and into his arms. Instead, he drew back. It was her decision as much as his.

Dawn froze. She hadn't expected the kiss, but knew she didn't want it to stop there. Lowering her arm, she looked at him. Her hand reached out, touching his face, brushing across his freshly shaven cheek and lingering at the cut near his eye. With the slightest pressure of her fingers she drew him down to her for a real kiss.

His arms slid beneath her, capturing her slender body in a powerful embrace. He'd never imagined she would feel so good. Her fingers moved through his hair, sending an army of sensations down his scalp. Every movement she made, he felt in the muscles of her bare back.

She kissed him, slowly testing the erratic pulse of sensations he created in her. He kissed with finely controlled passion, as if at any moment he might devour her. She yielded to his careful exploration, giving and then taking. The kiss was long, unhurried, a delicate exploration that grew to almost unbearable desire. Dawn felt the room slipping away. The only things around her were Luke, his arms, his kiss. Time disappeared in the magic of their feelings.

Luke had never held a woman so vitally alive. He'd caught her on the fringes of sleep, an unfair advantage that every masculine instinct urged him to press. Drawing back from her was like leaving the warmth of a wonderful fire for a plunge into an icy river, but he knew he had to do it.

Gently he broke the embrace and sat up. His hand brushed another strand of hair back from her cheek. "You've taken me by surprise."

Her smile was slow, easy. "I could say the same. The first time I met you, I thought you were going to kill me. Little did I know. . . ."

His lips brushed hers again, a promise deliberately left unfulfilled. "While you were asleep, I did some scouting around. There're some shops at the other side of the Quarter. We'd better hustle if we're going to make it."

"Make what? What are you talking about?" Her snooze had left her way behind him.

"I did a little work, and there is a Louis Manetti who has a regular seat at the track. He likes to party, and he isn't too careful of the company he keeps."

"So?"

"The company he's keeping tonight is yours."

She started to sit up, remembered her nude state beneath the sheet and sank back onto the pillow. "How did you arrange this?"

"With a few phone calls. Said you were in town with some cash to invest. Lots of innuendo and no fact. I mentioned a business deal that paid high, high dividends; lots of emphasis on that word. I made it clear you were looking for some racing action. What do you think?"

Dawn's frown said it all. "I don't think I'm going to be very good at playing the role of wealthy American."

"Well, just talk horses. Your knowledge of racing is what I'm banking on. Manetti has a weakness for horses. But he has an even greater weakness for winning, no matter what the means. I want him to want your expertise. My scheme is to make him need you."

"Me? Wouldn't it be simpler to sneak around the track and ask a few questions?"

"I don't have the rest of my life, Dawn. I'm in the middle of my breeding season."

"I didn't know you had a stud." She looked at him. "You never mentioned it."

"Well, I'm mentioning it now. And I need to get home. I figure you can get next to Manetti and find out more than any other way."

"You're right. And I suppose I will have to buy some clothes."

He stood up, but the good humor was missing from his face as he looked down at her. "If there were any other way..."

"We'll try it, Luke. That's all we can do. I can hold my own on the topic of racehorses. It's just that if things should shift, I don't know what I'd do. I'm not exactly an expert on hidden bank accounts and the like."

"You're a trainer from Mississippi who made a few good hits. I implied that you had a special gift, an ability to judge."

"And you?"

"I'll be down at the track, working on it from that angle."

She sighed. "This whole idea is so full of holes, we'll probably sink in the first ten minutes, but he can't exactly shoot us at a public track."

Luke went to the door. "I'll let you get dressed, and then we'll head to the shops."

"Now what exactly should a conniving horse trainer who has a weakness for gambling wear?" Dawn asked herself.

The solution was a tailored, coral silk pantsuit. While she made her selection, Luke found a shop that rented jewelry. With their purchases they hurried back to the suite and dressed.

"I feel silly going to all this trouble to go to a racetrack," Dawn said, nervously slipping a dangling diamond into her ear. "I'd rather be at the paddock with you."

"I'd rather have you there." He appraised the effect of the pantsuit with a look that was like a warm touch.

"Well, we're off."

"I had a rental agency send a car." He escorted her out of the apartment, across the courtyard and out the front door. The gleaming black, Mercedes roadster made her pause.

"It's the life-style of the rich and unfamous," he said with a laugh, holding the door for her. "I'll keep the top up."

Dawn bent to straighten the heel of her shoe. Just above her head something whished by, then struck a wall with a high-speed impact. Her eyes registered the bullet hole before her brain could work.

Luke heard the soft thud of the silencer, and when the bullet struck the building only inches from Dawn's head, he knew what it was. With a shove he pushed her into the front seat, ran around and got behind the wheel. He jerked the car into the flow of traffic with a suddenness that caused Dawn to fall across him. His hand held her there as he sent the car racing down the dark streets.

He hadn't seen the assailant. The attack was as unexpected and nearly as deadly as the ones that had preceded it. Had one of the men from Hot Springs tailed them? It seemed impossible.

Helping Dawn to a sitting position, he felt a surge of protective anger. "If Manetti's on to us, this could be more than dangerous, it could be deadly."

"If Manetti were on to us, he'd have us quietly driven upriver and sunk, as Orson mentioned." Dawn got her bearings and began to direct Luke through the traffic to Jefferson Downs track. "Besides, where can I go that's safe? They find us wherever we are. It's as if someone watched us and kept a detailed report."

Luke felt his stomach knot. She was right. Where could she go? They'd followed her to Tampa, to Hot Springs, now to New Orleans. Going home to Mississippi wouldn't make her safe, especially now the ante was upped with Roulette. There was no turning back.

"You could come home with me, to Kentucky."

Dawn felt tears sting her eyelids. Luke's offer was so generous, so spontaneous. "Thanks, but that wouldn't solve anything. We don't have Private Stock. We do have Roulette, and I'm not a step closer to finding Speed Dancer. All of these horses! What a mess."

"And one incredible woman." Luke's hand caressed her shoulders. "Let's give it another day. If we don't turn anything up, then we should consider going to Kentucky. We can call the Racing Commission and let them handle the whole mess."

"If we do that, we'll never find that filly." Dawn's voice was filled with worry. "They might even kill her if she gets too hot."

"They might kill us all."

Chapter Seven

Louis Manetti was not what Dawn expected. To be sure, he had the tall, dark good looks of the playboy he was reputed to be. In his expensive suit he cut an elegant figure. His "private" seats were indeed private, in a small club room complete with his own waiters and three other men who stood at the bar watching television screens and the track.

"Ms. Markey." The tuxedoed waiter with a noticeable bulge under his arm led her to Manetti's table.

"I hear you're interested in horses." He didn't hide his doubt. "Women are supposed to be bad luck at the track."

"The poorly informed often suffer misfortune." She took a seat at his table, accepting the champagne that a waiter held out to her.

"Are you here to bet?" Manetti's dark eyes sparkled.

Dawn didn't waver. "I'm here to invest, Mr. Manetti. I don't spend a lot of time away from my work, but I do like to explore certain activities, such as racing. Some people say I have an eye for the horses."

He nodded to the window, where they could see horses parading for the second race. "Pick the winner."

Dawn forced herself to appear supremely confident as she surveyed the field of nine. There were really only two horses that looked fit enough to win. But handicapping a race without any history of the horse, trainer or jockey was a fool's chore.

"Number three has the ability to win. That horse should finish first, but a lot depends on the jockey, on the desire of the owner and trainer to win." She gave him a level look. "I can evaluate the horses. It's the humans I can't always assess."

Manetti signaled the waiter with the champagne. When their glasses had been refilled, he ordered everyone else to leave.

"I take great pains to hide my interest in certain horses. How did you find out that Winner's Gold was my horse?" He didn't touch her. His glittering stare was forceful enough.

"I didn't know. The horse is the best in the field. Anyone with a trained eye could see it. But that doesn't make him a winner. Does he have heart? Does he quit? Will he run for your rider? And most importantly of all, has he been injured?" She sipped the champagne. "Answer those questions, Mr. Manetti, and I'll give you some odds."

"You wanted to meet me. Why?" He leaned back in his chair. "You want something. What is it?"

"I hear you often come across good horses. I want part of one. I'm willing to invest heavily, and I'm not particular about certain aspects of...the business. I've made some good decisions in the past." The gold of her rented Rolex picked up the candlelight and glittered as dangerously as his eyes. "I've saved some of my winnings, and the time is right for a stake."

"I might have a few leads." He leaned forward. "Expensive investments, though. I don't deal with small business loans."

"I have the cash, Mr. Manetti. My only requirement is that I see the horse before I deliver the money."

He shook his head. "That isn't possible. We often buy on advice. I see the animals, but I don't have time to let my investors view every horse I'm interested in."

"I want a Derby horse, Mr. Manetti. I want it badly enough that money isn't an object. And I want it this year."

"You're a very direct woman." He nodded to the window as the horses broke the gate. The number three horse came out last, getting snagged in the gate. Dawn felt her heart drop. She'd risked a lot on that horse, and it looked as though she'd lost.

"Bad break." Manetti drained his champagne glass.

"Don't give up so easily." Dawn forced herself to remain confident. In the backstretch the number three horse gained ground, pulling into fifth position. On the curve he inched closer, moving into third. But it was down the homestretch that he lengthened his stride and pulled into second, with his nose only inches behind the lead horse.

"He'll win." Dawn looked down at her hands on the table and smiled a small, supremely confident smile. "I told you so." She couldn't watch the end of the race; she was too nervous.

"He did it!" Manetti jumped up, his face alive with excitement. "I knew he could do it. One of Johnny D's boys tried to convince me the horse was a dud. I told that trainer to give him a chance. He had the look about him, didn't he?"

He turned to her, his hand touching her shoulder, almost in a caress. "And you knew it, too."

"I knew the horse could do it. Yes."

"I'm riding tomorrow at eleven. I'll send a driver to pick you up. Perhaps we could talk some business while we ride."

"Of course." She gathered her purse and stood. "Good luck with Winner's Gold, Mr. Manetti. Rest him for at least three weeks. He'll be sore on that right front leg."

She walked out of the room and past the group of men, who were still waiting just outside the door.

"I'M RIDING with him tomorrow at eleven." Dawn was breathless from hurrying down the stairs and into the parking lot, where Luke was already waiting in the car. "He isn't what I thought he'd be."

"No?" Luke had spent the last half hour with his own unpleasant thoughts. He'd grown protective of the woman who sat beside him, so elegant in the silky, coral pantsuit, so regal in posture and bearing. It had occurred to him that Manetti might find Dawn more interesting than simply as a horse handicapper. That thought had given him some bad moments as he'd scouted the paddock area of the track to no avail. All discreet questions about a filly had met only blank stares.

Dawn was so deep in her own thoughts that she failed to notice Luke's tenseness. "Manetti was, well, maybe more decent than I expected. I don't know. He wasn't as frightening as I thought he would be. I mean he didn't drag out a gun and point it at me or ask any hard questions about my alleged money or me."

"So he wasn't a movie gangster. That doesn't mean he can't be ruthless." Luke almost snapped out the words, and his hands tightened on the steering wheel as he drove them back toward the French Quarter.

"You're right. Did you find anything?" From the corner of her eye she cast him a speculative look. He was mad. Really mad. She'd only done what he'd asked, and with some degree of success. "Luke, what's wrong?"

"I don't like the idea of you riding with Manetti tomorrow. I can't protect you."

She heard his words, but it was the line of his jaw that told her the truth.

"You don't have to worry about protecting me. I don't think I'll be in any danger tomorrow. I'll be very careful." She leaned across the console and kissed his cheek. "I want to find Private Stock and get on with my life. I won't take unnecessary risks."

Slowly the tension left Luke's face. He reached an arm around her and gave her a hug. "Pretty transparent, huh?"

"Just a little. But it's nice to have someone worried about me."

"Manetti is classy, but never think that makes him safe."

Dawn smiled. "I don't underestimate him. I just don't think he's . . . I think the horses are more than just money. That's what I'm trying to say. He isn't in it just for the money."

"Believe me, if you threaten his fun or his money, he'll retaliate. Just find out what he knows about the filly and we can move on."

"Private Stock. Where could she be?" Dawn looked out the window at the lights and traffic. "Is she here, in this city? Maybe I'll catch a glimpse of her at Manetti's barn. I didn't even ask where it was."

"How about some dinner?"

"That's an excellent idea. I'm starved."

BUILT ON THE LEVEE overlooking the Mississippi River, the restaurant was small, elegant and very romantic. The river traffic passed before their table, the lights of one slow-moving paddleboat shimmering across the water. Dawn sighed with contentment as she wiped her mouth with the napkin and then placed it on the table.

"I'm very, very full," she admitted, taking a tiny sip of the delicious wine.

"Dessert?"

"You are a fiend." She shook her head. "What I'd really like to do is call Freddie. I have a sudden feeling that I'm neglecting the ranch. I also asked Freddie to check up on you. I thought you might be trying to kill me.''

Luke's expression changed from lighthearted to deadly serious. ''There's not much to find out about me. I breed and train jumpers near Lexington. Not much else to tell.'' He shrugged offhandedly. ''At least no more than anyone else.''

''I don't believe that.'' Dawn leaned forward, her eyes sparkling. ''I'll bet there's some wild and sordid tales about you. After watching your ability to get in trouble over the last two days, I'm certain you must have an intriguing past.''

''Nothing that would interest you.'' He smiled, but there was a tightness around his eyes. ''When we first met, you thought I was trying to kill you. You don't still think I'd hurt you?''

She locked her gaze into his, holding him with a look. ''No, Luke, I don't think you'd hurt me. I don't think you'd deliberately hurt anyone.''

''Is that a vote of confidence?'' He struggled to reestablish the lighthearted mood that had prevailed over the meal.

''Absolutely. You have my unshakable confiden—'' She faltered as she watched his expression alter again, an alert, wary quality replacing the humor. ''What is it?''

''Don't turn around, but remember that man at the Hot Springs airport? Well, he's coming out of the back of the restaurant.''

''He's in here?'' Dawn couldn't help the doubt in her voice.

''Yes. And he's watching this table.''

A tingle of apprehension glided down her spine. ''Everywhere we go, he turns up, and there's always danger. I'll bet he was the one who shot at us tonight.''

Luke felt a chill touch his back. The short man did turn up everywhere they went, and it was strange that he followed them so easily. There was one way to find out.

Somehow he had to get her to leave without him. The quarry was about to become the hunter, but Dawn had to play the bait, a role he'd unwillingly cast her in more than once. Guilt put the necessary edge on his next question.

"Don't you find it a little odd that after several attempts on your life, you haven't even been scratched?"

For a moment Dawn thought she'd misunderstood. One look at the coldness in Luke's eyes made her realize that her first reading of his statement had been true. He doubted her. "Are you saying that the attempts aren't real?"

"I'm saying that you're a very lucky person. Maybe you aren't just lucky. Maybe you're working with them."

"Don't forget that they tried to run you down with a truck, and you weren't hurt!" His accusation was so unexpected, so ridiculous that she struggled to order her thoughts.

"That man finds us wherever we go. I'm just beginning to wonder how, that's all." Luke forced the issue.

"And in wondering, you're wondering if maybe I'm telling him." She rose from the table, her face a pale oval devoid of color. "I thought we knew each other better than this. I thought we trusted each other." She turned and stalked across the restaurant floor.

Luke watched her leave, waiting until the small man dropped his busboy's apron and followed her out into the night.

He was on his feet with an agile lightness. Careful to be sure the small man didn't observe him, he followed, stalking the man who stalked Dawn. At the curb Dawn spoke nervously with the valet. The man radioed for a taxi for her.

The small man was between Luke and Dawn, ducked into the shadows of a sign. He watched Dawn eagerly, twice looking down at his watch. When the taxi arrived and Dawn left, he hurried away.

Treading like a cat, Luke followed. The small man crossed the street, making his way toward the crowded French Quarter. Keeping half a block behind, Luke dodged the tourists in shorts and sandals, stepped around road blockades, avoided the musicians who were performing on the street corners.

The small man hurried down Bourbon, heading straight for the end of the Quarter and Esplanade. Straight for Dawn.

Luke quickened his pace so that he drew nearer the man. He was in his early thirties, well built though short. His frame was slender, but there was a wiriness, a toughness in the way he moved. As the crowds began to thin and the surrounding area became more residential, Luke felt his excitement grow. He had every intention of catching the man and making him talk.

Bourbon ended at Esplanade, and just as Luke suspected, the man turned toward the hotel. Luke was very close behind him, only fifty yards away. Not once did his quarry even look back over his shoulder.

The man paused at the leaded glass door of John Morrow's House, his hand outstretched toward the knob as he looked up and down the street. Something made him hesitate, and he drew back into the shadows.

From around the corner a long, steel-gray limo cruised into the street. The windows were blackened and gave no clue as to the occupants. As it neared the hotel, it slowed at the curb for a long moment, then pulled away into the night.

Once the car was gone, the small man reappeared, a grim look casting his face into harsh angles. Like a wraith, he slipped through the door and was gone. Luke was left to follow him and ponder the mysterious behavior both of the man he'd followed and the occupants of the car. He could infer only one thing. They were not friendly with each other.

The lobby was completely empty, and Luke felt a chill of apprehension for Dawn. Had he endangered her life? Knowing that the smartest thing to do would be to wait and see what type of encounter occurred, Luke nonetheless found himself slipping toward the privacy fence of the rooms they shared. Once again he saw the small man, his body bent over the lock.

"Do you have an invitation?" Luke's question sounded as loud as a crack of thunder in the still night.

The short man whirled, his hand going to this jacket.

Luke's foot caught him in the elbow. "Not so fast. I've been trying to catch up with you for a few days." He grabbed the man's arm and twisted it sharply behind his back. "Now I think we're due for a chat." Pushing up on the arm, Luke forced the man back toward the lobby and into the street.

"My boss is gonna get you for this." The small man was panting from the pain, but his tone was threatening. "He don't play with no amateurs, and he's gonna see to it that you get out of our way."

On the street, Luke pushed the man into an alley. The night was all around them, close and dark.

"Who's your boss?"

The little man was incredulous as he turned to Luke. "Who's my boss? What kind of game are you playin'? You got his horse, and you ask what his name is? Buddy, you're cookin' for some serious intestinal disorders from me, Jack the Knife."

The man's words made no sense. Was he referring to Roulette? "What horse?" Luke still gripped the man's arm, and he lifted it a half inch higher. "And tell the truth!"

"What horse? That big bay you're running at your place. You think we're fools. We knew you had the horse all along. It seemed like a good place to chill out, until the heat was off. Based on your past, it was the perfect place. But now the boss is reconsidering, what with you asking all those questions about the filly. He sent me to warn you, and the broad. Go home. Mind your own affairs. Stay out of the way or the A team will be down here to show you a little gratitude.''

"What are you talking about?'' Luke released his grip slightly. "Is this about Roulette?''

The small man turned around, his face a blank. "The mare? Nah, the boss is finished with her. Too risky.'' He shifted his shoulder to work the cramp out of his arm. "Just go home.'' In a movement so sudden that Luke didn't react in time, the small man's arm shot out and caught Luke in the throat.

The choking sensation blocked all sense of time and place. Luke felt himself slipping down the wall to the dirty alleyway. "That's from me. And this—'' he drew back his foot and caught Luke squarely in the stomach "—is from the boss. Now get home and take that stupid woman with you, or it'll be worse.''

The sound of a shot came from a long distance away. Struggling to remain conscious, Luke was aware of the man sliding down beside him in the alley. Somehow he knew that Jack was dead. The small man didn't move at all, and there was no sound of life from him. Luke pulled himself against the wall, groping for the other man. His hand encountered a large, wet wound in the man's chest.

DAWN'S HAND SHOOK as she dialed the number for the ranch. It was late, but Freddie was notorious for staying up until the wee hours. He answered on the second ring.

"Hi, just checking in.'' She sounded upset and she knew it.

"I've been worried sick. Where are you?'' Freddie was as fussy as an old hen.

"New Orleans, and I'm fine. I've been all over the South, and I've managed to steal a horse. Have you heard anything from Orson?"

For an older man, Freddie maintained remarkable balance. "Nothing from Orson, and what horse?"

Dawn told him the story of Russian Roulette. "She's safe, Freddie. I don't know what we'll do, but I'm really calling to find out what you uncovered about Luke O'Neil."

The silence on the other end made Dawn tighten her grip on the phone. "What is it, Freddie?"

"Luke O'Neil has a long past in the horse world, Dawn. He was an Olympic hopeful."

Dawn drew in a breath. Freddie was hedging. "And what happened?"

"His horse was sold. It was a swindle and he was an innocent kid that got used. He didn't have time to train another horse, so he lost out. He was bitter, upset, and when the horse turned up lame after the first trials, there were rumors."

"Luke wouldn't do something like that!"

"I'm not making the accusation. I'm merely telling you what I found out."

"Sorry," Dawn managed to say. "I've seen him around horses. He isn't the type of man who would injure an animal for revenge. What happened after that?"

"He went into private work, training horses and riders for the national and international circuits."

"And he was good, right?" She knew that much about him.

"He was very good. His riders and horses were sweeping the events. Until the Maclay, five years ago."

Doom hung suspended in the long distance telephone wire. "What happened?"

"One of his horses went wild when it came into the ring. The rider, a young girl in her teens, lost control. The horse crashed a jump and the girl was seriously hurt. A back injury.''

"But that happens. No one could blame Luke for that. It's part of the business.'' Dawn felt herself defending him, even when she knew Freddie wasn't deliberately trying to make him appear to be the bad guy.

"Dawn, the horse had been injected with uppers. It was on the verge of collapse. The girl said Luke administered the shot. After that, he closed down his barn and disappeared. Over the last three years he's gradually been making a comeback. He has a new barn, a new string of horses and new students. But in a lot of circles, that old doubt never will heal. He's marked as a crook and a cheat.''

"I see.'' And she did, too clearly. Luke was elusive about his work, his horses. And his past. Now she could understand why. The allegations were serious.

"Dawn, he never made an attempt to defend himself. Not in either case.'' Freddie's voice was tender but determined. "Has he mentioned any of it to you?''

"No.'' And that was the part that concerned her most. The Luke she knew was incapable of committing a cruelty against a helpless animal. Not for revenge. Not to win. But why hadn't he told her something about it, unless he was trying to hide it?

"I think you need to come home, girl.''

"I can't, Freddie, I'm too involved.''

"With the horse, or with Luke O'Neil?''

The silence was Dawn's answer. "Freddie, he helped me steal a mare because I wouldn't leave her to be mistreated.''

"Dawn, my girl, I can't begin to assume to know what's in a man's heart, especially one I've never known. Maybe he has changed. Where is he?''

"Good question." Where, indeed, was Luke? And why had he acted so absurdly in the restaurant? "I guess I need to take a look around and see where he went."

"Promise me you'll be careful, girl. Don't let your heart lead you into trouble with a man you don't know."

"My heart?" Dawn bluffed, trying to hide her worry.

"It's all in your voice, Dawn. You care for him. I don't want you coming home heartbroken and useless, you hear?" The old bluster had returned.

"Thanks, Freddie. I'll talk with you tomorrow. I need to make arrangements for that horse."

"Leave her with Orson for the time being. He's got the best place, until things cool off and we can get all of this straight with the authorities."

She replaced the receiver. A replay of the scene in the restaurant spun through her mind as she changed into jeans. The more she thought about it, the more she felt as if Luke had tricked her into leaving. He'd wanted to follow the man who was watching them. That was it! Luke had used her for a decoy.

A nagging anxiety came with that revelation. Where was Luke? She'd been home at least half an hour. She hurried outside, determined to find him and make sure that his plan hadn't backfired on him.

She heard the echo of a gunshot as her hand touched the latch to the gate. She bolted through the garden, intent on one thing only, finding Luke O'Neil.

"LUKE!" Dawn's voice was edged with fear. He was nearby. She knew it without proof. And he was in danger. "Luke!"

In the narrow alley, Luke rocked forward, regaining his feet. His throat was too constricted to make a noise louder than a croak. He used the wall to steady himself as he forced his legs beneath him. With staggering steps, he turned out of the alley. He couldn't begin to unravel what had happened; he only knew that Dawn didn't need to see the body of the man who called himself Jack the Knife.

"Luke!" There was reproach in Dawn's voice as she finally saw him at the mouth of the alley. "Where have you been? I heard a gunshot." Dawn hurried toward him, grasping his elbow when he began to totter.

He tried to speak, but his voice was only a croak.

"What is it?" Worry replaced the reproach as she helped him toward the hotel door.

He couldn't talk, so he concentrated on walking and remaining upright. His throat was swollen, and he resisted the impulse to swallow. With a little more force, the blow would have been deadly.

They limped across the lobby, which was empty, a fact that Luke noticed with a growing sense of alarm. He'd come back later and check for the clerk. For the present, he wanted to get Dawn into a safe place, to see that she was tucked away behind locks. He couldn't shake the memory of the body sliding down the wall beside him, a dead man still moving.

When they were within the privacy fence, Luke insisted on locking the gate. Inside the door, he repeated the precautions. With each moment, he felt more and more stable. His throat hurt, but the first flash of excruciating pain was passing.

"Now, what happened?" Dawn held out a glass of straight bourbon.

He took a sip, finding the hot warmth both pleasurable and painful. The fiery liquor worked to relax the muscles, and he cleared his throat. He gave her a quick account of following the little man, and the discussion in the alleyway.

"Who shot him?" Dawn went to the heavily draped window and peeped out.

"I don't know, Dawn. We're pawns in some game, and I don't have any idea who's masterminding the moves." That much was true.

Still looking out the window, Dawn asked, "Is there anything in your past that might have led to this?" Freddie had opened the door on that Pandora's box of doubts, and she wanted to confront them head-on.

Reflected in the window, she saw Luke tense, then quickly bring his reaction under control.

"No, why do you ask?"

"I just wondered. From everything I know, we're innocents. I've tried and tried to think how we got involved in this. I mean the video was originally addressed to Ann, not me."

"And does she have a secret past?" Luke was grim as he stood there, his hand touching his throat.

"No."

"But you thought I might?"

"I thought there might be something you wanted to tell me, yes."

"Sorry, no family history, no excuses, and no more talk. I'm going to call the police and report that shooting." As he spoke, he picked up the telephone and dialed the emergency number, filing an anonymous report.

Dawn lingered in the room, wanting to press the issue of his past but undecided how best to approach it. She cast several glances at him, taking in the strain on his face, the concern that tightened his mouth. She cared for him. And she didn't want to believe that he was capable of such deceit.

The wail of a siren cut through the charged atmosphere of the room, and Luke suggested, "Let's walk down. Maybe we'll learn something."

She nodded and fell in beside him as they ventured once again across the private garden to the lobby. To Luke's relief, the young clerk was behind the counter, leisurely posting billings. He gave them a smile and a half salute.

"Big excitement outside," he commented.

"Yeah," Luke agreed, stepping into the street.

"Tell them it was a crank call." An officer stood in the alley, his bright light shining down the narrow pathway, illuminating the empty walls.

Luke started forward and Dawn's hand detained him.

"What happened, officer?" Dawn asked.

The policeman shook his head. "Damn crank calls. We get them every night. Someone reported a shooting. Of course, when we get here, there's nothing to be found. Not even a drop of blood." He shook his head again. "If I could catch the kook who thinks its funny reporting these things, I'd like to put him in jail for a long portion of his natural life."

In the headlights of the patrol car, Dawn and Luke looked at each other. The body had vanished.

Chapter Eight

"Are you certain he was dead?" Dawn sat across from Luke, her legs curled beneath her on the sofa.

"Positive. He was shot in the chest. I wouldn't have left him if he hadn't been dead." Luke sipped his drink, but he barely tasted it. "What happened to him? He didn't simply vanish."

"Whoever shot him came back and took him."

"But why?"

Dawn didn't try to answer. She avoided Luke's gaze as she busied herself making a fresh drink. After Freddie's revelations, she couldn't stop wondering why Luke wouldn't, or couldn't tell her about his past—and if he was telling her the truth now. She returned to the sofa, still avoiding eye contact.

Sensing her unease, Luke checked his watch. "You'd better get some rest. It's nearly three, and Manetti will be expecting you."

"You're right." She unfolded her legs and stood. "And you?"

"I'm going to finish this drink and then catch some shut-eye, too."

"See you in the morning." She went to her room and slowly closed the door. The horrible image of a man killed just outside her door stayed with her, as did her doubts about Luke. Why was he avoiding telling her about his past? She'd felt so close to him, had viewed him as the antithesis of the man Freddie described. She had to face the possibility, though, that something from Luke's past might have placed them in danger. They had suffered close calls, but now a man was dead.

Luke would surely tell her the whole truth, and soon. She consoled herself with that thought as she waited for sleep to claim her.

She awoke with the early morning, stretched and tried to return to sleep, but it was useless. She got up, showered, dressed and spent a few minutes with makeup and hairpins.

When she stepped into the living room, she found Luke, slumped on the sofa, asleep where he'd stopped.

"Coffee and *beignets*," she whispered in his ear. "Café du Monde."

"Are you delivering?" He kept his eyes closed as he asked.

"Not on your life. Let's go. We have plenty of time to have breakfast and get back here before Manetti sends his couriers for me."

Luke stretched his tall frame, shook off sleep and insisted on a shower. Ten minutes later, blond hair still wet, he stood at the door.

It was early morning, and the east end of Bourbon was still snoozing. As they drew closer and closer to the river, the traffic, pace and atmosphere became brisk. The Café du Monde was filled with businessmen and the early-season tourists. The fresh, hot French doughnuts coated in powdered sugar and the rich, chicory coffee laced with hot milk drew a bustling breakfast crowd.

Dawn chose to sit in the open-air section of the restaurant, where the early-morning nip made the hot coffee even more delicious.

"Promise me you'll be careful."

She looked up to find Luke's tired eyes watching her. "Of course I'll be careful."

He picked up the morning newspaper and buried his head in the local news. Though he searched carefully, he found no mention of a murder that might involve the man in the alley. The disappearance of the body had him very worried.

Behind the safety of the paper, he didn't bother to conceal the scowl that tightened his features. The man had made reference to his farm. There was no room for misinterpretation. The past had reawakened, and somehow Centaur Farms was in jeopardy.

He didn't have to look at Dawn's face to know she suspected something. No man could successfully hide his past, and he'd intended to tell her. But not right away. He'd wanted to build her trust before he confronted her with the facts, the circumstantial evidence of his past guilt. He had enough concerns with the present, where Dawn was involved, not to want to have to wage the old war of past charges and allegations.

During the night, one thing had become clear. The videotape of Private Stock related to his farm, his business. He was meant to be Dawn's adversary, not her partner. In linking up with her, he'd endangered them both. And he had no idea which direction the danger might approach from.

Shut out by Luke, Dawn watched the hundreds of people circling around them. Paranoia nipped at her like a small dog. Any one of them could be watching her. The short man, Jack, had certainly found it easy enough to trace her every move. And someone had been following him. Someone who killed him.

"I'm going to wander down to some of the art galleries and window-shop. I'll meet you back at the rooms at ten." She suddenly felt the need to be alone, to be free of Luke and his untold past. She wished she'd never asked Freddie to check up on him. Before she'd talked with Freddie, she'd felt a growing trust of Luke O'Neil. She'd come to expect honesty and integrity, had thought she saw those qualities in his intense, blue eyes. Now, sitting across from him, she knew she had to leave or press the issue of his past.

"Be careful." He lowered the paper long enough to stare directly into her eyes. His look was guarded. "When you get back, maybe we should talk about what has you so edgy."

"Maybe we will." She picked up her purse and maneuvered around the tightly packed tables until she was part of the crowd, away from Luke's disturbing gaze. But no matter how fast or far she walked, she could not escape her own thoughts.

At ten she was back in her room, digging through her clothes for breeches and a light sweater. Her stomach jittered with each slight noise. When she held out her hands, she had to force them to be steady. Not a good sign for a ride, and so much depended on convincing Manetti of her horse skills. Most horses were sensitive to the rider's mental state, and a nervous rider made for a fidgety mount.

As the minute hand on the clock swept around, Dawn realized Luke was not going to return. At five minutes of eleven she went to the lobby. A uniformed chauffeur was at the desk, waiting for her.

She followed him out and slid into the steel-gray limo, startled to find Louis Manetti sitting quietly on the other side of the wide seat.

"It's a wonderful morning for a ride." His voice was laced with warm pleasure.

"Yes, it is. I hope it's a good morning for business."

He was darkly handsome, dressed in tan breeches and a sparkling white shirt that contrasted with his skin and eyes. "My farm is near Mandeville, something of a drive. I thought it would give us time to talk, to get to that business you're so eager to begin." His smile was calculating.

"I'm sure I'll be very interested in what you have to say." Dawn forced herself back into the role that Luke had created for her.

"How does a horse trainer come up with money to invest?" Manetti flicked at a manicured nail.

"By betting wisely, and accumulating her funds. I haven't been a fool, Mr. Manetti. I'm not in a hurry to strike it rich. I am in a hurry, for my career, to have my name associated with a winner. That isn't too much for a working woman to ask, is it?" She challenged him with a slow smile.

"Not at all. Rather modest for a woman of your obvious talents." His own smile was lazy. "I may have the horse for you."

"Can I see...him?" Dawn caught herself in a half heartbeat of time.

"I'd like to see your check first. A hundred thousand, first installment."

"How many other investors?"

"Ten. A very elite group. Only four want their names associated. One of the benefits of including you is that you can be up front, in the winner's circle, so to speak." He gave her another easy smile. "Just as you dreamed."

"When do you need the money?"

"This afternoon. Tomorrow morning at the latest."

"But only if I can see the horse first. I've only my wits and good judgment, Mr. Manetti. I'm not questioning your abilities to choose a winner, but I must see for myself."

The car rolled smoothly through the city, entering the bridge that stretched across Lake Pontchartrain. Dawn felt a sudden apprehension when her thoughts drifted to Roulette, tucked safely away at Applegate Farm. Was it possible that Manetti had learned about the mare? Was this all a trick?

"Something wrong?" He was watching her closely and had obviously seen the shiver that touched her shoulders.

"This is a big moment for me, the realization of a dream. But you never said if I could see the horse."

He smiled. "You're very naive, Ms. Markey. But that has a certain degree of charm for a man like myself. Perhaps I will let you see the horse. After I have your check and it's cleared the bank."

Dawn held her breath, then exhaled. "I'm afraid that won't do. The horse first, and then, if I feel it's the right animal, you get my money. Somehow I don't think I could complain to the authorities if you took my money, because as we both know, I haven't paid a dime of taxes on it."

"You are naive, but certainly not stupid." Instead of being angry, Manetti was laughing. "And now I must insist that you call me Louis. I'm beginning to see the possibility of a place for you in my business, Ms. Markey. Let me consider it further."

They talked racing, comparing favorites, until the car turned between white fences and acres of green pastures. In the distance Dawn saw an elegant barn that structurally resembled Churchill Downs. The design was very telling of Louis Manetti's ambition.

"We own a little over a thousand acres, and we're standing several excellent stallions. Not Secretariat quality." He didn't flinch, but held her with a direct gaze. "Not yet. It will take some time to get there. We're very excited about a young stallion, a yearling we bought out of Kentucky last year. Man of War descendant."

As he talked, he led her into the barn. The brick floor was spotless, and the strong scent of pine cleaner filled the airy structure.

Manetti signaled to two stable hands, and they brought out horses into the hallway and began to groom and saddle them. Dawn noticed that the animals were well behaved but alert. The ride would be exhilarating.

In a matter of moments they were mounted and walking down the road between paddocks. The farm was beautiful, and Dawn felt her body relax as she adjusted to the rhythm of the horse.

When they were clear of the barn, Louis moved into a trot, then a canter. For half an hour, Dawn didn't have to worry about pretense; she could truly appreciate the ride and the well-trained horse. Manetti showed her the farm, circling to back pastures where streams wandered through the green acres, then moving on to uncut areas where the natural vegetation was thick and dense.

"It's a lovely place," Dawn said as they returned to the barn at a walk. "I can see where you've worked hard. Maybe this young stallion will be the horse you want."

"Maybe," Manetti said. "He has the breeding. Would you like to see him?"

Dawn agreed and they walked around the barn to a large paddock where a fiery, golden yearling tossed his head and pranced. Dawn couldn't help her smile. War Son, as he was called, was a beautiful creature, but had nothing to do with Private Stock or Speed Dancer.

"What do you think?"

"He's young, he's magnificent. So much depends on the next few years. On luck and keeping him sound. It's an incredible business, isn't it?"

"Indeed. Now what about that investment?"

"What about the horse?"

"I'm afraid the animal isn't here on these premises. We could go tomorrow. How about that? You bring the check, and I'll take you to see this racing creature. Then you can decide and we can transact our business. Or at least a portion of it. Remember, this check is only half the payment.

The remainder would be due in, say six weeks, just before the Derby.''

"Excellent," Dawn agreed, ignoring the pounding of her heart. She was getting closer and closer.

"My driver will return you to New Orleans. I have other business here that demands my attention. There's only one other thing." His lips smiled, but his eyes didn't. "Why was Jack the Knife following you last night?"

Dawn was glad the horse under her was sensible. She stiffened and the horse held himself steady. "Who is Jack the Knife?" She turned shielded eyes toward him.

"The man who died in the alley beside your building. I saw him following you, and I saw your friend following him. Why? Is there Chicago money behind you?" There wasn't a scrap of friendliness in his face as he leaned toward her. "Because if you're fronting for The Boss, it could be very dangerous. Especially with me. Understand?"

Dawn nodded, because her throat wouldn't work. She understood all too well. Louis Manetti didn't need a gun to make his threats effective. His eyes did all the work.

"I don't know who you're talking about. I don't know why that man has been following me."

"Keep it innocent, Ms. Markey. It's the best way to stay alive in this part of the country. And watch out for your bodyguard. His reputation precedes him."

He touched his heels to the horse and started away. At the end of the lane he stopped, then turned. "Tomorrow at ten. The car will pick you up."

Dawn walked back to the barn. Before she could begin to unsaddle, a groom arrived and the driver appeared at her elbow, ready for the trip back to New Orleans. She followed like an obedient puppy, only too eager to get back to Luke. Manetti had frightened her, but it was an emotion she was beginning to feel was second nature.

LUKE SPENT the morning waiting anxiously for Dawn to return. At noon he went to the lobby and found a seat that gave a view of Esplanade. Each minute that passed seemed stretched, pulled to a maximum amount of worry. When the door opened and Dawn entered, her face slightly pale and her dark hair rolled so neatly at the nape of her neck, he went to her without thinking. His large hands pressed against her shoulders, those delicate, expressive shoulders, and he pulled her to him and held her.

He could feel her heart beating against him, could smell the clean scent of her shampoo. One hand reached up and pulled the pins from her hair, allowing it to fall free to her shoulders.

"Everything okay?" he asked.

Caught in his embrace, Dawn could at last nod in the affirmative. It was okay, now that she was with Luke. The terror of Louis Manetti's gaze lessened. She was safe.

"Dawn?" He sensed her fear.

"He threatened me." The words bubbled up in her throat and she stopped. Drawing a deep breath, she stepped back and looked up at Luke. Though his blue eyes expressed worry, his hands held her, giving support and safety. "I'm okay. It's just that when he finally did threaten me he was so cold, so detached. I have to have $100,000 tomorrow, and he's going to show me the horse."

"Is it Private Stock?"

"I don't know. He never said. But it has to be, Luke." She saw doubt in his eyes. "Doesn't it? If it isn't, we're going to be in big, big trouble." She cast a look around the lobby. "Let's go to the room."

"How did he threaten you?" Luke held the gate for her.

"He asked if I was fronting for the boss. He said if I was, I was going to get hurt, that he didn't want this boss person involved in his business."

A tentacle of memory touched Luke, damp and gripping. "The man, Jack . . ."

"Jack the Knife," Dawn supplied. "That was his name and he worked for the boss."

"That's right!" Luke released her shoulders and paced the lobby quickly. "Jack said something about the boss. I couldn't breathe, so I wasn't paying real close attention, but it was something."

"Luke, the men in Hot Springs, did they say anything about the boss?" Dawn felt the puzzle shift. At last they had an incident that linked something together.

"I don't think so. They mentioned Manetti, about taking Private Stock to him. But no one else."

"Want to drive over to Applegate and check on Roulette?" Dawn lifted a shoulder in a question. "I'm worried about her. She was in bad shape. Maybe Orson can shed some light on Louis Manetti and his past. Orson likes to shoot the bull, and he seldom tells as much as he knows. That's why folks like him so much. But if I press him, maybe he'll help us out."

"Orson Rinter." Luke spoke the name softly. "Has he always been in racing?"

"Well, at least for the last few years. He isn't from the area. He's from up north somewhere. Pennsylvania, New York, somewhere like that. Since he's been here, racing has been his life. Who knows? A lot of people change." Dawn pulled a brush from her handbag and rearranged her thick hair, braiding it into two long plaits. "I'm ready."

"His name is familiar, and I thought maybe he'd worked in jumpers before. But I could have come across one of his horses. Lots of racers end up jumping fences."

"That's the truth," Dawn agreed as they left the hotel and walked quickly to the car. Her face brightened as she turned to him. "There's even the possibility that you might have seen my stallion, Speed Dancer. I hadn't thought of it before, but he might be on the jumper circuit. Of course, he'd have a different name. But I'm sure you'd recognize him."

"Did Manetti give you any clue where this prizewinning racehorse might be?" Luke started the car and merged into the traffic.

"None." The hopelessness of the search for Speed Dancer made her silent. The conversation lagged, and soon they were out of the city and nearing the Covington area. Rolling pastures and large oaks made for ideal horse country. To take her mind off her doubts, Dawn related some of the facts she knew about area farms.

"Orson hasn't really produced a top-quality horse, but he seems to come up with some pretty good mares. This may not be fair, but I always felt a little sorry for him. I mean, he's missed a few good opportunities. He had the mare that gave birth to the Pimlico track champion four years ago, and he lost her in a really foolish claiming race. You know, just bad breaks like that."

"But he seems happy enough." Luke took the turn Dawn indicated and saw the sign for Applegate Farms.

"Orson's an optimist. And he's been very kind to my boss, Ann Tate, since her trouble started years ago when her husband and Speed Dancer disappeared. He was Johnny-on-the-spot with help and encouragement."

"And everything worked out?" Luke had a sudden desire to reach over and unfasten her hair, but he restrained himself. For Dawn's good, he was going to have to put some distance between them.

"Everything's great now. Orson was a big help. He came over and sat with Easy. He's that kind of friend to Ann. He was also good friends with Cybil, and I think he was as shocked as the rest of us that she was mentally ill."

Luke pulled up at Orson's house and they got out. There was no sign of life, and Dawn went straight into the barn. "Orson won't care," she reassured him when he hesitated.

They found Roulette in a large, airy stall, already looking a hundred pounds heavier. The mare's warm, even dis-
position was evident as she came forward and offered her
nose for a pet.

"I'm positive she was bred to Speed Dancer, and Private
Stock is the result." Dawn stroked the mare as her gaze
drifted from the large, intelligent eyes to the mare's conformation. "What a perfect pair."

"Too bad Speed Dancer disappeared." Orson's sympa-
thetic voice came from behind them.

Dawn turned to him with a big smile. "Roulette looks so
much better already. Thanks for taking such good care of
her."

"What are you going to do with her?" Orson Rinter
propped an elbow on the stall door and nodded a greeting
at Luke.

"Another good question." Dawn lifted one shoulder.
"I'm open to ideas."

"Not from me." Orson laughed. "I'm afraid I still
haven't overcome my desire to own her myself. But then the
insurance companies are going to have a heyday with her.
Ownership will probably be tied up for years."

"That's true." Luke rubbed the mare's nose. "It seems
we've hauled her from one state to the next, from one bad
situation to another."

"If I were inclined to be crooked, I'd find some papers on
a dead horse, breed her to Easy Dancer over at Dancing
Water Ranch and see what kind of baby I got." Orson
tugged at Dawn's braid like a mischievous schoolboy. "But
I know that idea won't wash with this little Indian princess."

"Ann wouldn't go along with it, either," Dawn said with
a rueful smile. "It's tempting, like any other illegal scheme.
But unless you're feeling uncomfortable about keeping her,
maybe we could just leave this unresolved for a few more

days. I mean she's safe, she's happy and I feel she's in wonderful hands.''

For the first time the cheerful grin on Orson's face slipped. "Come on into the house, you two."

"What is it?" Luke tensed, his arm protectively shifting Dawn to his side so that he had a clear view of both entrances to the barn.

"Nothing life-threatening," Orson said, patting Luke's shoulder. "I had a strange phone call last night. It might interest you, or you might find it just coincidence. Let's go inside." Orson gave a quick look around the barn. "Discretion is never wasted."

They walked across the yard and onto the porch without further comment. Orson held the door while Dawn entered, followed by Luke.

"Go to the kitchen, hon," Orson directed Dawn. "There's fresh coffee and some pecan shortcake cookies that Mrs. Marble baked."

Dawn gave Luke's arm a squeeze and drew him down to her so she could whisper, "Mrs. Marble's a widow. She's been after Orson for the last three years. She sends him goodies all the time."

Luke's answering grin was still in place when they settled around the kitchen table and Orson filled heavy mugs with hot coffee. He puttered about, seeming to avoid the subject of his late-night phone call.

"Spill it," Dawn finally directed him, catching his hand and drawing him to the table to sit. "Who called?"

"Well, it was just strange. I hadn't heard from him since I first opened up. We're not exactly in the same league, you know."

"Who?" Dawn repeated.

"Louis Manetti. He called and asked if I knew you. He said you wanted to invest in a horse. He was wondering if you had any money, or if you were bluffing."

Chapter Nine

"Why would Manetti call you?" Luke pushed back from the table and stood. He took a protective stance behind Dawn, his hands resting on the back of her chair.

Dawn was glad she was sitting. At the mention of Manetti's name, her legs had gone rubbery. She was truly afraid of him, more so than she'd even admitted to herself.

"Luke, he didn't just call, he stopped by this afternoon."

Dawn remembered the look on Manetti's face when he'd left her with the horse. He said he had business to attend to. That business had been Orson, her friend.

"Did he see Roulette?" Luke asked the most important question.

"No, he didn't even go near the barn. He didn't seem as interested in any horse as he was in Dawn. He just gave me a scare, showing up like that." Orson took a clean, silk handkerchief from his pocket and touched his forehead several times.

"Why would Manetti come to you?"

"When I first came to Louisiana, Mr. Manetti and I talked. He was interested in a mare I had, and eventually acquired her." Orson continued talking, unaware of the look Dawn shot at Luke. "He was helpful, and we've seen each other occasionally at some meetings or at the track. My friendship with the people at Dancing Water Ranch is no secret, and I assumed that he called because of that.''

"What did you tell him?" Dawn found her voice a little shaky.

"I said you were an astute woman with an eye for horses. I said if you'd managed to make a little money on the side, you were smart enough not to go running around the country, blabbing about it."

Luke's grin was contagious. "Excellent work, Orson."

Dawn felt her anxiety ease slightly. Manetti was checking up on her, but that was a normal business precaution. She should have expected it. And she should have called Freddie and warned him!

"Orson, I need to use your phone. I'll bet Manetti has already called Dancing Water. There's no telling what Freddie might have said!" She rose as Luke pulled out her chair for her.

"Whoa, girl." Orson shook his head in a slow, determined fashion. "I'm a step ahead of you. I told Manetti that the man in charge of Dancing Water was an irritable old rascal. I sort of convinced him not to bother Freddie at all."

Dawn dropped back into her chair, a wide smile replacing her frown. "You're wonderful. How did you manage to think of everything?"

"I don't know what you're up to...." He held up a hand. "I don't want to know. But I do know Freddie, and if he thought someone was checking up on you, he'd be worried sick. He's too old to worry like that. But maybe you should give him a call and check in, just to see what's happening. Feel free to use the phone in the den, or go on back to my private study."

"Thanks." Dawn turned to Luke. "I should call him. Just to see if I have a job left after traipsing all over the country."

"Go ahead. Orson and I can always talk horses."

Dawn slipped out of the kitchen and made her way back to Orson's study. She closed the door and dialed the ranch.

"When are you getting yourself home?" Freddie was blunt.

"As soon as I can. We haven't found that filly, but I think I'm going to get a look at her tomorrow."

"Look at her! What good's that going to do? Looking won't help anything."

"Once I see her, I'll get her," Dawn promised him. "And Freddie. I'm fine. Don't worry. Have you had any interesting calls?'"

She waited, silently holding her breath. A large, glass container perched on the desk contained hundreds of matchbooks. She reached in, dragging out a handful to examine. Weeding through them, she discarded the mundane. The names of famous restaurants, bars and hotels, Arnaud's, Brennan's, Antoine's, were all familiar. Orson had acquired an impressive collection from New Orleans establishments. Elegant settings and fine cuisine were two of his weaknesses.

There was also one from John Morrow's House, a distinctive, brocaded cover with fine, antique lettering. A black one with heavy, gold embossing in the design of a horse's head caught her eye. The concept was striking, and Dawn flipped it over several times, wondering if Orson was getting ready to launch some new advertising gimmick. He was always talking about the need for name recognition for his ranch. The year before, he'd wasted several thousand dollars on monogrammed balloons.

"None!" Freddie's emphatic answer drew her back to the moment. "No phone calls. If you aren't home in two days, I'm coming over there looking for you. Understand?" Freddie was in one of his irascible moods.

"I do." She blew him a kiss as she flipped open the matches and hung up. Mr. D's was the only name. With a hint of disappointment, she dropped it back into the glass jug. She'd half expected to see Applegate Farms on it. She stood, stretching long. Dancing Water was secure, untouched by the series of events that had her ricocheting around like a rubber ball. That was something to be thankful for.

Returning to the kitchen, she stopped just outside the door.

"Were you ever in jumpers?" Luke's question was clear, direct.

"No. I've thought about it, especially since I haven't really made the name for myself in runners that I dreamed about. Down here, though, there's so many jumpers and not that big a market for a real quality horse. It's a tough decision."

"Yes, it is."

"You're not trying to convince Orson to breed jumpers, are you?" Dawn pushed open the door. "Luke isn't that involved in racing, but he breeds hunter-jumpers, right?"

Luke nodded, apparently eager to change the subject. "I do, but not on a big scale."

"You train, too, right?" Dawn pressed. Luke had to open up to her. Her trust depended on it.

"A few."

"And riders, too?"

"Yes, riders, too." He pushed his chair back from the table. "If you're satisfied that Roulette is doing good, we should leave. I want to go back to the track tonight."

"Not to see Manetti?" Dawn felt a chill.

"No, to the paddocks. A few more questions, a little more watching, maybe we'll get lucky."

"You guys still at that swank guest cottage?" Orson shook his head. "New Orleans can be a mighty romantic place."

"That's true, but horse thieves and killings sort of take the romance right out of the environment," Luke answered smoothly, giving Dawn time to collect herself. The flush that touched her cheeks was very pretty, and it cut him to the bone. The thought of the kiss they'd shared made him eager to hold her, to touch her. But he was convinced his past had endangered her, and he couldn't let her get any closer.

"You're a born meddler, Orson," Dawn said. "On that note, I'm ready to go back to New Orleans, Mr. O'Neil. We have work to do."

On the drive back, the long silence between Dawn and Luke grew strained. The past seemed to have driven a wedge between them.

They were almost at the tracks before Luke spoke. "I don't think Manetti will hurt you, Dawn. I think you got involved in this by mistake."

"Is there a reason he'd want to hurt you? Have you done something wrong?" It was as close as she could come to a point-blank question. She dared not look at him, for fear he might see the tears that had begun to collect in the corners of her eyes.

"If Manetti has a reason to hate me, I haven't been able to think of it. Not yet." Luke maneuvered the car skillfully. His gaze followed the shifting traffic, but his attention was on his carefully chosen words.

"If there was something, you'd tell me, wouldn't you?" Dawn felt foolish asking. She was practically begging him.

"There are things that I want to tell you."

"Then do it!" she pressed. "How can I trust you, if you aren't honest with me?" She felt her heartbeat triple. He was going to tell her. He was going to prove Freddie wrong and tell the truth about his past. She started to touch him, to offer the most basic encouragement and support.

"For right now, Dawn, it would be safer if you didn't trust anyone." His words were cold. "If you knew the whole truth, you'd be a bigger target. Manetti told you that innocence is your best defense. Manetti is a smart man." It took rigid control to be so harsh with her, but he had to keep her out of his path. Warning her would be futile. She was too brave to consider her own neck, so he had to do something to put distance between them.

He turned the car into the track's parking lot. He was out of the door and handing the valet the key before Dawn could ask anything else of him.

THE BETTING WINDOWS were lined twelve deep. Jefferson Downs had opened only that week, and the cool spring weather made the track irresistible for horse fanciers. Dressed in old jeans and sweaters, Dawn and Luke sauntered about the windows, listening, watching, hoping for some idle gesture or overheard word that might indicate the whereabouts of Private Stock. It took all of Dawn's concentration to keep up the casual front. She wanted to push Luke into a handy corner, to force him to come to terms with her and her doubts. He could instruct her to stay innocent, but it wasn't quite that simple.

"I'm going to the stable area. I might have better luck alone." Luke didn't look at Dawn as he spoke. He was cool, as if he barely knew her and she were a major inconvenience.

"Certainly." All traces of hurt were convincingly covered with a smile. "The idea of working alone has a great deal of appeal tonight. Good luck." She edged toward a window, her racing form gripped tightly. All around her the talk was of horses, and she was determined to lose herself in the crowd. Two men arguing caught her ear.

"Blue's Gray is the horse of the year, I'm telling you."

"He won't stand a chance, if the horse I know makes it to the track."

"Blue's Gray, to hell with whoever else races."

"You're a fool. I'm trying to give you a tip, and you won't even listen. My cousin works for the track. He said there's a filly comin' that will run circles around everything else on four legs."

"Bah! I hear this filly story every year. A filly hasn't got what it takes. They fade."

Dawn cast a furtive glance at the two men. They were in lightweight jackets, casual slacks, nothing significant. But her wild heartbeat told her that there was a slim possibility they were talking about Private Stock.

"Yeah?"

She looked up blankly at the man behind the betting window. His hands were above the buttons that would key her ticket. "Well?" he repeated. "You gonna bet?"

"Number six." She spoke without any idea of what horse she was betting on.

The man took her money and pushed her ticket toward her.

"Yeah?" He asked the man behind her.

Dawn lingered, hoping the two would mention the filly again, but their talk had turned to family grievances. They placed their bets, arguing as they went back to the floor seats. Dawn tailed them as closely as she dared.

For twenty minutes she strained to follow their conversation, as she pretended to read her racing form. When one man got up to place more bets, she decided to make a move.

"Could you help me with this form?" she asked the man who'd mentioned the filly. "I've been sitting here trying and trying, and I can't understand this."

"The simplest thing to do, if you don't follow the horses, is pick out a name you like, or a color." He was brusque and impatient. "Racing forms won't help, if you don't know the horses."

"But I want to learn," Dawn persisted.

"I'm telling you, lady, just follow your intuition. That'll work better in the long run."

"If there was a girl horse running, I'd just bet on her. That would make sense to me."

The man turned to her sharply. "Girl horse?"

"Isn't that right? The male horses are stallions and the girl horses are . . . fillies, right?"

"I don't know anything about girl horses." He snatched the form from her hand and looked at it closely. "There's two fillies in this race. See the *F*, that's for filly. *S* is stallion and *G* is gelding. Now if that answers your questions, I'd like to be left alone."

"I didn't mean to bother you." Dawn took the empty seat his friend had vacated. "I'm just learning horses. My father left me some money and I've never really had much chance to have fun. Some of my friends said I should throw a little away on the horses. They said it would do me good, so here I am, and I've only placed one two-dollar bet." She laughed at herself, shrugging her shoulders in a self-deprecating manner. "I can't seem to do it without at least trying to make a wise investment. But I'll go put a hundred dollars each on those two fillies. That should help." She started to rise, but the man reached out a hand and detained her.

"A hundred on each filly?"

"Well, I don't know which one is best. If I knew that, I'd be willing to go more. You see, I promised myself I'd spend at least five thousand on this trip. Sort of an exercise in selfishness, don't you think?"

"Your husband thinks this is a good idea?"

Dawn blushed prettily. "I don't have a husband. Since my father died, there's only me."

"You like betting the horses?"

Dawn felt the jaws of the fish closing on her bait. "If I knew more, or if I could find that one horse to really put my money on, then I'd be happier, I think. Some female horse."

"There's a match race cooking that you might be interested in." The man gave her another suspicious look.

"Match race?"

"Yeah, just two horses. One of them's a filly. Big horse with lots of power."

"Why only two horses?" Dawn widened her eyes. "There's usually nine or so, aren't there?"

"This is a private race. But if you're interested, and have some money to bet, I might be able to help you place a wager. In my name, of course. This is a strictly private affair."

"Would you do that?" She leaned slightly toward him. "At first I thought you were going to be rude. Now though, it seems you're a very nice man to take an interest in my needs. This match race sounds very exciting. When?"

"It's set for tomorrow."

"Here? What fun!"

The man hesitated. "Not here. There's a private track. It's a good track, just out of the way."

"How exciting! I didn't realize that was possible. How will I get there?"

"Uh, well, that's a problem. See, it's a private race and you can't go."

Dawn's face fell. "Well it won't be much fun to bet, if I can't watch the race. That would almost be like buying another CD. So impersonal, you know. I'm supposed to be having fun spending this money. That doesn't sound like much fun." She started to rise.

"It's at one of the old estates, used to be a sugarcane plantation. I could tell you how to get there, and you could watch from a distance. But you have to promise not to come to the track, okay?"

Dawn brightened immediately. "That's fine. I could do that, sort of sneak around to watch." She shivered deliciously. "This sounds more like it."

"It's Riverman's Run." He gave her quick directions. "Be there tomorrow at six. I'll find you and get the money. Five thousand, right? I'll make the bet and bring you the winnings. There's not a doubt that filly will tear the other horse up."

"The other horse is who?"

"Cajun Spice. He's a good runner, but not up to the filly."

"Cajun Spice." Dawn repeated the name, drawing a curious look from her new friend. She smiled. "It just sounds like something in a recipe."

He relaxed. "Yeah. See you tomorrow." He gave an uneasy look behind him and Dawn understood. He wanted her gone before his friend returned.

"Thanks for your help. You've really been a blessing to a poor woman who has so much to learn."

"You bet."

The man grinned, and Dawn felt as if she were talking with a shark. She turned away, eager to find Luke and relate her incredible good luck. If Manetti failed her in the morning, then she had the race at six. Surely one would yield Private Stock. Surely.

A BLOOD-BAY STALLION crested his neck and laid back his ears as a groom approached with his saddle.

"Easy, Bunyan," the groom cajoled. "It's me, Sam, so be nice."

Luke watched the groom edge toward the horse. The stallion was having none of it. With ears flat against his head in displeasure, he nipped at the groom, just catching his jacket.

"Now get back, old man!" The groom waved an angry fist at the horse. "You're too mean. You're going to end your days in a dog food can."

Unintimidated, the horse made another attack as soon as the groom stepped near.

"Need some help?" Luke asked.

"His temper's vile." The groom, a man in his forties, threw Luke a smile. "Bunyan and I have been playing at this war for several seasons now. He hates the saddle and he loves the race. But he can't do one without the other."

"Let me hold his head." Luke stepped forward and settled a hand on the horse's halter. While the groom rapidly cinched the tiny racing saddle tight, Luke kept a firm hold on the halter and spoke softly to the horse.

"All done, my boy." The groom patted the horse's neck. "He's so well mannered, except for the saddle. He dearly hates it. Makes me wonder what wonderful experience he might have had."

"Luke O'Neil." Luke held out his hand.

"Sam Sinclair." The groom took his hand in a firm grip. "Thanks for the help." One day old Bunyan's going to get me, and then he'll be sorry."

"And so will you. He's a strong animal."

"This'll be his last season. He'll go for claim or sale at the end of this year." Sam Sinclair shook his head.

"He'd make a nice jumper," Luke commented.

"I only hope he's that lucky." Sam didn't continue the thought. It was clear to Luke that each year a lot of horses passed through the track. "You have an animal running?"

"No, I raise jumpers."

"Looking over some prospects?"

"In a manner of speaking. I'm also looking for one horse in particular."

"Aren't we all?" Sam shook his head and laughed. "That one horse that will bring our ship in. That creature of fantasy."

Luke liked Sam Sinclair. The man had patience, humor and wit. "I've seen this horse, Sam. I know she exists. A big, bay filly by the name of Private Stock."

The humor drained slowly out of Sam's wrinkled face. "You're asking after the wrong horse, mister. She's a phantom that won't ever run on a regulation track. She's..." He looked in both directions. "She's not one to be talking or asking about."

"I have to find her," Luke insisted.

"Why don't you just go out and buy a gun and shoot yourself? That would be so much simpler, and probably a lot more pleasant than what's going to happen to you if you don't leave that horse alone." Sam's eyes were narrow and he leaned back against the paddock wall. "They'll kill you."

"They've already killed one man."

The news didn't appear to affect Sam. "I know they're capable of it. I saw the filly once, by accident. The story I got was that she was stolen, or her sire was stolen. The guy wasn't clear. But he was positive that the best way to handle it was to forget I'd ever seen her." For a moment the fear left Sam's face and was replaced by awe. "I've never seen an animal run the way she does. And she can go the distance. Watching her was like a dream."

"Where is she?" Luke touched Sam's shoulder with urgency.

"I don't know." Sam came back to himself, and once again looked up and down the area. "I don't want to know. I hear she's owned by some gangster. Has his own track, his own wine cellar, his own stables. His own army." He pointed a finger at Luke and pressed it into his chest. "And they use real bullets, so take some advice and find another horse to chase."

"I wish I could," Luke said. He'd felt too close, and now he was no closer at all. "There's nothing you could tell me that might help?"

Sam went back into the stall with Bunyan. He looked at Luke over the horse's withers. "Why are you looking for this horse?"

"Someone's involved me in something I don't like. I want to know who, and why."

"And if you find out?"

"I don't know. My future is at stake, everything I care about." Involuntarily he thought of Dawn. He'd certainly lose her if he didn't find out what had happened. He should have told her the truth in the beginning. Now it might be too late.

"There's a place over across Lake Pontchartrain. I don't recall the guy's name, but he's in tight with the wise guys from Chicago. He has horses. That's a good place to start."

"Manetti?" Luke asked. "Is that the name?"

Sam paused. "Naw, I don't know. I spend most of my time in California. New Orleans is a new track to me, so I'm not familiar. All I know is that filly is a ticket to death. But if it's any help, I hear they're going to run her soon."

"Thanks." Luke started to walk away.

"Listen. If you get in trouble, forget you talked to me. Okay?"

Something in the man's voice touched a raw nerve in Luke. He turned around. "I've already forgotten your name," he promised.

"Watch your back."

Chapter Ten

"He's a beautiful animal." Dawn couldn't keep the disappointment from her voice as she watched the black stallion stretch across the finish line.

"But not the right horse for you." Louis Manetti finished the sentence for her.

"I'm sorry." She crossed her legs. To her surprise, she was sitting in Manetti's private club at the Jefferson Downs track. The black stallion, Demon's Way, was running against another stallion in an unofficial, early-morning breeze.

"He's a magnificent horse. The best I've seen this year," Manetti countered.

Dawn looked at him, trying to read humor or satire in his face or voice. She saw nothing except honest puzzlement. "He's magnificent, but not the horse for me. I'm sorry." She started to rise.

Manetti's hand on her arm stopped her. "I get the feeling that you were expecting another horse. Perhaps you had a specific animal in mind?"

Dawn felt the blood rush to her head. Deceiving Manetti was like tormenting a snake. He seemed relaxed, but he was capable of striking a deadly blow in a matter of seconds.

"Of course not. If I knew the horse, then I wouldn't have to go through you, would I?"

"What game are you playing, Ms. Markey? I've debated that thought and come up with some interesting scenarios, but no definite answers. You seem to be what you say you are, a horse trainer in Mississippi. I've checked around. You have a good reputation, though I'm concerned about your choice of friends."

"What do you know about Luke?" She shifted to the edge of her chair.

"That he's been in trouble in the horse world before. His reputation is far from impeccable. Of course, there was no criminal charge." He smiled his slow, lazy smile. "That leads me to believe Mr. O'Neil is a smart man. Not ethical, but smart. That's often far more important."

Dawn felt her already taut nerves stretch a little farther. "Is there another horse you might recommend? I'd hoped to make my purchase for this year's Derby."

"The black will beat anything I've seen, and believe me, I've made it a point to see the horses from California to Canada. There's nothing on either coast that can touch him, and he's sound. He's never been injured." He looked at her. "And he's legal."

"Is there an alternative to 'legal' that I should be aware of?" Dawn held her breath.

"I warned you once, Ms. Markey. If you're poking around as a front for that criminal, you'll pay a very high price. I've considered the idea that you were spying for him. Is that possible?"

"You also told me that innocence was the perfect mask. I don't have to pretend. I don't know who you're talking about. But now that you mention duplicity, are you holding out on the better horse? Maybe you don't trust me enough to show me the best."

"You're a very bright woman." His lazy appraisal went from her head to her ankles. "Are you tired of training in

Mississippi? I could give you a chance to start in my business."

"No thanks. I'm an ambitious woman. I want my own stallion, my own business. Now, if you'll take me home..."

Manetti signaled to one of his men. "We'll meet again, Ms. Markey. Think about the black. You have until tomorrow. I respect your judgment of horseflesh, but Demon's Way will win the Derby. You can be a winner, too."

"I intend to." Dawn picked up her purse and preceded the driver out of the room.

The disappointment was so great that she was afraid she'd cry on the way back to the hotel. She'd been so certain Manetti was going to show her the filly. But he had no intention of taking an unknown into his inner circle. She'd been a fool to think otherwise, a silly fool to get her hopes up.

She rushed to the suite, high heels clicking across the lobby floor.

"Miss?" The clerk called after her. "I have a message for you."

Short of breath, she turned back and took the sealed envelope from his hand. She tore it open and read the contents. Unnoticed, the envelope slipped from her suddenly nerveless hand and fell to the floor.

The clerk was watching her with open interest, she could see. All around her the lobby was the same as always. But everything had nonetheless changed—her perception of her surroundings, even her ability to move her arms and legs.

"Miss?" The clerk started around the counter to her side. "Is something wrong?"

"No," she mumbled. She stumbled slightly, then felt his supporting hand on her arm. "Who left this?"

"I didn't see. It was pushed under the door." Disapproval was evident in his manner. "Can I get you some water?"

"No." She straightened her back. "I'm going to my room and I'll be fine."

She had to talk to Luke. She had to make a decision. The words of the note kept playing across her mind as she walked slowly to their rooms.

"Return home or Freddie will pay." The note was unsigned, typewritten. Attached to the page was a tiny clip of a flannel shirt, one of Freddie's favorites.

"Luke!" She called him softly as she entered the suite. She'd expected him to be waiting for her, anxious to hear her news. "Luke!" The stillness of the apartment made her stop in the den. Midday sun stole through the rooms, but they were as silent as a summer classroom.

She had to pack, to pull her things together and go back to Dancing Water. With Freddie and the ranch in danger, she had no choice. Luke could continue to hunt. She'd help him all she could, while protecting Freddie.

Hurriedly she threw her few belongings into her carryall. Her expectation of seeing Luke at any moment strained her nerves to the point where any slight noise on the street made her jump. When she was finished and there was still no sign of Luke, she went to his room to leave a note.

Reality struck hard at her stomach. Luke's things were gone, and so was he.

Stunned, she stood in the middle of the room. At first she didn't trust her eyes. She searched the closet for his luggage. The room was swept clean of anything that might indicate Luke had once been there. And there was no note to indicate where he might have gone.

She dropped onto the bed, too shaken to cry. She had a decision to make. Should she keep her appointment at six with the man she'd met at the track? Since she had no intention of giving Manetti $100,000, she hadn't worried about her lack of funds. But if she met her appointment at the track, she had to have the cash. There was that much available in the Dancing Water accounts, but could she dare risk it? Her head throbbed at the very idea of losing Ann's reserve cash. Could she risk Freddie? And could she leave, without trying every last avenue to find Private Stock and Speed Dancer?

Leaning on her elbows, she put her face into her hands. Luke O'Neil had simply vanished. If his belongings hadn't been taken, she would have been even more worried about him. As it was, it appeared he'd simply tired of the chase— or thought better of it. Several times he'd mentioned priorities at his own farm. She understood that. But he hadn't even left a note.

She stood and began checking the rooms to make sure she had everything picked up. Walking out, she took a look around. New Orleans was a romantic city. Her heart twisted, and she knew that her feelings for Luke had grown very strong—despite Freddie's warnings to the contrary.

At the desk she settled the account. The clerk hadn't seen Luke leave, and at her question he gave her a strange, probing look. He obviously thought she'd been abandoned and stuck with the bill, and indeed she felt slightly that way, as she hefted her bag and walked out into the sun.

LUKE GRUNTED as the luggage landed on top of his chest. He recognized the bag as his own. So they'd been to the suite and cleared out his things. What of Dawn? He shifted his head slightly from side to side. He was alone in the back of the van. The ropes that bound his hands and feet were painfully tight, restricting all movement to a mere fraction of a degree.

He tried to piece together what had happened, but he was still groggy from the effects of whatever drug they'd used to sedate him. Chloroform, he supposed, judging from the queasy way his stomach was reacting.

He'd been sitting in a rental car, drinking coffee and waiting for Dawn. When he'd followed her to the New Orleans track, he'd been more than a little surprised. He'd expected some private rendezvous with Manetti, a hidden place for an illegal horse. The public location afforded him a tiny measure of relief.

The arrangements with his bank for a cash advance were complete. If he needed the hundred thousand for Dawn to maintain her front with Manetti, it was available. He'd also purchased a gun. He was tired of being the only player in the game without a weapon.

Now, bumping from one side of the van to another, he realized that his precautions had been useless. He was a captive, and Dawn was on her own.

The van slowed and he relaxed his body, forcing his eyes to close. If he pretended to still be under the influence of the drug, he might learn something.

"Take him in the basement."

Luke had a vague recollection of that voice, but was too cautious to open his eyes and look at the man. He'd heard him before, though, and in the not too distant past.

"He won't get away this time."

At last the recognition registered. The speaker was the tall, thin man from Oakdale Stables in Hot Springs. A twinge almost made Luke jump, as rough hands grabbed him and dragged him from the van. He used all of his concentration to remain limp.

"Is he dead?"

The second voice was unfamiliar, a singsong accent that spoke of Caribbean islands. Luke peeked quickly and caught a flash of a man who could easily claim island heritage.

"He isn't dead. Not yet. But as soon as The Boss gives the word, it'll be my pleasure to make him as dead as yesterday's lunch meat." The tall thin man laughed.

"Why you so mean, Mr. Bertrane?" The islander was making conversation, as he let Luke's feet thump harshly against the pavement. "Why you kill this man, after all the trouble we go to to get him? Is he an evil man? Is he wicked?"

"Gele, you are a fool." The thin man laughed out loud. "I'll kill him because he's an inconvenience. So you just keep that in mind. When you get to be an inconvenience, The Boss will one day decide to have you thrown in the Mississippi."

"I swim real good, Mr. Bertrane."

"Not with a pound of lead in your gut." Bertrane's laugh was cruel. "You stay on my good side, and I'll see that The Boss gets only good reports about you."

"You a man of great influence, Mr. Bertrane. Very great influence."

Luke couldn't resist another peek, and to his surprise he found himself staring into the warm, dark eyes of the man called Gele. In that split second of contact, he realized that Gele's humor covered a deep contempt for the other man.

"I do have some power with The Boss." Bertrane continued talking, unaware that Luke had regained consciousness.

"I take him to the basement." Gele slid an arm under Luke and hoisted him unceremoniously over his shoulder. "The basement, right?"

"Good work, Gele. Good work."

Luke felt a wave of queasiness attack as he hung upside down over Gele's shoulder, but he had to control it. The islander had not given him away. The jolting steps down into the dank basement were almost his undoing. He didn't even groan as the wiry islander dropped him to the floor.

"What you do to make The Boss so mad, he let Benny Bertrane have you?"

Luke forced himself to a sitting position and opened his eyes. The darkness made him feel better, but he could hardly discern the features of the man who stood before him.

"I think I'm hunting for something he doesn't want me to find."

"Drugs, liquor, women, money, horses, which?"

"A horse."

In the dim light, Luke could see the smile on the other man's face.

"Gele likes horses. Very pretty. Lots of trouble."

"I like them, too, but I didn't plan on dying while in the middle of hunting one."

"The river is full of people with too many questions." Gele settled on the floor. "Mr. Bertrane has put a good number of them there, and then Louis Manetti gets the blame. Very clever for Mr. Bertrane. That's why he is so popular with The Boss."

Luke's stomach had settled considerably, and the last vestiges of the drugs were wearing off. There were questions to be asked, and Gele had plenty of answers.

"Who is this boss person that everyone talks about?"

"The man who pays my ticket. The man who runs the show. Put more simply, the man." Gele grinned.

"That's no help." Luke was beginning to like the infectious humor. He didn't trust the islander. At any moment he could decide that Luke was a detriment to his future. Then again, he knew that Gele hated Benny Bertrane with the pure, focused hatred that comes from a man who has suffered at another man's hands.

"What's Benny Bertrane to you?"

"Toad excrement. Unfortunately, he is The Boss's right-hand man. Your escape from Arkansas put Mr. Bertrane in a very bad light. You will pay for that. Bertrane will see that you are very sorry." There was no threat in Gele's words, only acceptance of the inevitable.

"Benny is your boss?"

"He is not often in New Orleans. If that were not so, perhaps I'd have to kill him."

Luke shifted, to allow the blood to circulate more freely into his legs. He'd been cramped in the van, too sedated to move. A tingling burn crept up his limbs, signaling the return of use. "Mind if I walk around?"

"Help yourself. Do not try to leave, or I will have to hurt you. I have no grudge, Mr. O'Neil. I wish only to preserve myself, my job. I have no wish to suffer, as you will when Mr. Bertrane returns."

The words were chilling, matched with Gele's certainty of what the future held. Luke carefully surveyed the dark room in which he was being held prisoner. There was a door to the outside, the one which they'd used to enter, and a second door up a flight of steps that obviously went into the house or office above. If only he'd been able to get a look at the neighborhood. For all he knew he could be at the docks, in downtown New Orleans, along the lake or in the ghettos.

"You are not far from the river." Gele volunteered the information readily. "We brought you from the track. The Boss has some questions you will answer, I believe."

"What about the woman?" Luke couldn't stop the jolt that struck at his heart.

"Ms. Markey is in the guardianship of Ricky. She is safe, for the moment."

His last three words were loaded with an ominous threat.

"For the moment? Are there plans to hurt Dawn?"

"She will find you gone, then go home herself. If that happens, she will be safe. If she persists in causing trouble, the fact that she is a pretty woman will not protect her. All who interfere pay the price. It has always been so."

"We're only looking for a horse, a bay filly."

Gele shook his head. "You were warned."

"The horse is..."

"Do not tell me any more." He rose as gracefully as a wild creature. "My wife and children remain in Jamaica. Until they are with me, I do not want to know the troubles of others. Don't you see?"

"I can see that someone is using the safety of your wife and children to blackmail you, and I'd be willing to bet it's Benny Bertrane."

"Mr. Bertrane is a ruthless man, and he is also very clever, as I said before. When my family is safe, perhaps he will pay for his cleverness in a way he never expected."

As ruthless as Luke knew Benny Bertrane to be, he understood that Gele was by far the more dangerous of the two men.

"Are you going to kill me?"

"No. That is reserved for Mr. Bertrane. I am only to watch you."

"There's nothing I can offer to make you let me go?"

"If you escape, I am a dead man, and my family will be tortured and then killed. There is nothing you can offer me."

Luke sank back onto his heels against the wall. It was an impossible situation. He and Gele were both caught in Manetti's web. He leaned against the wall, eyes roving the basement for an escape route. The islander had no gun, but he was alert. To surprise him, Luke needed a weapon. As his hand brushed the floor, his fingers found wood. Moving carefully, he traced the outline of a two-by-four that was as long as a bat. Though he had no desire to hurt the friendly Gele, he knew he had to make a move.

Before Gele could think to react, Luke lunged forward and swung. The board caught the islander on the side of the head. His face folding in an expression of disbelief, Gele fell over Luke's shoulder.

"I can't leave you for Bertrane to kill," Luke mumbled to the semiconscious man as he hauled him up the stairs.

The keys were still in the van's ignition, and Luke drove straight for the John Morrow House. He was twenty minutes away, and a clock at a bank showed that it was 4:00 p.m. If Dawn was waiting for him, he'd just have time to follow her out to the match race. If Dawn was safe, if she hadn't been abducted, if she hadn't found the filly, if, if, if. He drove faster and kept glancing back to make sure Gele didn't come to.

The islander was still unconscious when Luke parked in front of the hotel. He was halfway across the lobby when the clerk's voice stopped him.

"She checked out at two."

He turned to face the man, the same clerk who'd been on call the night Jack the Knife was murdered. "Did she say where she was going?"

"I'm not so certain she'd want you to know." He gave Luke a thoroughly disapproving look down his nose. "She paid the bill and left."

Luke held on to his temper by exerting all of his hard-won control. "Did she leave alone? Did she have any visitors, messages?"

A flicker of worry swept down the clerk's thick brows. "Perhaps you should ask the lady."

Luke took three long steps and grasped the clerk's tie and shirtfront. "Her life could be in danger. I have to find her."

"There was a message." The clerk fumbled behind the counter, his gaze fixed on Luke's angry countenance. "It's right here." He produced the crumpled letter. "I thought you'd sent it to her, to scare her away."

Smoothing out the letter, Luke read the typewritten warning with a sense of dread. Dawn was all alone, and someone dangerous was after her. There was no chance now that she'd leave the search for Private Stock behind. That warning was the last motivation Dawn needed to keep hunting until she found the filly, or until someone stopped her.

"The letter was pushed under the door. I almost threw it away, but then thought better and decided to give it to her."

"Thanks." Luke interrupted the clerk's flow of words and stalked out into the street.

Gele was slowly coming around when Luke slid into the back of the van. He shook the islander's arm. "Where is Bertrane staying?"

"My head is exploding." Gele pressed his palms to his temples. "You hit me with a club. You, too, are a clever man."

"Bertrane will hurt Dawn." Luke resisted the impulse to shake awareness into Gele. Every second was crucial, but he had to allow Gele time to pull himself together.

"They will not hurt the woman. Not until this evening." Gele's dark eyes were more focused, the corners of his lips touching up into a rueful smile. "You didn't leave Gele behind for Mr. Bertrane to kill."

"I thought about it, then decided I liked your accent too much." Luke grinned. "How do you know they won't hurt Dawn until this evening?"

"I heard them talk. They have set her up to go to that plantation. They have some surprise for her." He touched Luke's arm in a soft, stilling gesture. "I heard them say she would prove useful. I did not understand everything."

With his unexpected ally in the front seat, Luke drove toward the secluded plantation where Dawn was supposed to place the bet on the fast filly. It was obvious from what Gele had said that the whole episode was a plant. He raced through the possibilities. They could be intending to corner Dawn and capture her, or the plan might be to let her see the filly, and somehow use that information to further their own goals.

"Gele, who is this man you call The Boss?" It was a crucial bit of information.

"I have never heard his real name." Gele's singsong voice was sincere. "He does not live in this city, but he has many interests here. He is a gambler, with much money in Las Vegas. It is the horses that he loves. Horses, women and wine. He is also a man who knows how to hold a grudge for many years."

The last, chilling sentence sharpened something in Luke's memory. Dawn had questioned him about his past. There were plenty of things he hadn't wanted to tell her at the time, but none of them involved gambling or mobsters. But what of Ann Tate's background? There had been trouble at Dancing Water Ranch in the past. Serious trouble. And the videotape had been addressed to Ann, not Dawn.

"This woman, is she yours?" Gele's question was softly put.

"We aren't married, if that's what you're asking."

"But you care for her?"

"A great deal."

"Then I will help you, because I know what it is when the woman you love is in danger. My wife, Cecelia, will know and approve of what I do."

Luke put his hand on Gele's shoulder. "I'll take your help, and if there's anything I can do to help you in return, I will."

"We must be very careful, Mr. O'Neil. The men with Mr. Bertrane are cruel. They enjoy killing, even when it is not necessary. They will not hurt the woman as long as she is useful. After that—" he rolled his eyes "—she will swim with the fishes, just like they planned to do to you."

Chapter Eleven

Dawn parked on top of the small knoll, protected by a thick windbreak of camellias and azaleas. The dirt track, obviously a private affair, was clearly visible below her, yet she was concealed by the shrubs.

The lights around the course flared on, even though the sky was still alive with evening sun. Two horses were led onto the track. The jockeys were mounted, their silks fluttering in a soft breeze that had kicked in from the south.

Like a woman in a trance, Dawn got out of the car and stepped forward. She was unaware of her surroundings, of the time, of all extraneous thoughts or details. All of her attention was focused on a large, bay filly that danced from one side of the track to the other. A magnificent roan gelding, at least two inches taller, paced beside her. Both horses were eager to run, but Dawn saw only the bay filly.

"Private Stock." She whispered the name and realized suddenly how appropriate it was. The filly was a rare combination of genetics, conditioning and luck.

"You bring the money?" The man from Jefferson Downs came around her car.

"It's on the front seat." Dawn had no qualms about betting Ann's five thousand on the filly. There was no way she wouldn't win. All of the anxieties she'd suffered as she withdrew the money from the bank were gone with one look at the horse.

"I've put the bet in my name. After the race, just drive away and I'll bring you your winnings tomorrow."

At last Dawn turned her attention to the man. In the evening light he looked rumpled, greasy and reprehensible. "I'll wait here. You'll excuse me if I'm not quite as stupid as I act."

Instead of getting angry, he grinned. "I knew that business about wanting to bet on a girl horse was all a trick. I'm not so stupid, either. But what difference does it make, if we both earn a little on the game? That's the question I ask."

"A superb question. What's the filly's name, and who owns her?"

"I'm not in the business of answering questions for nothing."

"Bet the money and bring me back my original five thousand. I don't care about the winnings, if you give me the right answers."

The man settled on the fender of her car. "Ask away, lady. You seem to pay a very decent hourly wage."

"Who owns the horse?"

"Think you're going to buy her?" The man was condescending.

"Remember, I'm asking the questions." She knew she had to maintain control. Something about the man's attitude was unsettling. "Who owns her, and is she for sale?"

"She belongs to The Boss, lady, and once he owns something, he never turns it loose. Next question?"

"The Boss isn't exactly a specific name."

"Specific enough. He's a very powerful man. He controls this city, in more ways than one. Maybe, for your own good, it's better you don't know too much about him."

"Would his name be Louis Manetti?" Dawn pressed the point.

The man grinned. "The more you talk, the more I wonder that you're alive." He pointed down to the track. "The horses are getting ready to break."

Dawn laced her hands in front of her to keep from clenching them into fists. Both horses went eagerly into the gate, and in a matter of seconds the doors sprang open. The roan shot out, front legs reaching. Dawn clearly read the jockey's strategy to go for the lead and try to tire out Private Stock in the opening furlongs.

A smile of sheer pleasure tilted the corners of her mouth. Private Stock came out of the gate like royalty in a review. There was no hurry, not a wasted motion in her lean, powerful body. She followed the roan a half length behind, as refreshed as if she were on a spring stroll. At the turn she moved in beside him, and down the homestretch she opened wide, extending to her fullest.

"Magnificent." Dawn spoke out loud. Even the man beside her was struck silent for the last seconds of the race. Dawn watched the filly cross the finish line with a sense of total satisfaction. "Looks like you won your bet." The man shifted from foot to foot. "You sure you want to wait here? In a minute they'll kill the track lights, and it'll be dark."

The delicate, spring dusk had given way to a blue darkness that crept from the eastern horizon. The idea of waiting on the isolated knoll, not far from an old, abandoned plantation, wasn't very appealing. Neither was the thought of leaving Ann's ranch money in the hands of the man who stood before her.

"I'm not afraid of the dark. I'll wait. Don't make it too long, though, or I'll begin to think that I'm double-crossed." The humor was laced with warning. "I wasn't foolish enough to come here alone."

"Is that right?" The man sounded interested. "I didn't see anyone with you."

"That's the point. It wouldn't be much of a backup if you saw him." Dawn slipped into the car. "I'll wait here. Say, twenty minutes?"

"Thirty."

"I'll wait."

She watched him walk the long way to the track, glad to see him go, even if it meant waiting in the dark alone. If only Luke were nearby, watching out for her. She smothered the pang of betrayal that came with his name and turned her thoughts to the filly. Private Stock. She was in New Orleans, easily within touching distance. She'd told Freddie that once she saw her, she'd get her. That was a bold vow, and one she'd have to make good on. She cast about for a plan. She couldn't charge down to the stables single-handedly and demand the horse. She was reluctant to call the authorities. Roulette was safe, but Speed Dancer was still missing. A false step and she'd never find the stallion.

The lights on the track were suddenly doused, leaving the area in darkness. In a few moments she was able to detect the feeble light of a few stars. It was dark early, too soon for any illumination from the moon.

The loss of Luke's assistance jabbed painfully at her heart and mind. Working with him, she'd never felt over-whelmed. No matter what the odds, they'd always been able to think of a plan. Why had he left so suddenly, without even a goodbye note? As the initial feelings of betrayal began to recede, Dawn was struck by a terrible thought. What if he hadn't left voluntarily?

Footsteps on the gravel drew her attention, and she stepped from the car to gain an advantage. The tread was lighter than she'd expected, more assured. A figure approached, but she could barely make out the silhouette. The man was tall, well built.

"Ms. Markey?"

Louis Manetti's cultured voice came through the darkness.

"Mr. Manetti! What are you doing here?"

"The same thing you are." He spoke with urgency. "Why do you persist in putting yourself in such danger? For a horse?"

"I might ask you the same thing." She took a step toward him.

"Stop!" He started forward.

Dawn was determined to find out the truth. Louis Manetti was at the track with Private Stock. He was the key to finding Speed Dancer.

Her forward momentum was suddenly arrested as a strong hand clamped over her mouth and nose. A sickly-sweet smell made her gag. With all of her strength she turned and grasped the clothing of the man who held her. Her fingers caught at his pocket and she tore frantically. The cloth ripped, and then she slipped into a thick, warm fog.

"ARE YOU CERTAIN this is the place?" Luke could barely make out Gele's dark countenance in the van. They were at the plantation track, but there was no sign of life, not even a single light.

"This is it. I delivered the horse here this week. To Mr. Manetti's stalls."

"Louis Manetti?"

"He often brings green horses here for matches. Before he puts them on the public tracks. I understand it is a common practice. No big man wants a horse that doesn't finish properly." Gele's singsong logic was hard to argue with.

Luke parked the van in the shelter of camellia and azalea bushes. Below him, the oval track was barely discernible.

"She would have parked here." Gele spoke with authority.

"How can you be certain?"

"It is not uncommon for the track workers to bring friends to bet. It is a privilege of working for important men. These visitors are never allowed on the track, but this hill gives a proper view."

"The men who own the horses, they always know about these extra visitors?"

"Always."

So Dawn had been hoodwinked. He'd suspected it. All evening he'd felt a growing concern for her safety. No doubt Dawn thought he'd abandoned her, left without a word or a note. It was a perfect setup. Angry and hurt, Dawn's pride would not allow her to call his farm in Lexington. She'd never report him missing. When anyone began to suspect his absence, they'd check the bank records and find that he'd mortgaged his place to the hilt for a hundred thousand in cash. One look into his background, and the assumption would be that he'd taken the cash and run. No one would give it a second thought.

His fist struck the dash and he pushed open the van door. As he stepped to the ground, his foot encountered something and he tripped.

"Is there a flashlight in the van?" he called to Gele.

The islander emerged a moment later with a small plastic case. In the dim circle of light it cast on the ground, Luke quickly found a beige, high-heeled shoe. Dawn's shoe. He picked it up and noticed a book of matches. The rich, black paper was embossed with a heavy gold horse's head. Luke flipped open the matchbook. Below the name Mr. D's, a telephone number was scrawled.

Luke pocketed the matchbook, then held up the shoe for Gele to see. "This is Dawn's."

The islander took the light and searched the ground further. "It appears that a struggle took place here. The lady lost her shoe as she was being taken—" he pointed to the road that led down to the barns "—that way." Gele touched Luke's shoulder. "We should walk, very silently."

The road was empty, and the stables near the track seemed deserted as the two men hurried through the darkness. At the end of the stables, Gele paused. In the distance there was the sound of a horse shifting comfortably in a stall.

"The filly," Luke pronounced in a barely audible breath.

"Maybe, maybe not."

Luke started around the corner, then drew back suddenly. "There's a guard at the horse's stall." He peered around the corner slowly. A man was sitting in a chair, tilted back against the wooden wall. "He's asleep. We can take him."

"If he is the only one," Gele cautioned. "I must remind you that these are not stupid men. They do not take half measures."

The warning was not enough to slow Luke's determined charge. He was around the corner and bearing down on the man in the chair before Gele could reach out and stop him. Luke dived in a flying tackle, knocking out the chair from under the man. To his surprise, the guard didn't make a sound, but fell with his full weight on top of him.

"Sweet saints of preservation." Gele was at his side, pulling the man off him. "He is dead, Mr. Luke. This man is a dead man."

Luke could feel the deadweight atop him, the stiffness of the body. With Gele's help he was soon standing. "Did you bring that little flashlight?"

Gele snapped on the beam. Jack the Knife, white and bloodless, stared blankly at the night. Bound to his wrist was Dawn's other shoe. Luke retrieved the shoe and felt a small scrap of paper inside. His hopes soared at the thought that Dawn had been able to prepare a clue.

Gele held the light while he unfolded the paper. "I always collect my debts, and you, Luke O'Neil, owe me." The message was handwritten in the same bold scrawl that had addressed the videos. There was no signature.

Gele involuntarily backed up a step. His voice was frightened as he spoke. "They will kill you, Mr. Luke. You are a man marked for death. You must run away, if you want to live."

"I can't leave Dawn, Gele. You know that. But I won't ask you to involve yourself further. I'm afraid I've gotten you into enough trouble."

"I have done everything I know. The woman could be anywhere now. This man—" he pointed to Jack "—was highly respected. He could knife a person in a crowded elevator and get away. He was very useful to The Boss. Now he is dead. Soon we all will be."

"Take the van, Gele, and find a safe hiding place." Luke drew a pen from his pocket and on a scrap of the note he wrote his address. "Go to this place and tell them that you are my friend. You can stay there until I come home. Then I'll try and help you. Okay?"

"I will go there for a while, but then I must move on. They will hunt me now. They will not stop. My family..."

"I'm going to stop these people, Gele. They have to be stopped."

"Good luck." The islander put one gentle hand onto his shoulder, then turned and trotted off into the night.

Alone in the darkness with the lifeless body of Jack the Knife, Luke realized that his words had been spoken to give himself confidence as much as Gele. He didn't even know whom he was trying to stop. He had only the name The Boss, and the suspicion that The Boss and Louis Manetti were one and the same person.

Ignoring his distaste for the task, he made a quick check of the body. Inside the pocket of the jacket he found a book of matches with the same, distinctive black cover and gold horse's head. He tucked it away with the other pack he'd found and then moved down the stalls. A roan stallion was munching hay, but there was no sign of the bay filly, or of Dawn.

Leaving the empty track, Luke tried to line up his options. He could go straight to Manetti and make an accusation. That sounded like sure suicide. It was pointless to go back to John Morrow's. Dawn had checked out, taking all of her things. Even if she escaped, she wouldn't go back there. He reached into his pants pocket and drew out both matchbooks. One had a telephone number.

He broke into a run, covering the distance to the plantation in a short amount of time. The phone number might eventually lead him to the place where Dawn was hidden. Or it might lead him to another clue. The note left in Dawn's shoe implied that there was a motive behind his involvement. It wasn't happenstance that he'd been sent that tape. And so it appeared that the same would apply to Ann Tate. Possibilities rushed through his mind, only to be discarded, a second after consideration. There had to be a bond between Dawn, Ann, Private Stock and himself. A common denominator. Something from the past. He slowed as he approached the old mansion.

In the shadow of the enormous old house he stopped. Whatever life that had once been there was completely gone. Walking around the structure, he couldn't help thinking that the three stories could hide a wealth of secrets, or that one of the rooms would make a perfect prison for someone. Someone like Dawn.

He slipped away from the wide, front porch into a clump of crape myrtle trees. The small flashlight was in his hand, and his mind was made up to search the house, room by room. The feeling that he was being manipulated was strong, but still stronger was his concern for Dawn.

His footsteps thudded across the boards of the porch, and the front door opened as if it invited him inside. The flashlight did little to dispel the gloom that seemed to creep forward from every corner of the foyer. A scurrying sound alerted him to another living presence in the house. The place was likely a haven for rats and other creatures.

An elegance long past its prime was evident in the wall hangings, the curve of the stairs that led to the second floor. It didn't take much imagination to see the house as it must once have been. The glamour of the past didn't cover the present danger, though. Feeling his way down the wall, Luke turned all of his senses onto alert.

He went to the kitchen first, to check for signs of recent occupation. The weak beam of his light cut across an oak table, wooden counters. A thin layer of dust was everywhere, evenly distributed. No one had been in or near the kitchen for at least ten years.

The scurrying sound came again. He could well imagine a rat almost as big as he was. From the counter he picked up a wooden rolling pin, and as a second thought tucked a knife through his belt. He'd never imagined himself in the role of great explorer, but the feeling that Dawn was somewhere in the house persisted. Her shoe had been left for him to find. If she was being used as bait, then he'd certainly walked into the trap.

From the kitchen he went into a large, formal dining room, sitting rooms and a ballroom, but the first floor of the house yielded nothing. The rooms were sparsely furnished, and what little bit of furniture there was left was sadly going to ruin. He touched the velvet brocade of an old chair and felt it disintegrate in his hands.

When he was satisfied that there was no sign of anyone downstairs, he returned to the foyer. The flashlight was growing weaker, but in the dim glow he saw evidence of footsteps on the staircase. There were the footprints of two grown men, and the trail of something dragged between them.

Above him, the rat thumped and scurried. The biggest rat he'd ever heard.

His grip on the rolling pin tightened as he lifted it.

The noise grew louder, edged with an odd franticness. Something was trapped in a room of the house and couldn't get out. Something bigger than a rat.

Halfway up the stairs he stopped, one foot on the next step. A wild animal confined could be a serious adversary. A rabid animal was also a slim possibility. A tiny voice from his childhood warned of even worse things. As he started up the stairs again, a tight smile played at the corners of his mouth. The house was the classic setting for a haunting. For a split second he felt like every dumb actor called upon to explore a strange noise. As a teenager he'd watched such films and wondered at the stupidity of the character who went into the gloom. Yet here he was, doing the exact thing.

His danger was real, and behind it stood greedy, diabolical men. Whatever was rustling so frantically upstairs was human or animal, not supernatural.

Louder, more desperate now, the sounds came from a room to the left of the stairs. Luke felt a pang of sympathy for the creature trapped inside. It could hear him approach, sensing that danger was drawing ever nearer. With a little luck, he'd be able to free the creature without risking it or himself.

There was a loud bump, the sound of something heavy falling. A muffled sound came from the room, as if something struggled to speak. An iron rod of warning shot down his spine as he paused with his hand only inches from the doorknob.

Behind the closed door of the room there was only silence.

Instead of turning the knob, Luke drew back and kicked the solid oak door with all of his might. As it flew open, he dropped and rolled into the room. Behind him, the whack of a wooden club against the door frame let him know that he'd just missed playing a leading role in an ambush.

As he tumbled across the dirty floor, he caught a whirling view of Dawn, her eyes wide with fear and her mouth gagged. Hands and feet were bound to a chair. At the door, the muscular Ricky was struggling to his feet. The force of his swing had spun him into the door frame.

"You got me in big trouble with Benny and The Boss." Ricky was breathing hard, but his gaze was level on Luke. "I knew if I nabbed the girl, you'd come looking for her."

"I came looking for you." Luke took a deep breath as he crouched low and moved away from Dawn. Whatever happened, he didn't want her hurt. The club Ricky held was dangerous, shaped like a bat and made of solid wood. He knew from past experience that Ricky enjoyed introducing wood to muscle.

"We got business to settle. What'd you two do with that mare?"

"What mare?" Luke stalled, aware that Dawn would never tell about Roulette.

"Never mind. The Boss will find her. Nothin' ever escapes him for long. Nothin' and nobody."

Luke lunged, his body arching in the air as he lengthened himself for the full impact of the strike. He met Ricky's stomach with his shoulder, and both men fell out of the open doorway to the head of the stairs. Twined together, their punches hampered by the close contact, they rolled over and over toward the spiraling descent.

Bound and helpless in the chair, Dawn could only watch in horror as they thrashed at each other, each turn taking them to the edge of safety. She rocked forward in the chair, trying to free her hands. The gag was so tight that she could barely breathe.

Luke landed a solid blow to Ricky's jaw, but the stouter man seemed to absorb the shock without flinching. He drew back an elbow and connected with Luke's ribs.

His groan made her frantic, and she worked at the bonds until the skin on her wrists was raw.

With a sudden thrust of body weight, Ricky pushed Luke to the edge of the staircase. The last Dawn heard was a startled cry, then both men disappeared and there was the terrifying sound of bone and muscle crashing down the long, deadly flight of stairs.

Chapter Twelve

An ominous quiet settled over the old house. Unable to escape the unrelenting bonds, Dawn felt almost paralyzed by the beating of her own heart. Her imagination triggered an image of the horror that lay at the base of the last step. Both men had gone down the treacherous staircase. Too vividly she imagined Luke, sprawled on the hardwood floor, dying.

That thought sent a new jolt of adrenaline through her, and she renewed her efforts to free her hands. The rope, lengths of twine taken from bales of hay, was thin and tightly drawn. She forced herself to relax and attempt a calmer method. She had to keep her presence of mind. Luke's life depended on her.

Her struggles were interrupted by the sound of slow footsteps on the stairs. Numbness crept into her hands as she stilled them and listened. For a moment she thought she'd imagined it. Once again there was the distinct sound of leather on wood. A step closer, then two.

A split second of hope that Luke was coming for her died with the realization that it was more likely to be the cruel man she'd come to know as Benny Bertrane. She'd been grabbed by Ricky and Bertrane, the men from Oakdale Stables. Bertrane had disappeared shortly after she'd returned to consciousness from the chloroform they'd used to sedate her. It was probable that he'd returned, that it was his footsteps that were slowly ascending the stairs.

She tore at the ropes, but the knots held fast. Once again she set the chair rocking. She'd used the same technique to try and warn Luke of the danger he was walking into, but it had been ineffective.

Her anger reignited at the thought. Ricky had stood at the window, waiting for Luke to come to the old plantation. She was the goat, tethered in the middle of the woods to draw the lion. And Luke had come to rescue her, with no thought for his own safety. He hadn't left her. It was all part of the trap she'd been caught in. Her brief tenure as a hostage had taught her how little she mattered in the whole scheme. She was merely bait. Ricky and Benny Bertrane's interest in her had been minimal, a fact she hadn't had time to analyze properly.

The footsteps reached the top of the stairs, and she ceased the useless attempt to break free. Taking as deep a breath as the gag would allow, she held her head up to confront whatever came up the stairs.

"Dawn!" Luke was still hazy from the pounding on the stairs. He stumbled into the room and knelt beside her chair, his hands fumbling with the tight knots.

Unable to talk or move, Dawn didn't try to stop the tears of relief that gathered in her eyes. With a shake of her head she drew his attention to the gag.

He removed it quickly, his hand settling for a moment on her cheek. "Are you okay?" His fingertips caressed her skin.

"Yes." She could see that he was injured. A streak of blood ran down one arm, and his face was battered and already swelling. She wanted both to hide in his arms and comfort him, all at once.

"I thought at first that you'd left, just packed up and gone," she said as he struggled with the knots that held her.

"But as I sat here and watched Ricky, I knew that you hadn't left. I knew that they were waiting for you to come so they could hurt you. And that you would come because of me." The tears started down her cheeks. "There was nothing I could do, Luke. They were going to kill you, and it was because you wanted to help me."

The kitchen knife had fallen from his belt in the struggle in the hall. Now he retrieved it and released her with a quick cut. "Your wrists," he said as he gently held her hands. "When I found your shoe—" he kissed her hands softly. "—I couldn't even think what might have happened to you." He held up her wrists for a better look. "We need to take care of this."

"Your body," she answered, moving her fingers tentatively along his injured shoulder. "Did he stab you?" The question was almost too painful to ask, but she had to know. One thing she'd determined for certain; she wasn't going to be cheated out of a chance to talk with Luke. Whatever had happened, she was certain he could explain. He'd come hunting her. That was all she needed to know about him.

"It's a scrape." He touched her cheek again, making certain that she was real.

"And Ricky?"

"Dead. I think he must have broken his neck. We both went down together, rolling. When we landed, he was dead. I put him under the staircase."

"We'd better get out of here." Dawn lingered under his touch for a few seconds, reluctantly moving away. "The other one, Bertrane, will be back soon. When I heard you on the stairs, I thought it was him."

"Did they hurt you?" Luke followed her, unable to stop himself from touching her hair, caressing her shoulder, her neck. She was alive, uninjured. Wonder and relief combined in the need to hold her. He wrapped his arms around her, turning her slowly so that she faced him. His lips touched hers in a tender kiss that spoke of his concern. "Tell me the truth. Are you hurt?"

"No, just my pride. They tricked me. Manetti came up to me and distracted me, while that creep Ricky caught me from behind and put some awful-smelling stuff under my nose. The last thing I knew, Manetti was yelling some kind of instructions. When I came to, I was tied in that chair."

"Dawn!" Luke withdrew his arms as he stepped quickly to the window. "A pair of headlights are coming. We've got to get out of here."

Even as he spoke, lights drew up beside the old house and stopped. "Too late," Dawn whispered. "We're trapped."

"There must be another way out." Luke searched the barren room for something he could use as a rope. "We'll tie sheets together and go out the window."

"There are no sheets. There are no beds. Ricky took me all over the house. He enjoyed his game of torment while he had my hands tied. There's no place to hide." Defeat crept into her voice.

"Take it easy." Luke put a strong arm around her and gave her shoulders a tight squeeze. He wanted to hold her, to pull her into his arms, but he held himself in check. Dawn needed comforting, but she needed safety more. "Let's get out in the hallway. The house is dark, and we'll have that advantage."

His warm hand taking hers revived her natural confidence. She stepped beside him, her body once again alert and ready to deal with the danger that hid in every dark nook of the house.

They heard the front door creak open, then the sound of many feet on the wooden floor.

"Four people?" Dawn asked in a whisper.

"Three or four. It's hard to tell."

She released his hand and bent down, her hand clutching a piece of the old staircase.

"Hey!" Luke tried to grab her wrist. "What—?"

She shushed him with a hand on his mouth. "Diversion." She drew him with her to the banister. As he held her waist, she leaned over and threw the wood to the far back wall of the foyer.

"Ricky?" Bertrane's familiar voice rose in panic from the first floor. "Ricky! You better not be playing jokes. Answer me!"

Dawn moved closer to Luke, taking courage from his nearness. They hardly dared to breathe as they waited for the men downstairs to make a move.

"Something musta happened to Ricky. Check it out!" Bertrane ordered.

There was the sound of footsteps rushing in different directions, then silence.

"Three men," Luke said. "Two went to the kitchen, and the third is on the west side of the house."

"Let's give them a taste of their own medicine." Dawn started around the stairs.

"What do you mean?"

"We can hide in the dark, frightening them with surprise attacks. They won't know how many of us, or who we are. I have a slight advantage since I know this house, thanks to Ricky's little tour. Only the front door opens to the outside, but there's a servants' staircase down the back and a dumbwaiter. We can play their game on them, maybe even capture Bertrane. I've wanted a few minutes, to make him understand how Roulette felt."

An amused smile touched Luke's lips, but it was safely hidden in the darkness. Dawn wasn't concerned over her mistreatment, but the idea that Roulette had suffered still rankled.

"Maybe we should take the servants' staircase and not tempt fate. We can plan a better counterattack than annoyance tactics in the dark."

The wisdom of his words was hard to resist. "You don't think capturing Bertrane and making him talk is such a good idea?"

The wistful note in her voice made his smile stretch further. He could no longer resist the impulse to hold her. As his arms slipped around her waist, he felt her lift her face for his kiss.

"I did have one really bad hour or two when I thought you'd abandoned me," she whispered against his cheek.

"No faith in me," he replied, taking in the clean smell of her silky hair, the smoothness of her skin against his lips. "If I were going to leave you, it would have been with that horse you stole."

Her response was a long, explosive kiss. The house around them seemed to still for the length of the embrace, and then they both stepped back.

"This is one subject that deserves more comfortable surroundings," Luke said. "I'm not at my romantic best when three men are below me, all hoping to kill me."

Luke's droll humor was the perfect touch to remind them of the need for haste. Dawn's touch on his arm was tender, yet also urgent. "Follow me."

Treading silently past door after door, they slipped through the darkened house. Luke carried their only weapon, the kitchen knife. At last Dawn paused at the head of a flight of stairs. They could hear the sounds of the men on the first floor, still searching for them.

"They're going to be upset when they find Ricky," Luke reminded her. "We need to get out of this house as soon as possible, undetected. I don't even have a car."

Dawn tried to penetrate the total darkness of the stairs. It was a pit, a hole—into freedom or death. "Careful. It's narrow and steep.'' She fought down the fear that clutched at her.

With firm pressure on her arm, Luke insisted on leading the way. "I can take over from here."

Slowly, carefully, they moved down the staircase that was twice as steep as the one in the front of the house. The tickle of cobwebs was annoying at first, but in trying to keep her footing, Dawn soon forgot them.

"Where does this end up?" Luke asked, pausing for a moment to try to get his bearings.

"The kitchen. There's a narrow door by the refrigerator."

The darkness was so dense that Luke had to inch forward with one hand extended. At last he felt the smooth texture of a door beneath his fingers. Just beyond the door he heard someone approaching. His hand went to Dawn's shoulder to warn her.

Huddling close, ears pressed to the door, they listened.

"They must be upstairs. They aren't down here. Joe's been watching the stairs." Bertrane's distinctively harsh voice came through the wood only slightly blurred.

"Perhaps they've outsmarted you. I think the hunk of wood was a ruse." Louis Manetti spoke with his usual clipped elegance.

"Don't be too sure. We aren't that dumb. We manage to keep you busy enough."

Dawn pressed harder against the door. It sounded as if the men in the kitchen were moving furniture. Beside her, Luke was tensed and ready for anything.

One of the men uttered a loud exclamation, and then the noises stopped. Luke and Dawn remained pressed to the wood, listening as hard as possible. Minutes that seemed like hours dragged by, until Luke shifted his weight.

"Let's make a break for it." He inched open the door. Through the tiny crack they saw tables and chairs moved helter-skelter. On the floor by the window a pool of blood covered three tiles. There was no sign of anyone.

From the foyer startled voices echoed back to Luke and Dawn. "Hey! Get over here! Somebody's hurt him!"

"They've found Ricky," Luke cautioned Dawn.

There were the sounds of more footsteps and several more exclamations. "It sounds like they're all gathered beneath the stairs." Through the tiny crack in the door, Dawn couldn't be certain of anything.

"Go straight out the front door and to their car. I think if we get enough head start I can hot-wire it."

"Sounds better than going on foot!"

"Run for it!" He pushed her forward, then followed on her heels. Dawn's keen sense of direction took them unerringly through the kitchen, dining room and parlor to the front door.

The air rushing through her lungs blocked out the sound of everything else. She glanced back once, catching Luke's eye. His smile of confidence gave her another boost, and she slowed her Olympic sprint at the door to the foyer.

Manetti and his cohorts would be busy with Ricky, but the opening of the front door would surely attract their attention. In all likelihood they had guns. She felt Luke press close behind her, urging her forward. Instead of running, she took his hand and carefully edged across the foyer.

Near the staircase she heard the rumble of terse speech, but the words weren't distinguishable. Palms cold with sweat, she grasped the knob and turned. The door, so obliging before, stuck.

Luke's hand topped hers, and his additional strength was applied. Still the knob held firm.

The idea that Manetti had locked it occurred to her with a sickening thud in her abdomen. They'd have to break a window to escape, and that would draw deadly attention.

Luke shook her hand free of the knob and gave it a sudden twist. As gracefully as a dowager queen, the door swished open. Dawn was propelled onto the porch by Luke's power. He closed the door carefully behind him.

"Race you to the car?" Dawn offered the teasing challenge, knowing that neither of them needed extra motivation to run as fast as they'd ever tried.

"If I win, you walk." Luke leaped across the porch in one stride and disappeared. Caught unprepared, Dawn burst after him, legs churning for her life.

He was already on the floorboards of the car when she arrived. Settling into the seat, she turned back to watch the house. On the second floor, she could follow the flashlights of the killers as they searched.

"Luke, whose blood was that?"

"I don't know." His answer was curt as he worked with the car. "When I first went into the house I didn't see it. Maybe they had a scuffle among themselves."

"Bertrane's capable of stabbing his own mother," Dawn pointed out.

"Hey!" Bertrane's voice cried into the night. "They're out there with the car!"

Since she couldn't help, she remained silent in the passenger's seat. Luke was upside down near the steering column, curses slipping from his lips in a constant flow. "I've almost got it."

Dawn heard the pursuers coming across the wooden porch, pounding after them. She turned to look back. Now they were down the steps, two flashlights giving them the advantage of sight that she and Luke had lacked. But the lights also gave away their position. She opened the glove compartment and scrambled through the papers. Against the very back she felt the cold steel she sought. Her hand curled around the pistol and she brought it out, checking the cylinder to make sure it was loaded.

"I've got it!" The motor roared into life as Luke slid behind the wheel. His success was greeted by the first bullet fired by the men at the house.

"Just drive," Dawn managed to say. "I'm going to return fire."

"What?" Luke couldn't hide his astonishment, but Dawn didn't give him time to protest. She fired from the open window, the gun kicking so hard that she almost fell into Luke's side.

"Drive!" she commanded him. "I certainly can't save us with my marksmanship."

The gas pedal touched the floor and the new, luxury car answered with high spirits. Dawn squeezed off two more rounds, each time letting the gun knock her about the car. The bullets sailed harmlessly into the air, but they were effective enough to stop Bertrane and Manetti from following. She could see their flashlights extinguished.

"Drive like a madman," she counseled him. "Death on the highway is far better than what they had planned for us. If we have any luck at all, maybe a patrolman will pull us over."

"Warp speed, Captain."

Luke turned from the old plantation, taking the route Gele had shown him. As they fled through the night, he told Dawn about the islander and his unexpected help. He also told her about Jack the Knife.

"We're in way over our head, Dawn. How or why, I don't know."

"It's Manetti. Every time he shows up, we get in deeper trouble. And it's you, Luke. When Ricky and Bertrane had me, I got the distinct impression they only wanted me as bait for you. I'm insignificant to them."

Luke kept his eyes on the road, but his tense jaw gave away the strain he felt. "I should have told you about my past a long time ago."

Dawn felt apprehension gather in her stomach. After the anguish of wondering why he hadn't told her the truth, she was going to find out.

"It's very difficult for me to talk about. In fact, I've never told anyone else. Some things are better left behind, and that's what I thought I was going to do."

Compassion made her speak up. "Luke, I know about the charge that you drugged a horse and the rider was injured."

"Freddie told you, didn't he?" Luke shook his head. "I knew he wouldn't have much trouble dredging up that old story."

"I told Freddie I didn't believe it. The lust to win is one thing, but I can't believe you'd endanger a horse and rider."

Luke's strong hand dropped onto her knee. "You defended me? Without any evidence to the contrary?"

"All the evidence I needed was spending two days with you. You helped me rescue Roulette, when it would have been so much easier to leave her behind. You've risked your life to protect me. I've watched you, and you're a man who likes to win, but not at any cost."

To Dawn's surprise the car swerved suddenly to the side of the road and ground to a halt. "What is it?" She twisted in the seat, but there were no headlights behind them, only stretches of black, empty Louisiana highway.

"This isn't exactly my idea of proper surroundings, but I can't delay any longer." He reached across the seat, carefully drawing her into his arms. One hand wound into her thick hair, fingers tightening slightly as he moved her head back.

"You believed in me when my best friends, the people I'd worked with for years, didn't. I've fallen in love with you, Dawn. I knew it before, and now I have to tell you."

A car approached through the darkness, headlights illuminating Luke's face. His eyes glittered with intensity, and Dawn softly touched the swollen point on his cheek.

"Somehow I knew you'd never lie to me. I had my moments of doubt, to be sure, but I kept coming back to the man I knew, the man I watched and worked with. Luke, when we're out of this mess, we need to have a long, serious talk."

"Until then..." His lips took hers as the other car passed with a whoosh. Alone again in the darkness, they explored the power and pleasure of their kiss.

Shifting slightly, Luke drew her onto his lap so that she rested in his arms. One hand stroked her back, the length of thigh that was revealed by her skirt. "So delicate, yet so strong," he murmured against her neck.

At first overwhelmed by the power he exerted, Dawn yielded. As his touch spun dizzyingly along her body, she answered the challenge of his kiss. Her hands gripped his shoulders, kneading the muscles, calling for a deeper kiss.

Headlights in the rearview mirror forced them to break apart. Dawn held her hand on his chest, registering the rapid beat of his heart that exactly matched her own. They both tensed, but the car passed them without hesitation.

"We'd better go." Reluctance was obvious in Luke's voice.

"Where?"

"We can't go home, though I need to check in."

"Me, too. And I don't want to go to Orson's. No point in drawing unnecessary attention to Roulette. We're still not any closer to finding Private Stock."

"Not in the flesh, but we do know a lot more. The horse was here, and probably still is. And Louis Manetti is the man who knows where she is. Don't forget that."

"Louis Manetti." Dawn shook her head, one shoulder giving her characteristic shrug. "My first impression was dead wrong. He would have had you killed. My only question is, why?''

Edging the car back onto the road and picking up speed, Luke took a deep breath. "I started to tell you about my past. Now it's time. As you probably know, I was training for the Olympic team as a kid. I had this great horse, a true athlete. He was a mixed breed, but he had the heart and the intelligence to make it.''

Dawn's heart twisted as she listened. No matter how many horses he had in the future, she knew he would never get over the loss of this horse, his first.

"We trained like mad. The horse was donated by someone, anonymously. He was something of a joke; he was on the homely side. No one thought he could do it, except me. From the first moment our eyes met, I knew we could make the team. We had something special. No matter what I asked, that horse delivered.''

Memories of Speed Dancer flashed into Dawn's mind. She knew that special, once-in-a-lifetime connection. Now wasn't the time to mention it, though. Luke had his own memories to set to rest.

"Just before the team was supposed to pack for the trials, the captain got a call. The owner of my horse was taking him back. Somehow the horse had been donated on a limited basis, with a clause that indicated the owner could reclaim him at will. It was incredible. Nothing like that had ever happened before.''

"And with the changes in the rules, I'll bet it won't happen again.''

"No, it was a fluke. Anyway, the week before the competition, I watched my horse loaded into a trailer and hauled away. Then two weeks later the horse showed up on the Grand Prix tour. In the middle of a course he went lame. Somehow the rumor got started that I crippled the horse as an act of revenge, because he was taken from me.''

Dawn didn't want to distract Luke from his driving, but she reached across and touched his shoulder. "Don't bother denying it. I know you'd never do it."

"Well, time passed and I started over. I gave up the idea of riding on the team. I was older, just didn't have the heart for it. But I thought I had something to offer as a trainer. Maybe I could give some other kids a break. Then the business about the Maclay scandal walloped me. My entire barn deserted. For another few years I was treated as if I had the plague."

"The girl that was injured. Whatever happened? Did you sue her for slander?"

"Her spinal cord was severed at the neck. After a few weeks she recanted her story, but by then the damage was done. She didn't have any idea who drugged the horse, and the entire family was in such trauma that I didn't pursue it. I knew I wasn't guilty, and that was good enough for me. In some crazy, idealistic way I thought eventually people would recognize the truth." Most of the bitterness was gone from his laugh, but a fraction still lingered. "I was wrong."

"Is there anything in your past that might make Louis Manetti want to hurt you?" It was the question that had begun to nag at Dawn when she realized she was being used as a lure to get Luke.

"I've thought about that. Since I don't know your friend, Ann Tate, it's hard to find a common link in our past."

"Are you certain you don't know Ann?" Something in his voice made Dawn pursue the matter. "Maybe you met somewhere."

"Even so, why would Manetti want to bring Ann into this? From what you've said, she's had enough troubles. With her marriage, I thought maybe things would clear up for her."

"That's true," Dawn admitted. She felt she was on the verge of something, but it was still too elusive to grasp. "I guess the only way we're going to get any answers is to pin Manetti down. Or Bertrane!'' She spoke the name with such animosity that Luke could no longer suppress his amusement.

"You hate that guy."

"I hate bullies, and he's one. He even bullied Ricky, and Ricky was no charmer himself." She chuckled at her vehemence. "I don't often hold a grudge, but I feel that Benny Bertrane and I have something very personal to settle between us."

A sudden thought flashed into Luke's mind. His hand went to his shirt pocket. Both books of matches were still there. "I may have one more clue," he said. "When I was looking for you, I found a phone number. As soon as we find a place to settle down for the next few hours, I'll make a call."

"A phone number?" Dawn's excitement rose.

"It could be a tip."

Chapter Thirteen

Luke finally settled on a small motel on the outskirts of New Orleans. Where John Morrow's House had been elegantly private, The Palms was stamped with the attitude of another time. The neon sign, a palm tree shading a diving girl in a one-piece swimsuit, was pure fifties. An oleander hedge provided good coverage for the car. It was close to Lake Pontchartrain and horse country.

He took great care to check in and park without disturbing Dawn. She'd fallen into an exhausted sleep, and he didn't want to wake her. The view might give her the impression she'd stepped into a time warp, he thought grimly as he carried her into the room. She barely reacted when he placed her on the double bed.

There was no phone in the room, so he locked the door behind him and walked the short distance to an all-night convenience store. The neon blue of the phone booth was his target.

It was late, but he had no time to waste with concern for telephone etiquette. He got a handful of change from the cashier at the store, then pulled the matchbook from his pocket. He dialed the numbers, then counted rings.

On the fourteenth ring, a male voice answered. "Hello!"

Luke didn't respond. The voice was slightly familiar, but he couldn't place it.

"Hello!"

Again he waited, almost able to pinpoint who it was.

"Listen, you telephone nuisance. Either say something or hang up."

"Orson?" Luke couldn't believe it. "Is that you?"

"Well, who else would it be, since you've called Applegate Farms? Who is this?"

"Luke O'Neil."

There was a moment of complete shock from the other end of the line. "O'Neil? Is something wrong? Where are you? I've been worried silly, and Freddie is about to have a hemorrhage over at the ranch. You two are in serious trouble."

"That's an understatement." Worry made his voice gruff. "I hate to say it, but we may have dragged you into this, too." He fingered the matchbook, caught again by the intricate design.

"How so? Things have been quiet here. Except for Freddie calling every fifteen minutes. Is Dawn with you?"

"She's fine, for the moment. We're hiding from some thugs, and I have to tell you plainly, I found your phone number on one of them. They must know you're helping us."

"You don't say." Orson's tone was full of wonder. "My number?"

"It's in this book of matches."

"Matches?"

"Unusual book. Black, with gold horse's head embossed. Mr. D's on the flip."

"That scum Manetti." Orson broke into an uncharacteristic display of emotion. "He's up to something."

"Any idea what? Dawn and I were talking, and we think maybe some element from my past and Ann Tate's past has brought him after us."

"Nothing off the top of my head." There was a pause. "Since he called to check Dawn out, I haven't heard from him. That doesn't mean I won't!"

"I'm sorry we've dragged you into this, Orson. We never should have brought that mare to you."

"Roulette is fine, fattening up nicely. You did the right thing, Luke. Don't ever regret that. You did exactly the right thing. But what are you going to do now?"

"Go after Manetti."

"Be careful, Luke. Maybe you should send Dawn over here to stay with me."

The idea held a lot of appeal, but at last Luke rejected it. "I'd have to tie her up, you know that."

"Yes, I suppose that's true enough. What shall I tell Freddie?"

"Tell him we're fine. We've seen Private Stock, but we haven't been able to keep up with her." His voice lightened. "Dawn says she's the fastest thing on four legs ever."

"I have no doubt of that. Dawn has the eye for horses. If she ever decided to go into handicapping, she'd be good at it."

"I'll do my best to keep her safe, Orson. If Roulette gets too hot, maybe you could arrange to have her shipped somewhere else."

"If that happens, the mare will be taken care of completely. Rest easy on that count, Luke. Now where are you staying?"

"We're in a dive for the moment, but we'll be moving again as soon as we catch a few hours' sleep. Then it's an open question. But we'll stay in touch."

"Do that. And I'll call Freddie for Dawn."

Luke replaced the receiver with a sense of both relief and foreboding. If he'd brought down disaster onto Orson Rinter, then he'd involved an innocent man. But Dawn was innocent, too. And she had more than enough worries on her mind.

His hand clutched the matchbook, wadding it into a knot. He dropped it into the trash can. One thing Dawn didn't need was a guilt trip over involving Orson. If he could save her that little bit of anxiety, then he would.

He walked back to the room, slipped inside and stretched out beside Dawn on the bed. She was sleeping soundly, her chest rising and falling in a relaxed rhythm. Moving so that he didn't awaken her, he leaned down and kissed her cheek. She was cool, soft. The mattress gave beneath his weight, settling her snugly against him. His body curled protectively around her before he, too, fell into a sound sleep.

"I SUPPOSE room service is out of the question." Dawn stood over the bed, her dark hair dripping from the shower. "I'd settle for a clean shirt, slacks and sneakers." Her clothes were a sad, rumpled reminder of the night before.

"You look nice, all wet from the shower." Luke stretched. "What time is it?"

"Early. Just after nine." She shrugged. "I didn't think we had any morning appointments, so I decided to let you sleep."

He sat up on the edge of the bed. "How long have you been up?"

"Plenty long to wonder about that phone number. I've been about to pop to try it. Where is it?"

"I tried it last night, while you were asleep." He stood up and stretched again, bending over and loosening his back. "It was a bookie. Apparently Manetti likes to cover all angles."

"A bookie." Dawn didn't try to hide her disappointment. "That was our one lead. Now what are we going to do?"

"I need to check in at home. Ramone's not going to be happy with me. What is it?" He saw the sudden worry wash over her face.

"I lost Ann's money! I was betting her five thousand on Private Stock, and that creep ran off with my money. Every penny of it. What am I going to tell Ann?" Her anxiety was evident. "I feel like I've betrayed her trust."

Luke pulled her down beside him, so that she nestled in his arms. "Dawn, you did what you thought was right. You can't blame yourself for that."

"I took money that wasn't mine. Money that had been entrusted to my safekeeping, and I lost it. That's... embezzlement!" She stood up, but Luke pulled her back down.

"The money isn't lost. At least not permanently. When we get Private Stock, we'll make sure Manetti comes clean with your money, too."

His words were logical, but Dawn felt far too bad to let them comfort her. "I didn't give the money to Manetti, I gave it to some flunky to bet for me. It was all part of their lovely trap. I'm sure that scumbag took my money and never mentioned it. He thought they'd kill me and he'd just keep the five grand."

Luke didn't want to add to her anxiety by agreeing with her. Five grand were nothing to a man like Manetti, but to one of his toadies the money would be a nice bonus.

"We'll get it back, Dawn. When we get the rest of this mess straight, we'll get that corrected, too."

She relaxed against his arm, her damp hair cool on his shoulder.

"What are we going to do?" A forlorn note crept into her voice despite all of her efforts.

Luke eased backward, pulling her with him. "Think. We have to come up with some idea of what's happening to us and why." He knew that was true, but his mind was more absorbed in the feel of her against him. Her body was a contradiction. Beneath the soft skin and feminine gestures was a framework of wiry muscle. As his hand soothed her back, he explored her lean frame. Her shoulders were square, her back strong, but her waist was as slender as that of a teenager. As his fingers inched lower, he could feel a resilience, a strength in her body that required unexpected control from him.

Dawn responded with passion. His hand on her body was a fiery luxury. She wanted to feel his lips claim hers, but she was reluctant to rush a single second of his touch. She moved her hand across the masculine planes of his face to feather through his thick, blond hair. Each second magnified the attraction, the heat that surged between them. She met the gaze of his piercing blue eyes, read in them the promise of his desire.

With her fingers twined in his hair, she slowly drew his head to her own. The first contact of the kiss was light, teasing. He drew back, then returned to her neck. Pushing aside the flap of her blouse, he found the point of her collarbone with his lips.

The sensations that raced through her were magnetic, but not unanticipated. She'd longed for his touch, his caresses. She wanted to explore him and give him pleasure. Her nimble fingers quickly worked the buttons of his shirt, gaining access to his chest. Beneath her hands his muscles were warm, exciting.

She felt the tantalizing touch of his fingers on her bare leg, moving deftly up her calf to the back of her knee, tracing a line farther up her thigh. She caught her breath and saw that he watched her. Her smile was the invitation he was waiting for.

When he kissed her, she knew he was staking his claim. In one naked look they reached an understanding. Their wants and needs were mutual, their love and dreams accepted.

There was no need for haste or hesitation. Throughout the long hours of the morning and early afternoon, they loved and slept. When they finally showered and dressed to leave, Dawn looked at the small room with fondness.

"It looks better than I thought," she said, rising on tip-toe to give Luke a kiss on his chin. "If I weren't starving, I'd suggest we stay a little longer."

Laughing, he caught her in his arms and swung her back down onto the bed. "I could be persuaded to stay."

Dawn brushed a stray lock of hair from his forehead as he towered over her. "We could call for pizza delivery." She wanted him again with a passion as strong as she'd ever experienced.

Desire filled the blue depths of his eyes, but he slowly rolled to the side of the bed. "I'm afraid to stay here any longer," he said. "We'd better stay on the move."

Knowing he was right, Dawn sat up and smoothed her skirt. "We'd better get some clothes before it's too late."

"And other things, like a razor." He stood and held out his hand to help her up. Dawn followed him to the door, then turned back for one last look at the small room. Her smile told him that her memories were delightful.

"Now for a clothing store."

"Maybe we could go over to Orson's to hide." Dawn's voice rose with excitement at the idea. "That would be the perfect place. We could hide and check on Roulette."

"It might be better if we stayed away from Applegate." Luke kept his voice even. "Orson's been a good friend to help us out. I'd hate to put him in any more danger. Besides, we need to see if we can trace Manetti or that filly. It's time we put an end to this business."

"So what do you suggest?"

"Clothes, and then a return to the plantation. That's where we lost the trail of the filly, and that's where I feel we'll find a clue."

The plan was better than anything Dawn could think of. She slipped into the car they'd taken from the plantation and waited for Luke to complete the hot-wiring.

"What about this car?" she asked, glancing dubiously at it. "It's hot, isn't it?"

"Stolen from gangsters. They probably stole it first." He grinned. "My auto theft talents have certainly been exercised since I met you. We'll keep it a few days. I've gotten attached to these black windows."

Dawn laughed, feeling like a criminal in the dark interior of the car. They drove to a mall and made the necessary purchases. In her new clothes, she attacked the pizza they ordered at a small place just outside the mall.

"Hungry?" Luke teased her.

"More than I thought," she agreed. "You haven't done bad," she commented. As she put her napkin onto the table, she gave him a confident smile. "I'm ready for that old plantation now."

"I'm ready to resolve this mess, so we can resolve some personal matters," Luke answered as they left the restaurant.

Dawn clutched the bag that held their old clothes. "On the way, maybe we should incinerate these clothes."

"Just toss them in the back seat." He took the bundle from her hand and dropped it over the seat. "We only have a couple of hours of daylight left, and we need to examine that plantation track."

They left the interstate and turned onto the two-lane highway. Dawn felt a creeping chill move over her as she sighted trees and landmarks that reminded her of her earlier trip.

"I was so naive, coming here," she said aloud. "I thought I could bet the money, see the filly and then do something. As it was, I was just foolish."

Luke could tell the five thousand she'd lost were still troubling her. "We'll find out where Private Stock was taken. That'll make you feel better."

His concern made her spirits rise. She touched his leg, drawing her fingers across the tough fabric of the new jeans. The car slowed, and she scanned the area as Luke parked in the same spot on the protected knoll.

"This is where I found your shoe," he said, getting out. The signs of a scuffle were still evident on the ground.

He took her hand as he started down the back of the track. The area was clean, well maintained. On the opposite side lay a grandstand, a private dining and bar area, and farther on, the stables. The facility was designed for no more than five horses.

"Small but tidy operation." Dawn's words echoed his thoughts.

"Maybe it would be better if you waited here." Luke touched her cheek with sudden tenderness.

"Why?"

"Jack the Knife. If the body's still around . . ."

"Right. I'll explore down this way, around the jockeys' space."

"Meet you back here in fifteen minutes. And be careful." Luke kissed her forehead and clutched her against his chest for a moment.

"I'm naive, but I can handle myself," she reminded him with a quirky grin. "But I love it when you act concerned."

He trotted off toward the stalls. Dawn watched him until he disappeared around the corner of the barn before turning to her own assignment. To her surprise, the door wasn't locked. She pushed it open and snapped on the lights. The room, complete with several racing saddles, bridles, bandages and different-colored silks, was small but well kept. The floor was freshly swept. Pictures covered the walls; determined men on big mounts. There seemed to be nothing of real interest, but her natural love of horses took her closer to examine the photos.

There were greats and unknowns, equine and human. She admired the images of long Thoroughbred bodies stretched for the finish line, and the skill demonstrated by a jockey's hands as he held his horse together in a squeeze. The racing world was exciting, even in black and white photos.

Of less interest were the standard winner's circle shots. Mostly in color, they showed a restrained horse and a relieved jockey. They lacked the drama of the race pictures. A large, bay mare caught her attention, and she moved along the wall. The inscription read, "Russian Roulette, Jefferson Downs, 1983. Owner Patrice Deluchi, jockey Jackson Demar."

The mare wasn't Louisiana-bred, but it seemed that she'd been brought to the track to break out.

Taking the picture off the wall so that she could examine it better, Dawn held it under the light. Something in the set of the jockey's shoulders made her look at him more closely. She recognized him. In the years that had passed, he'd aged considerably, but he was Jack the Knife. The picture started to slip from her hand, but she caught it and carefully replaced it.

Jack the Knife had been a jockey. Until . . . ? What could have happened, for him to develop a taste for being a professional hit man? She stepped back from the picture, as if it could burn her. Now that she had the jockey's name, she looked around the room and found he'd made the winner's circle on several other mounts. One in particular caught her eye. It was a 1982 photograph of Jackson Demar on a big gray. He'd won the race on an animal owned by Louis Manetti. She stared at the picture. A happy, carefree Manetti held the winner's cup in one hand and the stallion's reins in the other, as Jackson Demar perched on top, a happy grin on his face.

They had obviously had a long-term relationship. And once riding was out of the question, then Jackson Demar had developed new skills. Talents that Manetti had needed to keep his business operations in line.

The rest of the room gave her no more clues, so she went out, eager to find Luke and share her discoveries. She was back under the stands when he arrived, puffing slightly.

"There's no sign of Jack the Knife anywhere. They must pick that body up and carry it all over town for special occasions." His cynical remark was offset with an apologetic smile.

"I found something." Rewarded with another smile, she related the details of the photos of Jack the Knife and his longtime association with Louis Manetti.

"Good work," Luke said. "We're getting things pieced together. We should write down those dates and the horses. The Jockey Club might be able to help us with some more detail on Jackson Demar. I've got some paper in my shirt pocket in the car."

"That old shirt?" She wrinkled her nose. "That old, dirty shirt?"

"I'll be right back."

"You check out the rest of the buildings. I'll go get the paper and a pen."

He kissed her quickly on the cheek, then the neck, at last moving to her lips. "You're a great detective, but it sure does cut into our romantic life."

"Maybe we should go back to The Palms tonight." She kissed his chin and backed away, then turned and started to run. It seemed that at last they might be making headway. It was almost too much to hope for, after the dead ends and danger they'd confronted.

She reached the car and pulled the clothes from the back seat. Running her hands into the pockets of his shirt, she felt a small square and pulled it out. The matches were vaguely familiar. She looked at the black cover, the gold horse's head. A vague sense of unease touched her stomach.

She'd seen that design before. Orson Rinter had several books in his collection jar! Luke and Orson didn't frequent the same restaurants. Luke didn't smoke, and wasn't likely to have picked up the matches from Orson's study. It was a puzzling coincidence. She stared at the design, another memory stirring.

The flags!

She'd been unable to decipher the black and gold flag that was flying at the Florida track on the video of Private Stock. But it could easily have been the gold horse's head on a black background.

Dread tingled up her spine. Orson said he'd eaten with Louis Manetti a few times in New Orleans. Mr. D's was obviously the place. An old maid about his momentary obsessions, Orson had taken the matches for his collection. But where did Luke get them? Where? Unless it was from Manetti himself.

Chapter Fourteen

Dawn found the sheets of paper taken from The Palms in his other pocket. She held them a moment, undecided what to do. Only that afternoon they'd shared the most intimate secrets. Her faith in him had been complete. Now a single piece of evidence made her wonder. His initial reluctance to discuss his past came back to her. He'd told the truth—but only after he knew she'd already discovered it. And every step she'd taken since Tampa had been shadowed by an agent of Manetti. Luke had been at her side, too.

The facts said he was capable of working for Manetti. Her heart rebelled at the thought.

Down the road was the old plantation house where she'd been held prisoner. Luke had come to her rescue with no thought for his own safety. Or had he known that he wasn't in danger? She hadn't seen Ricky's dead body. Luke had hidden it beneath the stairs. She'd never seen Jack the Knife's body. Only Luke had seen him die, and then later found the body twenty miles away, holding her shoe. As far as she knew, both men could still be alive and uninjured.

She couldn't stop the sickness that rolled through her stomach, but didn't give in to it. Clutching the paper, she tried to find a clear, coherent thought. Luke was a good man. He was kind. She'd seen him demonstrate those characteristics again and again. Unless it was all a ruse. Unless he was using her.

The first trace of a smile lifted the corner of her mouth. Using her for what? That was the obvious question. And there was no answer. She had nothing that Luke or Louis Manetti wanted. *She* owned no horses, controlled no money or public opinion. She started back to the stable area, relief growing with each step. There was no reason for Luke to double-cross her. Her own paranoia was her enemy, not Luke O'Neil.

At the thought that Luke would be worried about her, she hastened her pace. He'd also laugh at her if he knew what she'd been thinking, but she had no intention of telling him. Such dark thoughts were better left unspoken, especially to the man she loved.

"Find the paper?" Luke stepped from the jockey room and signaled her inside. "This is fascinating. To think that a man could go from jockey to killer."

"The track's a tough business."

"No worse than the show ring or Wall Street. There's corruption everywhere, and temptation on every corner."

She smiled at the lighthearted tone he used. "Luke, do you remember the Private Stock video pretty well?"

Jotting down the information from the pictures, he answered without stopping. "Like my mother's face. Why?"

"Well, I was thinking about the second flag, the one neither of us could identify."

"And?"

"It hadn't really occurred to me until just now, but Louis Manetti had some matchbooks with a horse's head on a black cover. Do you think that was his flag?"

Luke looked up at her, then quickly dropped his gaze back to the paper. "You may be right." He folded the sheet and tucked it into his pocket, giving her his full attention. "I remember the flag, but I could never get a good look at the insignia. I found the Tampa track flag without too much difficulty, and I'd forgotten about the other.''

"Me, too. Until today." She stepped away from him as her fears returned. If he was innocent, surely he'd mention that he, too, had seen the matchbooks. She gave him one last, hopeful look.

"Is something wrong?"

"No. Well, it's just that I forgot to call Freddie. You know, I should let him know I'm safe, with you."

Her heart was pounding so loudly that she thought he'd hear, but he didn't seem to notice. He was examining the other pictures in the room.

"Let's find a phone and then something else to eat. That pizza was great, but I'm starved again."

"Yeah, me too." She thought he'd certainly hear the false note in her voice. If she had to eat a bite, she'd be sick. If she had to look at Luke again, she'd begin to cry. Hoping to prod him into remembering, she tried one more question. "Have you ever smoked?"

He turned around so that he faced her. Puzzlement settled over his face. "Why are you asking that?"

"I don't know. I just wondered all of a sudden. Lots of people once smoked and quit." She sounded like a bimbo, she knew. "I never smoked." She almost bit her tongue to stop the deluge of drivel.

"Dawn, is something wrong?"

He stepped to her and it took all of her control not to flinch. She opened the door. "I'm ready if you are."

Luke kept his hands at his side, amazed at the change that had occurred in the woman who stood before him. She was pale as a ghost, her thick, black hair a somber frame for her drawn features. Nervousness had affected even the way she talked. Something had happened when she went to the car, but he had no idea what.

"Did you see someone on the hill?" he probed gently.

"Was I supposed to?" She snapped without thinking. "I'm sorry. I didn't mean to sound so harsh."

"Let's get out of here." Bringing her back to the place where she'd been abducted had been a bad idea. He put a hand onto her shoulder and felt her shudder. A gargantuanly bad idea. Maybe the worst idea he'd ever had in his life, and he'd had some real whoppers. Something about the set of her shoulders made him hesitant to offer any additional comfort. She'd pulled back from his touch, a fact that cut him deeply, even though he knew it was a reaction to what she'd been through, not to him. She practically trotted to the car and had the seat belt buckled before he could get into the driver's seat. Avoiding the road beside the plantation, he drove back to the highway.

"How about a cheerful Cajun place, something with some zydeco music and spicy food?"

"Wonderful." She didn't care where he stopped the car, as long as there was a telephone to call Orson. The matches! If Luke was working for Manetti, then Manetti knew about Roulette. He knew about Orson's part in everything. She had to warn her friend.

After several miles of silence, Luke found a place that promised atmosphere, music and spicy food. When they were seated at the table, he forced the conversation, talking of trivial things. He made one reference to the small room at The Palms, but Dawn's reaction convinced him it wasn't a topic she wanted to discuss. He couldn't help noticing the way she looked around the room, going from table to table and then back again, as if she expected to see someone she knew.

"Order for me, please." She stood abruptly, knocking the table with her thighs. "I have to go to the ladies' room." She couldn't stop herself from sounding like a prisoner, explaining every move, giving herself an alibi.

Casting her a disturbed look, Luke picked up the menu. Every move he made seem to add to her case of nerves. He concentrated on the menu and pointedly avoided watching her leave the table.

In the alcove near the bathroom Dawn found two pay telephones. She placed a collect call to Orson's number and prayed that he'd answer.

"Yo!" He sounded winded.

"It's Dawn!"

"What's up, girl? I hope you called Freddie, 'cause he's after your behind."

"Take Roulette somewhere and hide her, Orson. Then you'd better get out of town for a few days."

"Hold on there. My farm's running smooth. I haven't seen any creditors at my door. What's wrong?"

She took a breath. "Luke may be working with Manetti." The words tore at her throat, but she forced them out. "I can't be certain, but he may be. If he is, then you're in a lot of danger."

"You think Luke O'Neil is on Manetti's payroll?" Orson dropped all bluster. "That's impossible. Whatever's given you that idea?"

Dawn wiped at the tears that had begun to move slowly down her face. "It may be nothing, but then again, I couldn't take the chance with you. Since Ann first met you, you've been a true friend to us. Orson, promise me that you'll be careful." Her voice broke and she swallowed hard to keep the tears at a minimal level.

"I promise, Dawn. Do you think maybe you should come out here? We could all leave together." His voice rose. "That's it! Get Luke to bring you to Applegate. Together we can keep an eye on him and make sure he's right. I think he's a decent man, despite all the trouble he's had in the past. Get him out here, and time will tell us the truth."

The sense of Orson's words helped calm her. It was the perfect solution. They could check on Roulette, and Orson could help her find Luke's true character.

"Expect us late tonight. I think I can talk Luke into it. If I don't, then send out the Mounties."

"I'll call Freddie and tell him you're coming here. I think he's been in touch with Ann, and now the two of them are worried about you."

"That's all I need." Dawn was recovering some of her equilibrium. "Those two are enough to send me into the arms of the enemy."

As she spoke, she felt someone staring at her. Luke stood in the doorway of the alcove, his expression unreadable.

"I'll talk with you later, Freddie. I'm fine, and I'll be in touch when I speak with Luke. Probably late tonight." She replaced the receiver, before a startled Orson could protest.

"I had to call Freddie. He's been worried sick."

"I was worried, too, when you didn't come back to the table."

"As soon as we finish dinner, could we go to Applegate?" Dawn looked down at the bare, oak floor. "Freddie said he'd spoken with Orson. Roulette may be sick. I'm terribly worried about her." She forced her gaze up and met his eyes. Somehow she found the backbone not to flinch at her direct lie.

"How sick?"

"Freddie said she'd suddenly taken a turn toward colic. She was so depleted, maybe she's reacting to protein. It doesn't sound fatal, but I'd feel so much better if I could see her."

Dawn's expression was so distraught that Luke could not deny her. "If it means that much to you. I'm sure Orson is capable of caring for the mare, so don't worry so much." He let his fingers thread through her hair, marveling again at the silkiness, at the way the slightest touch could make him want her so.

"You're too kind." She meant to speak with a tinge of irony, but the words caught in her throat and she felt tears suddenly threaten. He did seem kind. His entire face showed nothing except concern for her, and his touch was tender, caring, so sincere.

"I'm not kind." He took her words at face value. "I care for you, Dawn. You look like you're being pulled in half. If seeing Roulette will make you easier, then it's a simple enough task to complete. And I can also make sure that Orson is okay. I've had some misgivings about involving him. He's such a decent guy, and no match for the likes of Louis Manetti."

"We should return to the table." Dawn had to get out of the close confines of the alcove. Luke's behavior was making her crazy. She was beginning to believe he cared about her. She'd been up and down that scale of reasoning so often that she was incapable of coming to any conclusions. She needed solitude, and time. And Applegate Farms promised both.

As soon as they were seated, the waitress brought them hot platters of blackened redfish, spicy rice, stewed okra and tomatoes and Cajun corn bread. Dawn's appetite was listless, but the delicious aroma of the food teased her into sampling it. One taste and she found that she was hungrier than she thought. Applegate was little more than an hour away, and Orson was like a larger, slightly distant relative of Freddie. Her worries about Luke had even subverted her concerns about the five thousand dollars. She swallowed a bite of the highly seasoned fish and tried to imagine Ann Tate's reaction. Anger? No, not anger. Shock. Ann would be shocked and horrified. That would be about it. Shock and horror. It wasn't a pretty picture to think about.

"You're visualizing the German invasion of Poland." Luke was leaning on one elbow, watching her face.

"No, I'm not." She answered spontaneously, a flush touching her face at her own response.

"The Khmer Rouge camps?"

"Luke!" She wiped her mouth and put the napkin onto the table.

"It has to be something terrible, because you looked absolutely anguished. I was just trying to think of things that might deserve such a woeful expression."

She smiled despite herself. "Actually I was thinking about Ann."

"And the dreaded five thousand?" Her one smile had taken tons of worry from her face, and he pushed for another light moment.

"You'd score high on ESP." That thought made her slightly uncomfortable, but she didn't let it show. "Ann won't be angry, she'll be shocked. Shocked and horrified." She laughed as she said it all. "I guess that is a little melodramatic."

"A little. Are you ready?"

"Definitely."

They rose simultaneously and left. At the car, Dawn turned. "Would you like me to drive?"

"I was hoping you might try to rest. You've looked so shaky all evening."

"I'm not a bit tired." The dark suspicion leaped forward again. If she went to sleep, she might wake up somewhere she didn't know. "I feel like driving. I think it would make me feel better."

Luke's face was questioning. "I know I could use the time for a nap, if you don't care."

"Wonderful idea." She got behind the wheel and quickly matched the wires that woke up the powerful engine. "Let's go."

Luke slept most of the way to the farm. He woke as she turned beneath the high, arched gate that was a new addition. Dawn slowed to admire the handiwork of the sign. Orson and his constant pursuit of recognition. The sign was lovely, but a little ornate for such a small operation. Well, every man deserved his big dreams. Orson's were certainly harmless enough.

At the front of the house she tooted the horn, then jumped out and ran up the steps before Orson could open the door. He was almost knocked down by her weight flying into his arms.

"How's Roulette? I told Luke you thought she had a light colic, and he agreed to bring me to see her." She pinched him lightly behind his back.

"The mare perked up when she heard you were coming, Dawn." Orson put an arm around her and squeezed. "She's out in the barn, waiting for you to take her a carrot."

"I'll get one from the fridge. It was just like Freddie to relay that information. He knew I'd hurry over here, and I think he wanted you to make sure I was alive and fine."

"You seem alive to me." Orson winked at Luke. "A little wan, but certainly alive."

"She needs to rest, but nothing would do her except that she checked on Roulette." Luke nodded his head, indicating he wished to speak with Orson alone.

"Dawn, go on out to see that horse. Luke and I'll have a drink and follow you."

Her first impulse was to resist, but she saw the glint in Orson's eye. She'd tipped him off about the possibility of Luke's involvement with Manetti. Orson could handle himself. And he just might have a plan for testing Luke.

She went to the kitchen, found several carrots, and trotted past the two men toward the barn. She didn't look back, but strained nonetheless to hear what they were discussing. Luke and Orson were only a few inches apart, and whatever they were talking about had both of them intensely interested. Wishing she had bionic ears, she went on to the barn.

"Does she suspect?" Orson asked, his face a mask of worry.

"No. But she's been upset all afternoon. If she thought you were in danger, she'd really pressure herself."

"The thing to do is convince her to go home and let Ann handle it from here. What you said about the money is going to be hard. Ann has never had a big cushion, and five thousand is a lot in her shoes. On the other hand, the ranch is doing great, and her new husband is successful. It won't be a death knell by any stretch of the imagination. Dawn's done enough. It's time for Ann to get involved, and Freddie says she's at the ranch, ready to take over."

Luke shook his head. "No way is Dawn going to stop in midstream. You've known her longer than I have. She's bullheaded when it comes to this horse thing."

"'Course, if we could just find that stallion, she'd forget all about the filly." Orson rubbed his chin. When he looked up, Luke had turned away to look out toward the barn.

"Do you think it would help, if we could assure her that Speed Dancer was safe and well treated?"

"How could we do that, when we don't know if he's even alive? I mean, the filly is three. That stud could have been killed four years ago."

"Would evidence of his safety mean anything to Dawn?"

"She cares for that horse in a special way. It's a bond that happens sometimes between a human and an animal. I've seen it with dogs, cats, birds, even wild creatures. It doesn't happen often, and it's a rare thing. With Dawn, that stallion became a part of her. Knowing that he was safe and cared for would go a long way toward making her give up this dangerous quest."

Orson took a deep breath and wiped a hand across his forehead. "If I give up the horse business, I could get a job as a televangelist. I can certainly talk enough."

Luke slapped him on the shoulder and laughed. "Or a politician. Or a television commentator."

"You seem like your spirits have picked up. Is there a reason?"

"You've given me an idea. It's too young to talk about, but it's got some merit. More than anything I want to see Dawn safe. I'll keep looking for that filly, if that's what she wants, but I want her home and safe."

Orson leaned against the porch and stared into the night that had fallen. "I don't want Dawn to hear this, but you should know. It isn't her place to be chasing this filly. Ann's a tolerant woman, and she won't hold Dawn responsible for what's happened so far, but it's time she got on back to the ranch, back to her job and responsibilities. Freddie Weston is too old for Dawn to run off and leave him with his work and hers, too."

"I'll talk with her. You do it, too. And I have a plan." Luke refused to say more. "I'm going to the barn and see Roulette. I think Dawn's horse attractions are contagious. I've gotten rather fond of that mare, just from listening to Dawn talk about her."

"I'd be fonder, if I thought I had a chance to get her bred to Speed Dancer." Orson grinned. "I've got to see if there's any of Mrs. Marble's shepherd's pie left."

"We ate," Luke reminded him.

"I did, too. But a snack is never a bad idea. Especially when Latavia Marble has rolled the dough." He patted his stomach, then went back inside.

Alone in the night, Luke listened to the sound of horses settling down. He'd forgotten how much he loved the noises of a horse farm at night. The animals occasionally called to each other, but the more subtle sounds of a feed bucket being snuffled or the slow munching of hay were the things he loved. And the smells. Grains and earth, horses and leather. He took it all in, then walked through the darkness to the barn.

Dawn hadn't bothered with a light. He didn't see her at first as he paused in the door, but in a moment he heard her. She was soothing the mare, speaking in a low murmur of indistinguishable words. He listened attentively, but was still unable to detect what she was saying. He walked closer.

The sound was almost a song, but there were no words that he understood, only a rhythm and a comforting pattern of noises.

"It's a lullaby my grandmother taught me." Dawn spoke to him. She'd heard him approaching. "She said it would calm nervous animals, tame them, essentially."

"And does it?"

"The horses seem to like it." In the darkness she suddenly felt sad. She'd been singing to the horse, but the words had been meant to comfort herself. Luke O'Neil troubled her heart. She'd have given much to have her grandmother materialize on the spot and give her assessment of Luke.

"I came out here to talk with you. I want you to do something for me, Dawn."

"What might that be?" All of her wariness rose to the surface.

"Go home. Let me continue the search."

"Forget that plan. You can abandon me, but I'll keep looking. If Speed Dancer is out there, Private Stock is the way to find him. Now that I believe in my heart that he's alive, I'll never quit looking."

"Would you go home, just for a rest? Let Ann take up the search for a few days, while you take care of yourself."

Dawn stroked the mare's neck. "No, Luke. Ann can look if she wants, but I'm not quitting."

"Your job may be in jeopardy. Orson said . . ."

"Hang Orson and his worrying. If Ann fires me, I'll get another job. Maybe even with Louis Manetti. I'll bet I could find that filly then." She spoke in sudden anger, then regretted her words. She seldom lost her temper, but each slip always cost her a great deal.

Silence stretched between them. Dawn could tell that he hadn't moved. He was still ten yards away. Too close, and too far.

"Luke!" Orson's voice came to them, pitched high with anxiety.

"What?" Luke answered.

"Telephone!"

"Damn!" He started toward the house.

"Who knows you're here?" Dawn's question was edged with fear.

Luke stopped in midstride. "No one. I told no one."

"Luke!" Orson called again. "Hurry up. It's Louis Manetti, and he says if you want Private Stock, you'd better hurry."

Dawn and Luke began running together. Their feet pounded the ground, then the porch and finally the rug as they ran to the phone. Orson sat at the kitchen table, his hand scurrying across the page as he made elaborate notes.

"I'm here!" Luke reached for the phone.

Orson looked up. "He said he didn't have time to wait, but I took down everything he said for you to do."

Chapter Fifteen

"How did Manetti know you were here?" Dawn pressed herself against the kitchen wall. Her legs were suddenly shaky. "No one should have known." She transferred her wide-eyed stare to the portly man. "Orson, you didn't tell anyone we were coming, did you?" Slowly replacing the receiver, Orson shifted his gaze from Dawn to Luke. "Manetti's a smart man. He knows plenty, Dawn. He could have called out here on an assumption, or he could have had you followed."

"Or Luke could have called him and told him." She was too overwrought to heed caution. Anger followed the shock and she rounded on Luke. "When did you call him?"

"Dawn, that's a serious thing to say to Luke." Orson stood up and moved toward her, placing his body between them as a physical barrier. His face was lined with worry, and he avoided looking at either of them.

"It's a serious charge, I know that." Her words were icy clear. "If he's guilty, then he's done me a serious wrong." Dawn braced her back against the wall to keep her body straight.

Voicing the accusation made it worse. And Luke did nothing but stand silently beside the kitchen table. He didn't move or speak.

"Did you call Manetti?" She meant to have an answer.

At last Luke looked at her. Though she was standing erect, she gave the impression of an enraged cat ready to pounce. Her brown eyes, usually warmed with amber lights, were black and never wavered from his face. Distrust was evident in her expression, and he recognized it as the same emotion that had troubled her earlier that evening.

Her peculiar behavior came back to him, and he tried to trace the course of events. She'd gone to the car to get the notepaper. When she came back, she'd seen or heard something that made her distrust him. He had to find out what. Nothing in the car could have given away the secret he kept. Whatever had happened, he had to make her see that his actions had never jeopardized her.

"Do you believe I could have endangered your life?" He spoke softly, appealing to her with his voice and eyes. "Look at me and tell me that you believe I'd do something that would hurt you."

"Have you told me the whole truth?" She held firm and didn't look away. Her heart felt as if it would shatter, but she forced the issue. "What are you keeping from me?"

Something inside Dawn crumpled as the seconds ticked away. She dropped her gaze to her feet before Luke answered.

"I've never betrayed you to Manetti." Watching the hope die on her face was almost more than Luke could bear, but he could tell her no more. If she acted on the knowledge he had, it might endanger both her and everything else he cared for.

"Where does Manetti want to meet?" She addressed the question to Orson. Before he could answer, she turned back to Luke. "I'm going to find that filly and Speed Dancer. I'll do whatever I have to. Don't get in my way, or I'll go over you. And once our business is complete, I won't remember your name."

"I need a drink," Orson said to the room in general. "I'll make us all a bourbon." He left the room with as much speed as possible.

"Dawn, I didn't . . ."

"There may be a fine line between 'betray' and 'deceive' in your vocabulary, Luke, but there isn't in mine. I've never been less than a hundred percent with you. I made a mistake." She started for the door, wanting the buffer of Orson's company.

"I didn't betray you." Luke's solid grip caught her upper arm. Even through her sweater, she was conscious of the power of his touch. "Whatever else I might have done, I never did anything to jeopardize you, the future, or that horse you're so concerned about."

"Right now, I'm not in the mood to split hairs." His hand on her arm was twice as painful now. His grip was unwanted, his touch a reminder of the pleasure she had known with him.

In her eyes he saw the hurt, the depth of pain he'd given her. Only a few hours before, her eyes had reflected a deep and trusting love. "I wanted to tell you everything, but it wasn't possible. It isn't. Not until I find out who's at the bottom of all of this. I promise you one thing. Soon you'll know the truth and you'll see that I didn't betray you. You weren't wrong to love me."

"You'll never be able to convince me of that." She brushed past him and followed Orson to the den. He was pouring three stout drinks and she took one. "Where is Manetti, and where is that horse?"

Orson looked up to make sure Luke was also in the den. He handed him a drink, the ice clinking against the glass. "We don't have a lot of time. This is going to be a very delicate operation, and we're going to have to call Ann to help out."

"Ann?" Dawn's voice carried a protest. "Why?"

"Manetti insists." Orson shrugged his shoulders. "He declined to say why. He only said that without Ann, the filly will disappear forever. He wants her to drop the money."

"Money?" Luke perched on the arm of a plump sofa. "Back up, Orson. What's going on?"

"Manetti has the filly, and she's gotten too hot for him. He's willing to give her to Ann. But it's going to cost, and it has to be according to his directions."

"This sounds like a trap." Luke put his drink onto a table and paced the room. "Why Ann? Why not me?"

"Maybe he doesn't trust you, either." Dawn tossed the words at him like a sharpened weapon, but she couldn't stop the tears that began to fill her eyes. She turned to the empty fireplace and fought to compose herself.

"Manetti is a peculiar man. He's taken with Dawn's abilities. He said so on the phone." Orson drained his glass and poured another. "He said he wants Dawn to go to the racetrack near that old house where she bet on the race. The five thousand she lost will be hidden in the jockeys' room. She can retrieve it, while Ann makes the drop of the money. Luke, you're to drive the horse van to a spot he designates, to pick up the filly as soon as he receives the money."

"How much?" Luke retrieved his glass and took a long swallow.

"Half a million." Orson spoke so softly that the words had a sledgehammer effect.

"That's ridiculous. Where are we going to get that kind of money?" Dawn put her untouched drink onto the mantel and looked at Orson. "The only way we could get that much would be to mortgage Dancing Water or Applegate."

"Applegate is already mortgaged, to the last foot of fencing." Orson gave Dawn a sad smile. "I couldn't raise a penny on this place. If something doesn't turn around, they'll foreclose on me by Christmas."

"Orson." The word came out in a whoosh. "I had no idea. You always act as if everything is fine."

He shook his head and sipped his drink slowly, carefully. "What's the point in complaining? You and Ann had your hands full at Dancing Water. I have a few good mares I need to breed, maybe even to that rascal Easy Dancer. You know how it is. You keep waiting for spring, for the new crop of babies, knowing that one will be that special creature, the Triple Crown potential." He smiled, and it was painful to watch.

Dawn went to him and hugged his wide frame. "Ann'll give you those breedings, and we'll keep the mares over at Dancing Water. She'd do anything to help. You know that."

"I do." Orson disentangled himself from her arms. "But a man likes to do certain things for himself. This farm was mine, and I wanted to make it run without favors."

"But you've always been so generous to us," Dawn protested.

Orson turned to Luke. "Women, always full of sympathy and kindness. Just the worst thing at a time like this." He smiled at both of them. "Well, my problems are bad, but we've got to make a decision on Private Stock. If we don't get her, I don't know what'll happen to her. Manetti's desperate to dump her."

"She isn't proven and she isn't papered. How could she possibly be worth five thousand, much less five hundred thousand?" Luke maintained his rigid posture near the sofa.

Orson swirled his glass, making the ice cubes rattle. "Manetti says he can validate the breeding to Speed Dancer."

The words were like a jolt of adrenaline to Dawn. She forced herself to hold steady. "He knows where Speed Dancer is?"

"Says he does." Orson continued to stare into his drink. "He said the stud's safe and reclaimable. He's with someone he trusts to take good care of him."

"Where is he? Did he say where?" Dawn grasped Orson's arm, as if to help him talk faster.

Orson glanced at Dawn, then at Luke. "He said that after the ransom for Private Stock is paid, Luke O'Neil will tell us where to find the stallion."

It took a few seconds for Orson's words to register. "You know, don't you?" Dawn felt the floor slide, but she knew it was only her emotions. Her horrible suspicion became certainty as she saw the guilt in Luke's face. "You know where Speed Dancer is. You've known from the very first."

"I wanted to tell you. There are reasons I couldn't. Can't," he amended. "For the safety of the horse."

"I don't believe you." Dawn felt more helpless than she'd ever felt in her life. "Don't tell me any more excuses, any more lies. I'd ask where Speed Dancer is, but you'd only lie again! If I knew where to find him, I'd go now! And leave you to Manetti!"

"Speed Dancer is well treated and healthy. He doesn't lack for attention or care," Luke answered softly.

Dawn turned her back on him. "Orson, how much time?"

"Tomorrow night. I'm going to call Ann, that is if Luke agrees to make the drop. We all know it could be fatal."

"Manetti would never let anything happen to his right-hand man." Dawn's bitterness was extreme. "I'm going out to the barn for a few minutes. Would you wait to call Ann? Ten minutes couldn't make much difference."

"I'll wait." Orson sounded as defeated as she did. "But Ann's going to have to move fast, Dawn. Will she do it?"

"If she can. To get the filly and Speed Dancer, she might be able to swing it at the bank. But only if we can prove the filly is Roulette's offspring." As she talked, some animation came back into her face. "With registration papers, that filly could make it to the Derby in May."

"If she's in any condition." Luke launched his comment into the room. "Half a million is a lot of money for a horse that could have crippled herself. You can't trust a man like Manetti."

The harshness in his voice unsettled Dawn, but her first reaction was anger. "I should trust someone like you?"

"Dawn, why should Manetti suddenly decide to sell the filly? Think about it. We've been chasing her all over the South. He could keep her hidden for the rest of her life."

"But he can't race her without those registration papers," Orson pointed out. "She's no good to him except for match races, and it would take some time to earn out half a million with the risk each race of crippling her."

There was no arguing with Orson, and Luke knew it was useless to appeal to Dawn. She'd never consider anything he said.

"I'll be back in a few minutes." Dawn hurried out of the room and ran across the porch into the clear Louisiana night. Roulette was the comfort she sought. Whatever else had come of her harrowing days with Luke O'Neil, she'd at least been able to do some good for the mare. As she stepped into the barn, she was greeted by several soft whinnies. The low tones of Roulette were easy to distinguish in the third stall.

The mare's muzzle was soft and gentle. She reached her head over the stall and pressed against Dawn's arm. Responding in kind, Dawn stroked her neck, running her fingers through the straight, black mane.

"I didn't betray you, Dawn."

Luke's voice didn't startle her. He was so much a part of her thoughts that she wasn't surprised he'd followed her into the night. Her first burst of anger had washed through her, and misery was beginning to take hold.

"Will you deliver the money?" She had no one else to ask. If Manetti demanded that Luke do it, then it was him or nothing.

"I think it's a mistake, but I'll do it."

"Ann will make an effort to raise the money. Jefferson Stuart will help her. Jeff's an old friend. He helped pass the horse-racing bill in Mississippi. He and Ann have a long history of friendship, and I'll bet he comes through with some cash." She spoke to fill the darkness, to stall the pain that waited to surround her.

"No matter where she gets the money, it isn't a smart idea. I think with a little more time, we can find the filly."

"And Speed Dancer?"

The question seemed to echo. Luke made no effort to answer, and Dawn pressed her forehead into Roulette's neck. All along she'd suspected Luke knew something about the stallion. From the first day she met him, there'd been a reticence whenever the stud's name was mentioned. She should have paid more attention, been more guarded. Instead, she'd taken him in as her greatest confidant, her lover.

"You can't believe me now, but one day soon you'll see that I haven't done anything to make you hate me. I told you that I loved you, and I meant it. Work with me, Dawn. I need your help, if we're going to get that filly alive."

Wary of his plea, Dawn tried to resist. Something in his voice made her hesitate to reject him completely.

"What do you want me to do?"

"Go along with Manetti's proposal. Get the money, get Ann and let's plan the drop and retrieval of the filly. Something doesn't sit right with me. I can't believe Manetti would sell the filly because he's scared. He likes horses, he likes owning the best. That's his trademark and the way he conducts business. He'd never let Private Stock go. His ego would never allow it, unless..."

"Unless she's been injured since I saw her race." Dawn thought she couldn't feel worse, but suddenly she did. The idea of Private Stock crippled made her stomach tighten.

"That's a possibility we must face."

"It doesn't matter. We want her, anyway." Dawn knew she spoke without Ann's authority.

"For half a million?"

"If that's what it takes."

Luke took a tentative step toward her, then stopped. She didn't need any more pressure. If only she'd let him, he'd hold her and give her a moment of comfort. She wouldn't allow it. He had to face the fact that she might never again seek his arms.

"Let's go back inside and get the full story from Orson. We need to know every detail, every syllable that Manetti uttered. Then we'll formulate the best plan and call Dancing Water."

Reluctant to follow Luke's lead at all, Dawn walked wordlessly beside him. She had no miracle schemes that would save the day. She had only an iron determination and a wary heart.

"Well?" Orson had been pacing the floor, but he stopped when he heard them enter the room.

"We'll accept Manetti's offer. Call Ann." Luke looked directly at Dawn as she stood at the door. "Let's get going."

Chapter Sixteen

The final hours of the night drifted by in slow motion. At last the sun turned the eastern horizon gray, then pink. Dawn rose from her chair by the window and showered, slipping into the clean shirt Orson had given her. If she ever got back to Mississippi and her own apartment, her own clothes and brushes and linens, she vowed she'd never leave again.

The thought of coffee made her uneasy stomach whirl, so she found orange juice in the refrigerator and took out a glass to a cowhide rocker on the front porch. Applegate was lovely in the morning light. She propped her feet on the rail of the porch and tipped herself back in the old chair, sipping the juice and trying not to think.

"I was hoping someone else would be up." Luke walked out, freshly shaven but still looking worn and ragged.

"I'm not going along with Manetti's plan." Dawn had come to her decision somewhere between sunrise and arriving on the porch.

"I'm willing to listen to anything reasonable."

She turned to him, slightly amazed. She'd expected great resistance, and he was giving none. She recalled his remarks about disliking Manetti's plan, and for a moment she allowed herself the luxury of believing him. Remembering past experiences, she erected a guard. "Why are you so agreeable?"

"I'm only reaffirming my original sentiments, and I haven't agreed to your plan." He eased himself down onto the floor beside her chair.

"I don't need your approval. . . ."

"But you do need my help." His sudden coolness stopped her short. "Tell me what you were thinking."

"I'm going with you to pick up Private Stock. Ann can take my place at the jockeys' room and find the money."

"Orson said Manetti insisted that Ann accompany me."

"Something about that really bothers me. Why would Manetti want you and Ann together? I think this may be a trap. Something in the past, something that ties you and Ann."

Luke leaned back on an elbow, striking a nonchalant pose, but in the brightening morning, Dawn saw the sudden tension that tightened his mouth, deepening the furrows between his eyes.

"Who would want to hurt Ann?" His question was calm, but his fingers still circled her ankle, establishing a light hold.

His touch made her want to jump up. He was the one withholding something, not her. He had secrets; she'd been completely open. "Maybe you should ask Ann that question." She tried to rise, but he refused to release her leg.

"This isn't an argument between us. Ann could get hurt if you don't tell me what you know."

"I told you the truth the first day we met." She felt his grip relax and jerked her leg away, but kept her seat. Beside her, Luke rose slowly until he stood in front of her.

"Tell me again."

His eyes were tired, but blue as a spring sky. Dawn watched every expression that flickered through them as she talked. "Last February Cybil Matheson, Ann's vet, tried to hurt Easy Dancer.'' She spoke each word as if she were talking to a young child. ''At that time, we found out that four years ago Cybil murdered Ann's husband and stole Speed Dancer. Cybil was insanely jealous of Ann. She's in an institution now, unable to talk about the past. The doctors say there's no way to reach her.''

''And there was no trace of the horse?''

''We thought Robert, Ann's husband, had stolen the horse. We looked, but there wasn't a trace of either of them. Robert was dead, and for all anyone knew, Speed Dancer, too.'' Her voice trailed off.

''No ransom was ever requested on Speed Dancer?''

''Never. He simply disappeared. There was no sign or word of him until that video arrived, with Private Stock so obviously his daughter. All of those years, I felt he was alive. I thought of him as living.''

''No one suspected that Cybil might have had a partner?''

''Of course not. Cybil was mentally disturbed. She loved Robert, and she killed him and buried him in an abandoned churchyard. That isn't the behavior of a rational person.''

''I agree, but she must have had some help.''

''There was a construction company owner, a man who drank too much. She killed him, too.'' Dawn shook her head. She hadn't thought of Bill Harper in months. The whole episode had been such a tragedy.

''No one else?'' Luke sounded as if he didn't believe her.

''No one that we knew or heard of. Cybil was a very smart woman. What are you getting at?''

''That Cybil was working with someone else. The other person took Speed Dancer and sold him.''

''Cybil could have done that herself. After Robert died, she did steal the horse to try and sabotage Ann's ranch.''

Despite herself, Dawn was getting caught up by Luke's reasoning.

"Then who is after Ann? We both agree that it seems to be a setup for her, maybe for both of us. If Speed Dancer is the link, then it's conceivable that Cybil had a helper." Luke brought his theory round with a sudden twist.

Dawn rocked forward and rose from the chair without any resistance from Luke. Instead of going inside, she paced the length of the porch, then returned. Her mind was churning with possibilities. In her best calculations, all of the bad guys who'd tried to hurt Ann, Easy Dancer and Dancing Water were behind bars, or in the case of Cybil, in a hospital.

Even with these preoccupations, she was aware of the upheaval he caused in her emotions. She forced herself to focus on the cool morning, the familiar atmosphere of a farm. Listening to the sounds of the horses waking and the grooms getting ready to feed, she realized how Luke had crept into her life. He'd gotten all woven in with the horses in her mind and heart. He'd become a part of her dream.

"I knew Cybil."

His declaration pushed all other thoughts from her mind.

"Why didn't you say so at first?" Anger once again sparked through her. "How many other things didn't you tell me?"

"Cybil worked on my farm when she was a vet student. She interned there. She spoke of Ann and Dancing Water often, with great fondness, and something more."

Dawn was mesmerized by what he was saying, but she was also furious. Caught between wanting to hear him or yell at him, she finally governed her tongue by gripping the rail with both fists.

"Cybil was insanely jealous of Ann. She hid it well, always remarking on Ann's kindness, her generosity. I watched her, and I could see that it was eating away at her.

But I never thought she'd become unbalanced. She was a great vet, really good with the horses. One of the best diagnosticians I've ever seen. After her internship she went away, and as Freddie told you, shortly thereafter my life fell apart. A few years later, I heard she'd gone back to Mississippi. I was shocked. After all, I knew she'd gotten great offers in California and Kentucky, but then, Cybil was always doing things that shocked me.''

"Why didn't you tell me this earlier?"

"I didn't think that it related to Private Stock. Now I'm certain that it does."

Luke decided to take a chance. His right hand covered her left on the rail. He felt her struggle for a moment, then relax. Very carefully he picked up her hand and held it.

"Cybil made some dubious friends in the horse business. She was a beautiful woman with a lot of talent. When she was working in Kentucky as a student, she ran with a pretty fast crowd. I always thought she was smart enough to handle it, but now I'm beginning to wonder."

Dawn's heart was pounding. Whether it was from the touch of his hand or the information he was so carelessly dropping at her feet she couldn't tell. "What kind of men?"

"Louis Manetti was one of them. He was handsome, wealthy, extravagant and very much attracted to Cybil. I remember he came to my ranch to see her once."

"Manetti and Cybil." Dawn could see the attraction. Manetti liked bright, talented women. Cybil certainly had fitted that bill. And Cybil had liked self-confident men. The fact that Louis Manetti also had money wouldn't have hurt. Money would have symbolized power for her.

"Nothing ever came of it," Luke continued. "Cybil brushed him off. She never really got involved with any of the men who pursued her. Whenever I asked, she just said her heart belonged to someone else. Who that someone was, she never told me and I never asked."

"Ann's husband, Robert Tisdale." Dawn supplied the information readily. "So you think Manetti may have helped her pull this whole scam off, and then stole Speed Dancer from her?"

"I think that's a strong possibility."

"Then why involve Ann? Why send the video, when he had the filly and Cybil was conveniently out of the picture?" Luke's theory had a lot of possibilities, but there were so many loose ends.

"That's what we have to find out." Luke ignored the obvious. Revenge was a word he didn't want to use in front of Dawn, especially when the motive wasn't clear to him.

"You think Ann is in real danger, don't you?" Dawn felt as if she were prying further facts out of him.

He didn't want to frighten her, nor did he want to minimize what he saw as a real risk. "Let's just say that I think swapping roles is a good idea. I know I can rely on you in a pinch, and Ann would more than likely be a lot safer away from Manetti."

Dawn considered the idea. Luke was right, and it also went along with her own plan—to watch him closely.

"I LEAVE for a simple honeymoon, and you trade in your horse training license for a private detective's badge." Still talking, Ann Tate Roper got out of the silver truck. Her smile reflected a deep happiness, and some concern for Dawn.

"I intended to be in Tampa for one night." Dawn had heard the approach of the truck and horse trailer and walked down the long, willow-lined driveway to meet Ann before anyone else at Applegate got there. "I took the five thousand out of the bank and bet it on Private Stock. I lost the money."

"Freddie told me." Ann pushed her short hair back from her face. "He also showed me the video of the filly. You did the right thing."

Ann's smile finally vanquished the worry on Dawn's face. "I was hoping you'd say that."

"We have to get Speed Dancer back, and that filly. At least until we can figure out the best thing to do."

"The best thing to do is put her in the Derby." Dawn's convictions were so strong that she didn't have room for any doubt.

"I've always respected your horse sense, even though I still say Easy Dancer will prove to be the best stud."

"Don't bet the farm on it." Dawn's smile widened to a grin.

"Now, you're beginning to look like the cocky, confident, intolerable Dawn Markey I've grown to know and love." Ann put a comforting arm around Dawn's shoulders. "While I've been mooning around in marital bliss, you've had a pretty rough time. And Freddie hasn't had a picnic. He's been worried sick about you. He's ranting and raving about Luke O'Neil and his wicked past."

"I know."

"What's the story?"

"The jury's still out." Dawn didn't want to talk about it. Her own opinion wasn't solid.

"I see. I don't need a crystal ball to fathom the depths of that comment. The only thing I'm going to say from personal experience is that you can't assess a man's intentions or character based on limited knowledge. Give him a chance to explain himself."

"And if he won't?"

"Then if he's worth it, give him the benefit of the doubt. Hop in. I see Orson on the porch waiting for us." She got back into the truck and cranked up as Dawn climbed into the passenger seat.

"Ann, whatever Luke says, just go along with it." Dawn looked straight ahead, watching Orson and Luke on the porch. "I don't have time to go into it now, but I think you may be in real danger, and Luke and I agree that we should keep you away from Private Stock."

Ann pulled into the parking space near the house. "Matt will be down from Atlanta tomorrow. I thought about calling him, but I didn't realize..."

"Let your husband take care of his business. There's nothing he could do. Louis Manetti has stacked the deck, and another person might topple it. We can handle it."

"Ann!" Orson hurried down the steps, nimble and spry for a man of his girth. "We have a lot to go over. Let's go inside."

"I'd like a look at Roulette first, if you don't mind." Ann got out of the truck, taking Luke's hand as Dawn made the introductions.

"Believe it or not, but I've heard about you through the years. I'm glad to meet you." Luke assessed the tall woman with her short hair, charm and coolheaded air. She was probably a good person to have on his side. He felt his chance of success notch a little higher.

"She's in here." Dawn led the way to the barn and brought Roulette out of her stall.

Ann's sharp intake of breath was the confirmation Dawn sought. "There's no doubt, is there?"

"None. It's incredible that someone could pull such a scam on the Racing Commission, not to mention the insurance company. But this mare is Russian Roulette. They killed another horse." Ann walked up to her and ran a hand down her neck.

"Let's get the details for tonight ironed out." Orson was obviously worried. "I don't like any of this, and I want to be sure that everyone is as safe as possible." Like a mother hen, he herded them all into the house.

The afternoon hours seeped slowly away as he outlined Manetti's instructions and then followed through with maps and details. According to the instructions Orson had written down, Ann and Luke would drive the empty trailer to the designated stables near the racetrack.

"I know that old barn. It hasn't been used in a while. Manetti said the horse would be in the third stall." Orson read instructions from the notepad where he'd jotted them down.

"I wish I'd talked with Manetti." Luke was anxiously moving back and forth across the kitchen. "This sounds like a perfect trap. We bring the money, and drive blind into a situation where we can't escape without going back the same way we drove in. What if he gets the money and then decides to kill us?"

"It's not the best situation, but Manetti insisted. I tried to get him to change the location, but he wouldn't listen to reason. And he was adamant that Ann accompany you."

Dawn shot Luke a questioning glance. He nodded, a subtle movement that was lost on everyone else in the room.

"Well, if that's what the man wants, I'm not afraid." Ann propped her elbows on the table. "I've mortgaged Dancing Water to the hilt, and I couldn't have raised the rest without Jeff. He came through with nearly a third of the cash."

"I knew he would." Dawn left her perch at the sink and sat down at the table. "What will I do, Orson?"

"You're to go to Riverman's Run. The five thousand will be hidden in the jockeys' dressing room. When you find it, return here, to Applegate. I assume someone will be watching you to make sure you are there."

"Or maybe to kill me." Dawn couldn't help the cynicism. "If Manetti is so interested in returning the five thousand, why doesn't he just take it out of the half million he's forcing Ann to pay to get her own stallion back?"

"Because," Luke said, also taking a seat, "that would be far too simple, and it wouldn't keep you out of his hair. I suspect, Ms. Markey, that you have become quite a thorn in his flesh."

Dawn grinned. "I hope so. A sharp thorn, in very deep."

"I hate to spoil the plot, but why don't we simply call the police and let them pick Manetti up?" Ann asked.

"He'd never tell where the filly is. He knows we want her, and that's the ace he's going to play." Orson put his hands, palm down, onto the table as he talked. "This man plays on your weaknesses. He finds out what you want, and then he uses that against you. Just to keep me busy, I have to drive to his warehouse and meet one of his cronies."

"We have to do it his way, or we may lose the horse." Dawn checked the time. "I think we need to eat, and then get ready to go."

"Ah, food." Orson rose. "Ann, help me throw something together. I've neglected Mrs. Marble, and I'm afraid she's retaliating by holding out on her delectable sweets. She's something of a talent in the kitchen, but the price is so high." Looking tired, but determined to be cheerful, he left the room and Ann followed.

"I'd like to speak with you." Luke touched Dawn's arm and she went with him into the den. He closed the door behind them, then returned to stand directly in front of her.

"Trust me tonight. Whatever I say, simply trust me. Tomorrow, when all of this is behind us, I'll answer any question you have."

"Why can't you tell me now? Why can't you trust *me*?"

"Two words, that's all I can say." His hands clasped her shoulders. "Speed Dancer."

In his eyes Dawn saw so much more. The direct, blue gaze was sure, steady, dependable. He never wavered. "I'm trusting you with my life." She gauged his reaction and was pleased to see that one corner of his mouth twitched into a smile.

"Always the girl for melodrama, but I have to tell you, I'm putting my life in your hands tonight, too. One wrong move on your part and I could be killed. We're in this together."

For the first time in what seemed like an eternity, Dawn felt her hopes surge. "You'd better not count on sleeping tomorrow night. You've got a million questions to answer."

"And you have my word, I'll answer each one to your total satisfaction."

"I FIND IT disgusting that I have to go to the docks, so far from all the action," Orson grumbled as he cleared the table. Everyone stood to help, but he waved them aside. "Leave this stuff. It'll keep until I return." He picked up his keys. "Good luck."

"We'll be fine." Ann gave him a hug. "We'll get that filly, find out the scoop on Speed Dancer, and be back before you get too worried."

Luke went to the door, waving Orson off. "Remember, if none of us are back by midnight, call the state troopers."

Orson started to speak, then, completely out of character, he merely nodded. He tore off down the drive in his truck.

Before the dust settled, Dawn turned to Ann. "There's been a change in plans." She gave her friend the keys to the car. "I'm going with Luke."

"What's going on?" Ann looked from one to the other.

"For you." Dawn handed her friend a close-fitting cap. "We're changing places."

"Why?" Ann was clearly mystified. "I thought we were following Manetti's plans to the T."

"As far as he knows, we are. But Dawn and I think the bottom line may be that Manetti wants to hurt you, Ann. There's no practical reason to insist that you be here tonight. Unless he plans to hurt you."

"But he may hurt Dawn. Besides, I can handle him. He couldn't be worse than that gangster who burned down my barn and tried to kill Ronnie and Jeff."

"Manetti's capable of anything," Luke cautioned her. "Dawn and I know him, we know a little more what to expect, and we know how to work together as a team." Automatically he reached out for Dawn, his fingers brushing lightly across her arm.

"I don't know." Ann was obviously reluctant to accept the change.

"It's the only way, Ann. Believe me. We've gone over it again and again. We didn't tell Orson, because we were afraid Manetti might call him again. You know Orson. He might slip up and let on that we'd decided to change the plan."

"I don't like this." Now Ann was balking.

"You have to listen to us. It's the best way, for all of us."

Ann looked from one tense, white face to the other. "Okay. You've been in this longer, and I've always respected Dawn's ability to assess a dangerous situation. I'll go to the old estate and find the money."

"If anyone else is there, try to avoid them, to stall them. We'll need as much time as you can get for us."

"I'll do my best." Ann impulsively hugged Dawn, holding her tightly for a moment. "I told you years ago, when Speed Dancer injured his leg and you insisted on moving out to the barn, that one day that horse would put your life on the line." Dawn felt herself squeezed harder. "I hope this isn't the night, Dawn Markey. I hope this isn't the night."

Chapter Seventeen

The money, all cash, as Orson said Manetti had directed, was in an old feed sack on the floorboards of the trucks. Dawn tucked it beneath her legs and turned so that she could talk more comfortably with Luke.

"I'm scared," she admitted.

"You'd be a fool if you weren't." Reaching across the seat, he pulled her close to him for a hug. "Now, let's get serious. We'll drive in. I figure they'll have someone at the gate, watching to make sure we're both in the truck. Halfway down the drive I'll slow." He reached up and flipped the switch on the overhead light so that it wouldn't come on when the door opened. "Roll out the door and hit the dirt. Let the horse trailer block you. Okay?"

"Got it. If one of Manetti's men is anywhere around, I'll find him."

Luke nodded. He had to get Dawn out of the truck as soon as possible. The way he viewed it, Manetti would strike as the truck stopped. The gangster would think that he and Ann Tate Roper were trapped inside. Luke grinned. Manetti would have a small surprise.

"You have a gun. Does Ann?"

"She brought her own. After everything that happened this year at Dancing Water, I think she's quite adept at handling guns." Dawn laughed mirthlessly. "Matt gave her shooting lessons as one of her wedding presents."

"Not romantic, but very practical."

"I think maybe Matt suspected there would be another chapter to this story. Who would have thought Cybil was manipulated by a mobster?" Dawn's shoulders came up in a tiny shrug. "Boy, when Ann and Jeff took on that racing issue, they made some serious enemies. Matt must have sensed this when he whisked her away on that long honeymoon in such a hurry."

Luke watched the characteristic twitch of her shoulder and pulled her in for another hug. "Do you have any preference for a honeymoon?"

Dawn knew he was teasing her, trying to lighten the tension that built with each mile that passed. At the main highway, they watched Ann turn in the opposite direction. For a long time Dawn didn't say anything, then she answered. "The Derby. That would be the perfect honeymoon, with Private Stock wearing the Dancing Water colors."

Luke laughed. "I was foolish enough to think maybe you'd say Tahiti, someplace where there would be privacy, sand, water and no horses."

"That was foolish." Dawn impulsively kissed his cheek and then slid over to her side of the seat. "We're getting close. I think I should act like Ann instead of like me."

Her hands, always quick and agile, rolled her hair into a tight bun that gave the impression of a short style similar to Ann's. She pulled up the collar of the dark jacket Orson had loaned her and reached into the pocket to check the small, snub-nosed gun.

"Sure you're okay with that?" Luke felt a whirl of apprehension at the sight of the deadly weapon in her small hand.

"I hate them. But I feel better with it than without it."

"We're not far away now. I've been watching, and there doesn't seem to be anyone following us." The rearview mirror had grown ominously blank as they'd gone farther and farther down the isolated highway. "Manetti sure knows every forgotten and abandoned site in the state of Louisiana."

"That's the turn." Dawn saw the mailbox Orson had described. Her heart thumped painfully and she drew a long, deep breath. The silver truck and trailer coasted into the drive like a ghostly conveyance. Ahead was darkness, cut only by the twin beams of the headlights. As the truck swung around, Dawn saw an old-fashioned barn with an enormous loft for hay storage.

The truck slowed and she had no more time to look. Just as she'd discussed it with Luke, she opened the door and threw herself to the ground, rolling. All of her falls from horses had taught her to hit the dirt with a degree of limberness. When she sat up, she scrabbled her way to the edge of the barn and ducked behind a wooden door.

In the truck, Luke edged slowly down the barn, giving Dawn time to find a good viewpoint. It was up to her to protect his back, and some inner sense told him that he definitely needed support. The whole deal was wrong. Huge and listing slightly to the right, the old barn seemed to harbor nothing but danger. Luke knew his imagination was getting the better of him, but he didn't like the plan and he didn't like the location.

At the far end of the barn he turned the truck so that he was facing out, then killed the motor.

One foot had barely touched the ground when he heard the noise behind him.

"You're pretty slick, aren't you?" Benny Bertrane asked.

"Hello, Benny. I can't say I've missed you." Luke had expected a double cross. "Where's the filly?"

"Oh, I'd say about a thousand miles from here." Benny laughed, pressing the nose of a gun into Luke's back. "Want to move away from the truck, so the little lady can get out?"

Luke stepped aside, giving a thousand silent thanks that Dawn was already out. At least she had a chance; maybe she was even his last hope.

Benny reached into the car, coming back with an angry gesture. "Where's Ann Tate?"

"She got tired of riding, so I let her out about ten miles back."

Bertrane brought the butt of the gun toward Luke's jaw. Ducking, Luke caught only a deflected blow, but felt the vicious cruelty with which Bertrane had aimed the strike.

"Up against the truck!" Bertrane had the gun pointed at Luke's head again. "You think you're so clever. We saw the girl in the truck. We know she's here, and she won't get out alive."

Bertrane's hand slipped into Luke's belt and removed the gun he'd tucked there. "Where's the money?"

"No horse, no money."

Bertrane's elbow came at Luke's side, slamming in with enough force to knock the breath out of him.

"I asked a question. Where's the money?"

"I want to see Manetti."

Bertrane's laughter was light, as if he'd heard the funniest joke in the world. "Manetti? That's a good one. Would you like to see Gele, your Jamaican friend?"

Luke felt an almost uncontrollable rush of anger. The islander had helped him, saved his life. "Where is he?"

"Well, he thought he was going to escape to the great island of his dreams. But his concern for his family was his undoing. We caught up with him this morning, lurking around the docks, waiting for a ship to Jamaica. He's had a very, very bad day."

Luke started to swing around, but Bertrane pressed the gun into his neck. "I wouldn't make any rash moves. Since you won't give me the woman, and I know the money's somewhere in the truck or horse trailer, why don't we take a little walk into that old barn? Gele will be mighty glad to see a friendly face."

Prodded by the gun, Luke walked into the darkness of the barn. Bertrane flipped on an overhead light that dangled by a thin cord, illuminating one corner of the ancient building. Suspended from a beam, his feet about three inches from the ground, was the islander. His tall, slender body was sweating, and the marks of blows and kicks were all over him.

"Gele!" Luke rushed forward, and before Bertrane could halt him, had unknotted the rope that held the Jamaican captive in the air. The islander hit the floor with a groan of thanks.

"My arms were coming out of the sockets," he said in his singsong voice. "I was wondering what type of work a man with no arms could do."

"I wouldn't let the future worry me too much." Bertrane was both angry and amused. "The Boss isn't going to give you much time to plan."

Luke cast several quick glances around the barn, but there was no sign of Dawn. He had a pounding sensation of fear that another of Manetti's henchmen had captured her and was holding her somewhere else.

"The filly ain't here." Bertrane settled on an old bale of hay, gun covering Luke and Gele. "We're just passing the time until we find Ann. Then there's going to be an unfortunate fire." He reached into his pocket and drew out a book of matches. Even in the poor light of the barn, Luke recognized the distinctive black cover with the gold horse's head.

"So Manetti's too much of a coward to do his own murders. I guess that's why he keeps gofers like you around. Someone to do the dirty work while he rakes in the money."

"Manetti?" Bertrane laughed again. "I don't mind being a gofer. I make pretty good money, and besides, I enjoy my work." He struck a match and dropped it into the hay at his feet. The dry grass caught instantly, jumping into a blaze. Still laughing, Bertrane stepped on it. "This place will go like a tinderbox. Maybe you guys will be lucky and die of the smoke, before the flames actually get to you."

Luke started to say something, but Gele stopped him with a soft touch on his shoulder. "I know Mr. Bertrane. Let him talk." The islander's rhythmic voice was softer than a whisper.

"I think I have made a mistake and I would like to work for The Boss again." Gele spoke louder, stepping slightly forward to address Bertrane.

"Too bad." Bertrane never even looked up. "One mistake is all it takes in this business. I—"

A piercing scream from above them cut through the barn. Bertrane jumped to his feet, and when he looked up, Luke dived at him, cutting his legs out from under him. A startled grunt escaped his lips, and he fell backward over the bale, his gun flying out of his hand. With one perfectly aimed blow, Luke knocked him senseless. He turned to the islander to offer assistance.

"Go!" Gele was on his knees, his hands still tied, but he was working at the knot. He motioned toward Bertrane. "If he makes a move, I will knock him out again."

Luke took him at his word and dashed toward the darkened end of the barn. The scream had come from the loft. He found the ladder and slowly began to climb. It was Dawn's voice, so frightened and alarmed that it had been like a knife in his heart. She wasn't a screamer. As he edged to the floor of the loft, he paused to listen. There wasn't a sound. Not even the rustle of mice.

DAWN CLUNG to the wall of the barn, letting her eyes adjust to the darkness. A half moon cast some light, but not enough for excellent vision. She watched the truck cruising down the barn, going as slowly as possible, circling before it stopped. A darker shadow disengaged itself as she listened, she heard Benny Bertrane's hated voice. When the gofer struck Luke, it was all she could do to keep from rushing forward, gun in hand. Common sense made her wait. She had to find out if there were others around. It would do no good to rush to Luke's rescue, only to be captured by another henchman.

Backing carefully, her eyes still on the scene at the truck, she eased into the old barn. It was a farming barn, used to store equipment, feed, hay and a few head of livestock. Even as she entered, she knew Private Stock wasn't there. There were no sounds or smells of horses. The trap was obvious; Luke had been right all along. She hefted the gun, trying to get comfortable with the feel of the deadly weapon in her hand. Would she use it on another person? She hoped it wouldn't come to that.

Her foot struck a wooden handle, and she bent and picked up an iron rake. It was unwieldy, but had some potential. She carried it with her as she slunk through the barn. At the far end she heard the soft moans of a man in pain. Once again she fought down the impulse to rush forward and offer assistance. Manetti was capable of any type of trap. She had to use her head, not her emotions.

The groaning man seemed to be the only living presence in the barn, and she withdrew. Finding the ladder to the loft, Dawn decided on a higher vantage point. From that angle, if she had to use the gun, she'd have the best possible shot. The rubber soles of her shoes were silent on the ladder rungs. Carrying the rake and gun was awkward, but she managed it without making a sound.

The smell of old hay, long abandoned, wasn't pleasant, but it was familiar. She pulled herself into the loft and crept on hands and knees toward the far end, the place where she'd heard the man moaning.

She was almost in position when she heard Luke and Bertrane entering. Peering over the edge, she caught sight of the scene below as Bertrane flipped on the light. Her eyes widened in horror as she saw the Jamaican hanging from the beam, his arms obviously hurting.

She remembered the cruelty Bertrane had used against Luke, and the terrible condition of Russian Roulette at Oakdale. Instead of ten minutes alone, she wanted twenty. They would be the longest twenty minutes of Benny Bertrane's miserable life. She saw Luke look toward the loft and wanted to make an encouraging gesture, but was afraid to draw any attention her way. She'd convinced herself that the barn was empty of all enemies except Bertrane. In another few moments she could make her move. She crept closer to the edge, her hands sifting through the hay to make sure the floor beneath was solid. Her fingers struck something stiff and cool.

Dropping the rake, she reached deep into the hay. Her fingers circled something larger than her hand. She felt deeper, following the object until she realized it was getting bigger. She slipped the gun into her pocket and worked with both hands, pushing the hay aside.

The light was poor, but she worked fast. The worst suspicions were forming in her mind. Afraid to go further but knowing she had to, she pushed the straw aside. The sight was so unexpected that she couldn't stop the scream. Louis Manetti, a garrote wrapped around his neck, stared blankly at the ceiling.

Before she could draw a breath, a large hand was clamped over her mouth. She was jerked backward with force. Her hair tumbled about her shoulders, and the man who held her shook her like a rag doll, his hand clasping her mouth and nose all the time so that she couldn't breathe or make a sound.

"You had to meddle, didn't you? Why, Dawn? Why couldn't you let it go? He never wanted you. He wanted Ann and Luke!"

Orson's voice was thick with desperation. "I tried to fix it so you wouldn't get hurt. I sent you across town, hoping you'd do as you were told. But no! You had to keep on and keep on. Warnings weren't enough. He said he'd kill you, if you got in his way one more time. He meant it. And he will. Luke and Ann are dead! And now you are, too!"

With every fiber of muscle, Dawn bucked and twisted. Her oxygen supply was rapidly diminishing, and she felt blackness hovering beyond. She had to breathe. She had to get away from him. But his grip was incredibly strong. She'd never dreamed Orson had so much strength.

Jerking her head, she was able to loosen his grip on her nose. Dragging in as much air as she could, she opened her mouth and clamped down on his finger. From out of the darkness his other hand smashed into her and she sank slowly to her knees, stunned.

Her vision was still bleary, but she saw Orson reach into his pocket and draw out a gun. He pointed it at her temple and cocked it.

"Don't make me do it. I will, you know. I don't have a choice anymore."

"Orson?" She spoke as if she didn't recognize him. The horror of Louis Manetti's corpse, the blow, her discovery of Orson's role, all had left her disoriented. "What are you doing?"

"I owe him so much. He owns me, don't you see? He has for years and years, even before I came here." His voice was a whisper.

"Orson," she spoke again, slightly louder. She had to make him understand that Manetti was dead. Everything would be fine if Orson knew that.

"Shut up!" He moved the gun closer. "One more word and you're dead. Then Luke will follow." He wiped his forehead with the back of his hand, sweating profusely, even though the barn was cool. "He'll be here any minute. He's going to be very angry when he finds out that Ann Tate has escaped him. He's determined, though. Since he got out of prison, he's thought of nothing but revenge. First Luke O'Neil, then Ann Tate, Jefferson Stuart, and finally Jeff's wife, Veronica Sheffield. See, he knew that Jeff would give Ann part of the half million. That was the beginning of his revenge. The money was only the beginning."

Dawn wanted to talk, but the gun was a reminder to keep her mouth shut. Somehow she had to tell Orson that Manetti was dead. She looked at the big man. The face that was usually so jovial and kind was a mask of fear and desperation.

If she could reach the Orson she knew, the man who was kind and cared for her, then she might have a chance. Orson had come to the area just as Ann and Jeff were growing serious about horse racing in Mississippi. He'd set up his breeding farm in Covington and encouraged Ann in her pursuit of legalized racing. A lot of the Louisiana racers hadn't been keen on a competing track so close in Mississippi, but Orson had been very helpful. He'd been involved, on the fringes but involved, in some of the preliminary plans.

Her thoughts were interrupted by the sound of Luke moving through the barn below. His step on the ladder was soft, but unmistakably his. Fear pounded against her temples. Eyes shifting from the gun barrel to the hole in the floor where Luke's head would appear, she tensed, ready to warn him.

"Don't, or I'll kill him as soon as he sticks his head up." Orson swung the gun from her to the loft entrance.

"We'll leave. You can have the money, the horses, everything. Just let us out of here." Dawn tried to reach him. "You don't have to kill us. Manetti's already dead. You can have it all, Orson."

"All?" His tone was harsh. "I'll be lucky if I live." He motioned her into silence as Luke drew nearer.

Indecision made Dawn clamp her jaw. She wanted to yell at Luke, to warn him, but if she did, all Orson had to do was walk to the entrance and shoot down. Clinging to the ladder, Luke would be a sitting duck.

"Dawn?" Luke's voice was soft, concerned.

"Run, Luke! Get away!" She rushed at Orson, flying into his bulky body with all of her strength. She'd left the rake partially covered in the straw, and she stomped on it now, making the handle fly up like a booby trap. The wooden handle slammed Orson on the shoulder.

He was caught off guard, but he recovered quickly. She was no match for his size. With an angry gesture he shoved her away and stepped to the hole in the floor.

"Hello, Luke." He pointed the gun directly at Luke's forehead. "Come on up and join us."

Of all the things Luke had expected, Orson Rinter wasn't one. Luke took in Orson's sweaty forehead, the tremble in his hand as he held the gun. He wasn't a man who could stand a lot more pushing. He was at the limit, capable of anything. Very slowly Luke eased himself up the ladder and into the loft. Dawn, uninjured, immediately went to his side, her hands touching his arms, his shoulders, giving and seeking comfort.

"You had to keep dragging her into it, didn't you?" Orson addressed the question to Luke. "There was nothing I could do about you, or Ann. You were going to die. But I tried to save Dawn. She wasn't part of it. She could have lived, but you wouldn't quit. Now all of you will die."

"Ann's safe. She didn't go to the old, abandoned track. She went to..."

"Don't bother with the lies, Dawn. At this moment—" Orson looked at his watch "—she's riding in the back of a car, headed this way."

"Mr. Luke, Mr. Luke!" Gele's voice echoed eerily in the loft, seeming to float along the high, darkened rafters.

Realizing that the islander couldn't know what was happening in the loft, Luke took a risk.

"Run, Gele! Run!" He bellowed the order so there could be no doubt in the islander's mind. "Get the police!"

Dawn cast a fearful look at Orson, but he made no move to stop Luke. "Let the Jamaican go," he said. "The Boss would kill him, but then, it isn't a long-standing grudge like the one he bears for you." He pointed the revolver at Luke, shaking the barrel slightly. "Gele can run for three hours before he finds a working telephone. By the time he gets help, you'll be ashes and I'll be gone. Long gone. There will be no trace of this place, except smoldering timbers. It's the perfect setup."

Watching the slight tremble of the gun, Dawn knew Orson was talking to keep his courage up. Gele was gone, and soon Bertrane would be waking. She signaled Luke with a flip of one finger. He saw her and gave a slight shake of his head.

Impatience made her want to rush at Orson. They had to do something before Bertrane recovered. He was the meanest man she'd ever met, and though Orson might not be able to pull the trigger on her, she knew Benny Bertrane would do it, and enjoy the act.

"You set me up with that injection at the Maclay, didn't you?" Luke was watching Orson with a new intensity. "You gave that child's horse the speed, trying to frame me."

"It wasn't my idea." Orson had the grace to shake his head. "I didn't know the kid would hurt herself. The Boss only wanted to ruin your reputation as a trainer. He had to get even."

"For what?" Luke almost shouted, but quickly got his voice under control.

"That horse you trained for the Olympics, the one you went back and lamed. That was his horse. He bought him, and he wanted to put him in the ring. He wanted to get even with you for that."

"I never touched that horse. He was sound the day he left my care. I thought it was a dirty trick to play, taking the animal back after I'd spent a year getting him in shape and trained. But no matter. I wouldn't hurt the horse to get even."

Something in Luke's voice must have struck Orson as genuine. "You didn't?"

Luke shook his head.

"You're the one who told Freddie about Luke's past, aren't you?" Dawn put her hand to her forehead as the truth struck. "No wonder the only stories Freddie got were bad ones."

"I tried to scare him enough, so that he'd get you home. He was plenty worried, but you wouldn't listen. You wouldn't listen to reason. Now—" Orson swung the gun around the barn "—there's no way to help you. I did everything I knew how."

"Let us go, Orson. Manetti's dead." Dawn eased back to the mound of straw behind her and kicked it away, revealing a portion of Manetti's body. "You *can* let us go."

"He's bringing Ann." Orson spoke as if he hadn't heard her. "He thought you'd try a trick. He was right, and as soon as he gets here with Roulette, you'll all die."

"Roulette?" Dawn felt a tremor of fear. If Orson meant what she thought he meant, she could see the frame. She and Luke and Ann would die in a barn fire, some sort of double cross among the three of them. In the horse world, Luke already had the reputation of being dishonest. If Russian Roulette's body—and Dawn was certain some good Samaritan would notify the authorities to check the break in the horse's leg—were found with them, it would appear they'd pulled the insurance scam and were all three involved in some illegal business.

"Where's Private Stock?" She snapped the question at Orson.

"She's at Luke's ranch, with her sire." Orson watched Dawn carefully. "I wondered when he was going to tell you the truth. I almost did a few times, but I was afraid you'd want to know how I knew. So Luke never told you?"

"Her sire?" Dawn clenched her fist. "Speed Dancer?" It was too much to believe. She forgot about Orson and his gun. She turned to Luke, wanting an explanation. He remained silent.

"That's what makes the whole setup so perfect." Orson wasn't gloating. "Luke has had the stallion ever since The Boss arranged for him to go to the sale as an unregistered stud." Orson looked at Luke. "You should have known something was wrong, when you were allowed to pick up an animal like that for twenty thousand. Even without papers, a fool could see that he was worth lots more."

"Only for someone like me. He couldn't race without papers, and I did suspect he had a past."

"You've had Speed Dancer all along?" Dawn's temper rose so fast, she thought she'd pop. "All this time, and you didn't tell me?"

"It doesn't matter now, Dawn." Orson's reminder was almost gentle. "Once the authorities discover the filly and the stud, then you and Luke and Ann will be branded as criminals, caught in their own game of fraud. And you won't be around to defend yourselves."

Chapter Eighteen

Dawn's angry recriminations were silenced by the sound of a car approaching. She cast Luke a long, hard look, then turned back to Orson.

"If that's Ann, you can't let them hurt her. She's been your friend, Orson. Through thick and thin she's been there for you. Whatever you think of Luke and me, you can't let them hurt Ann."

"I have to. She's the one who put The Boss in jail. She helped Jeff get the racetrack through. She wouldn't leave well enough alone, not even when she was warned." Orson shook his head wearily. "She's a lot like you. Neither of you know when to back off."

"Orson, Ann would risk her life for you!"

"I can't do anything. He was going to kill her from the very first, along with Luke, Jeff and Ronnie. You're the one I could have saved, and you wouldn't let me. Now it's too late for you."

Two car doors slammed.

Luke heard the first stirrings of Benny Bertrane as he returned to consciousness on the floor of the barn. He'd hoped that Dawn could talk some sense into Orson, but that hope was fading fast. Someone had a hold on the portly horseman, and Luke didn't have any idea who. It wasn't Louis Manetti, that much was certain.

Luke had a sudden idea. "Did you kill Manetti?"

"Benny did it."

"But why? Wasn't he with you?"

"Manetti? He got in the way once too often." Orson shrugged, a larger, grosser imitation of the gesture Dawn used so effectively. "He wanted that filly as bad as you did, Dawn. He killed Jack the Knife that night in the alley. Benny vowed then to kill him, and when he gave us trouble up at the old plantation, Benny did it."

The image of the pool of blood on the kitchen tile came back to Dawn with a sudden vividness that made her blanch.

"Orson?" A deep, authoritative voice called through the barn. "Where are you?"

"Up in the loft, with O'Neil and Dawn Markey."

"Get up, Bertrane!" the voice ordered, and the sound of flesh meeting flesh followed. "Bertrane, you're virtually worthless. I leave you in charge of one man, and I come back to find you napping in the hay. And you, Mrs. Roper, keep moving!"

Dawn felt her last hopes crash as she realized that Ann was, indeed, captured.

"I can't climb the ladder with my hands tied!" Ann's voice was sharp and clear. A moment of silence was followed by a bitter, "Thanks."

Dawn waited until her friend's head cleared the loft floor, then she went to offer assistance, pulling her into the hay.

Ann scorched Orson with a look. "I've been hearing some interesting things about you, Orson. All of those friendly visits. You were nothing more than a spy for that scum!" She pointed contemptuously down the ladder, where there was the sound of another person coming up.

The man who appeared at the loft was short, heavyset and dressed in a gray, pin-striped suit. An unlit cigar was clenched between his teeth. Small, black eyes surveyed the group. "Good work, Orson," he said around the cigar. "At last I have them all together. It's taken time. Time and planning. But it's been worth the effort."

He smiled at them, obviously enjoying center ring. "Allow me to introduce myself. Johnny Deluchi."

"The Boss," Luke said turning to Dawn. "Remember the photo of Jack the Knife as a jockey. The horse owner was Deluchi—Mr. D!"

"That's right, O'Neil." Deluchi was pleased. "You're a smart man, but you should have been smart enough not to cross me."

"Jeff will kill you," Ann interjected.

"I doubt it. You see, the influential Mr. Stuart and his lovely wife, that snooping reporter Veronica Sheffield, will have their own set of misfortunes in the very near future."

"You couldn't buy—or frighten—Jeff when you wanted to kill the horse racing bill in Mississippi. He put you behind bars. How did you get out?"

"Good behavior, and lots of gifts to the parole board." Deluchi smiled. He pulled out a matchbook, the distinctive black cover catching Dawn's eye.

"You didn't stop us from getting racing in Mississippi," Dawn challenged him, hoping to keep him talking.

"No, I didn't." Deluchi sighed. "So I had to think up a new tactic. Those long months in prison gave me plenty of time to figure out how to get even, and get what I want. Revenge is a very empty package if opened alone." He puffed a curl of smoke into the air, tapping the ashes into the dry hay. The straw smoldered brightly.

Deluchi was enjoying himself, relishing his moment. "But you must see the beauty of my plan. I kill you all, implicating Jeff in the scandal of Roulette, Private Stock and Speed Dancer. The filly and stallion will go on the auction block soon enough. I'll purchase them. And I'll also arrange it so that I own Dancing Water Ranch in the very near future. I couldn't stop horse racing in Mississippi, so I'll own it."

His laughter rang through the barn, a sinister sound that made Dawn want to run.

"Bertrane! Whatever are you doing down there? Go down the driveway and get Roulette." All of the pleasure was gone from Deluchi's voice as he shouted down the order.

There was a moan in response. "I'm sick."

"Get that horse, or I'll come down there and put you out of your misery." There was no kidding in Deluchi's voice.

"Yes, sir." Bertrane sounded suitably submissive.

"Whatever you're getting out of this, is it worth it, Orson?" Dawn inched in slightly closer. "Think of Ann. Think of the hours you've spent together. She thought of you as an uncle."

"Stop it!" Ann and Deluchi spoke simultaneously.

"Still so full of pride." Deluchi almost sounded impressed. "You won't allow your friend to beg for you. It's just as well, Orson can only do what I tell him. I own him, his very soul." Deluchi laughed. "Shall I tell them, Orson, how deep your debt goes?"

"There's no need for that." Orson shifted his weight. He still held the gun on them.

"They should know. I bought Orson by degrees, just as I bought another of your friends, Cybil Matheson. First her schooling, then..."

"Cybil is insane." Ann was clearly indignant. "Anyone can manipulate a person who's mentally unstable. That's no great accomplishment."

"That's where you're wrong. Cybil was a weapon begging for good use. I simply directed her anger, her insanity."

"Then in a sense you're responsible for Robert Tisdale's death," Dawn counterattacked, hoping to break Deluchi's concentration. Orson was shifting anxiously, his attention on what Deluchi was saying, rather than on Luke.

"He was incidental. I never expected Cybil to kill him. I wanted the horse. I thought by taking Speed Dancer I could cripple Ann's future in horse racing. I merely wanted to stop you then, not kill you." In the dim light his eyes were bright. "It wasn't until you joined forces with Senator Stuart that I decided I had to kill you, Ann."

"That's enough talk." Orson waved the gun. "Let's get it over with."

"But I didn't tell them, Orson, that you'll be getting the half million dollars so conveniently left in the feed sack in Ann's truck."

"Orson!" Dawn drew his attention. "You're not doing this for money?"

"It isn't the money!" Orson finally exploded. "He threatened to tell the police about the horses. He knew me in Kentucky, when I was taking stolen horses from the track and reselling them as unregistered jumpers. That's when he made me set Luke up with the drugged horse at the show. I thought I was through with him, but when I came here and started running some horses through the farm, he showed up again." An edge of desperation was in Orson's voice now.

"If you're going to tell them, tell the whole truth," Deluchi interrupted smoothly. "There was a little problem with a horse, and someone ended up floating in the river. Louis Manetti was blamed, but it was actually Orson, the gentle giant, who struck the fatal blow."

Orson was sickly pale, his eyes strained and jittery. "The Boss helped cover the accident. In return, he asked me to get real friendly with Ann, to keep up with the plans for the horse racing bill. So I did. It didn't seem so bad until Ann's barn burned. Then I suspected he was behind it all."

"You suspected, but you never did anything." Deluchi laughed again. "You were very cheap, Orson. Very cheap.

Now that all of our little secrets are told, kill Mr. O'Neil first. Then the ladies.''

Instinctively Dawn drew closer to Luke, but he forcefully pushed her aside. The whole time he'd been scanning the loft. The lighting was bad, the end of the barn disappearing in total darkness. His options for movement were limited. There was the hatch where the ladder came into the hayloft or the edge of the loft. Both were a good thirty-foot drop.

His focus returned to the gun in Orson's hand, to the sound of the hammer being pulled back.

"Don't let him make you a cold-blooded murderer." Dawn held out a hand to Orson. "What you've done isn't all that bad. The man you killed, it was an accident, maybe self-defense!"

"Kill Mr. O'Neil." Deluchi reached into his jacket and pulled out a small, efficient-looking handgun. "Or I will kill Ms. Markey. Now!" The last word was an order.

Orson leveled the gun at Luke's chest, his finger slowly tightening on the trigger. Dawn made a move to rush forward, but Ann's quick hand restrained her.

"Not so fast, Mr. Boss!"

The singsong words seemed to come from midair at the darkened end of the barn. The explosion of a gun roared and flashed orange. Johnny Deluchi sank to his knees, an amazed expression on his face. The hand that once held the gun was a mass of blood.

"Now you Mr. Heavy Man, drop the gun. Gele will not hesitate to shoot you, too."

With some degree of relief, Orson dropped the pistol into the hay. Luke had it in his hand only a second later.

"Gele, where are you?"

"Since Mr. Bertrane seemed to like me hanging in the air so much, I decided to try it on my own." With those words the Jamaican pulled himself farther into the loft door at the end of the barn. He was hanging by a rope and pulley once used to load hay into the loft. With natural grace he stepped into the straw and came forward. "Everyone is okay, yes?"

"Yes. We're doing very well." Orson spoke as he sat down in the hay. "Better than I have any right to be."

Luke kept the gun on Deluchi and slipped to Dawn's side, his arm circling her. "Are you sure you aren't hurt?"

"Are you kidding? It takes more than a little excitement to get me injured." Dawn blinked back the tears as she talked. Bravado was the best thing she had to offer to ward off the swell of relief, pain, fear, anger and anxiety that had rolled into one big wail and threatened to flatten her. Only Luke's strong arm kept her standing, but that was a fact she didn't want to tell him.

"Ann?" Luke asked, still holding Dawn.

"I'm fine. Shaken, but fine. I guess it's all a little hard to believe." She looked at Orson, then quickly turned away.

"Ann?" Orson spoke with none of his usual bluster. He was beaten, defeated. "I wouldn't have hurt you or Dawn. I couldn't have. I couldn't even have shot Luke."

"That's good to know." Ann couldn't suppress her sarcasm.

"Gele, where's Bertrane?" Luke had forgotten the other gofer.

"He is very busy, Mr. Luke. He is tied up with his work." The islander grinned, and though Luke didn't fully understand the answer, he knew enough to determine that Bertrane was no threat.

"Let's get the police here," Ann said. "I'd hate for Mr. Deluchi to bleed to death. I'm hoping that his next trial will also probe into the workings of the parole board and several other aspects of the penal system. I can see that Jeff is going to have his hands full in the days ahead."

With Luke leading the way and Gele bringing up the rear, they descended from the loft. Outside the barn, Luke found

Bertrane tightly trussed and hanging upside down from a tree. He started to cut the rope, but Dawn's hand deterred him.

"Leave him." She wiggled the gag in his mouth to make sure it was tight.

"What?" Luke looked at her.

"For Roulette. For me. For Gele and you and all the meanness he's done. Leave him."

Luke shrugged and started off. Dawn leaned down, just at Bertrane's ear. "You'll be the very last thing I remember to tell the cops about." She untied Roulette from the tree and hurried to catch up with Ann and Luke. Orson lumbered in front of them, already ten years older than he'd seemed only that morning.

IN SEPARATE PADDOCKS the filly and stallion raced along the fence line.

"It's like a mirror image, isn't it?" Dawn took a deep breath of the pure, Kentucky spring air. The silver truck and trailer from Dancing Water were parked in the driveway. She'd come to Centaur Farm to retrieve Speed Dancer. The fate of the filly, Private Stock, was still unsettled. Until the courts ruled, she would remain in Kentucky.

Luke rested a booted leg on the fence, his cotton shirt open to the sun. "They shouldn't be separated, you know. I'd prefer it if you could take the filly, too."

"I'd prefer it if you'd been able to tell me the truth." Dawn finally spoke the words that had been on her mind since the night, two weeks before, when Johnny Deluchi, Orson Rinter and Benny Bertrane had been taken to jail on a long, complicated list of charges. Neither rest, recuperation nor intensive work at Dancing Water had been able to make her forget that Luke had lied to her about Speed Dancer. In those two weeks she'd learned the depth of her love for Luke O'Neil—and of the pain that he'd deliberately caused her.

Luke turned away from her, looking back as Private Stock kicked up her heels and dashed madly to the end of her paddock. Speed Dancer pursued her with relish.

When his silence had stretched for a full minute, Dawn recoiled the lead rope and sighed. She gave a low whistle.

Four long years had passed since Speed Dancer had heard her special call. Her hopes were well hidden as she waited, lead rope twisting in her hand.

At the first note, Speed Dancer skidded to a stop. His pointed ears twisted backward and forward, testing the wind for the sound.

Dawn whistled again.

The stallion turned once, spied her and then ran full tilt toward the fence. He stopped, his nostrils quivering as he smelled her outstretched hand.

Dawn held perfectly still.

The stallion sniffed her hand, her arm and face, then reared, his dark forelock thrown magnificently over his right eye as his feet touched the ground. An earsplitting whinny ripped from his throat, and then he tore twice around the paddock, coming back to thrust his muzzle into Dawn's chest.

"Hey, boy," she whispered, stroking his neck. "You look great." No matter what the cost, she was determined not to cry. Speed Dancer deserved smiles, not tears.

Luke stood aside, watching the reunion that had been such a long time in coming. "He knows you," he said. "I never doubted that he would, but a lot of people wouldn't believe this."

"A lot of people don't know anything about horses." The happiness of touching Speed Dancer was marred by her conflicting feelings for Luke. As she could see with her own eyes, Speed Dancer was in excellent condition. He'd never been fitter, better groomed or fed. He was happy, confident. The years he'd spent at Centaur as Luke's breeding stallion hadn't hurt him at all.

What hurt was Luke's lie, or evasion of the truth, as he chose to call it. She swallowed hard and put a smile on her face.

"You've done a wonderful job with him, Luke. No one could have done any better. It's hard to believe he's actually going home."

"Dawn, could we talk for a moment before you leave?"

"I don't think so." She felt the threat of tears again. "It's a long drive, and Ann will be worried."

"We'll call her. Stay for dinner tonight." He reached for her hand on the rail and lifted it. "Please."

"Luke, it won't do any good."

"Give me a chance."

Her common sense told her to leave, but she wanted to listen to her heart instead. "Through it all, I had my doubts at different times. Somehow, though, I could never bring myself to believe you were capable of doing anything cruel. Then in the end I find out that you are. All of this time I've been wondering if Speed Dancer was alive or dead, healthy or injured, and you could have told me the truth. You could have saved me such anguish."

"Stay for dinner. Maybe I can't explain it, but at least give me a chance. After everything else, is one dinner that unreasonable?"

"Yes." He'd had plenty of opportunities to tell. She thought about the afternoon they'd spent in the time-warped little motel. He could have told her then. He could have told her anything then. "It would be better if I left."

Luke didn't try to argue. "You can take Speed Dancer and go back to Mississippi, but it won't end here. It isn't that easy." He opened the gate so that she could enter and snap the lead line onto the stallion's halter.

"Mr. O'Neil! Telephone for Ms. Markey!" Ramone, the farm supervisor, called from the office.

Dawn turned and waited for Luke as he refastened the gate. "There's a private phone in the house, and it's a little more comfortable."

He showed her to a neatly arranged office. Photos of hundreds of horses lined the walls, magnificent animals cresting jumps that looked to be at least seven feet tall. Glancing at the photos, she answered the phone.

"Dawn, it's Ann. Don't come home yet. There's a chance we'll get a ruling on Private Stock. By tomorrow you may be able to bring her home, too."

"I can't stay here." Panic touched her voice. Centaur Farms was a hundred miles from anywhere that would have a hotel. It was way in the Kentucky hills.

"It's only a night. Ramone said Luke wouldn't mind putting you up. It'll save another long drive, and we'd like to get them home together, don't you think?"

"Of course." What else could she say? "Call me in the morning when you get the judge's ruling. As soon as possible." She replaced the phone.

"Good news?" Luke was waiting at the front door.

"I have to stay over. Is there a place I could get a room?"

"Don't be childish, Dawn. Stay here. You've made your feelings clear and I won't press you. I gather the judge is due to rule on Private Stock?"

"By tomorrow morning."

"Ann should have the filly. The people who originally owned Russian Roulette, what happened to them?"

"The insurance company filed charges of fraud against them. They were involved with Deluchi. The whole house of cards tumbled, and Ann was allowed to purchase the mare from the insurance company. She's going to have a good life, plenty of rest and care."

"And a few more babies?"

"Without a doubt." For the first time that morning Dawn smiled. "I still would give anything to see Private Stock at the Derby. As a three-year-old, this is her year."

"She's in shape," Luke agreed. "It's a matter of registering her, I suppose."

"Legal technicalities, I believe is the way it's phrased." Her grin widened. "But as long as I know she could win it, that's all that really matters, right?"

"You've never been wrong about a horse yet."

Luke deliberately kept the conversation away from personal matters. He had one chance with Dawn, one explanation. Ann had given him the reprieve, now the rest was up to him.

When the cook signaled them for dinner, Luke took her arm to escort her into the room. Her skin felt charged with electricity. He seated her, then took his place.

"You keep glancing at your watch. Are you expecting a guest or something?" She'd seen him check the time repeatedly.

"No, just a habit. I'm behind on everything here. I suppose I'm trying to readjust to being home."

"It's hard." Dawn had to keep the conversation alive. Watching Luke across the table, candles lighted and reflecting in his eyes, was more than any woman should have to bear. "What will you do without the stallion?"

"Dawn, we need to talk." Luke dropped all pretense of casual conversation. "I wasn't going to do this at dinner, but I can't let you leave without making one final attempt. I didn't tell you about Speed Dancer at first, because I didn't trust you. That's a fact. Later, when I did trust you, it seemed a dangerous thing to tell you."

"Dangerous? What could have been more dangerous than not knowing?"

Luke stood up and walked around the table. He knelt beside her, his hand reaching for her hair and then falling short. "I thought from the beginning that the link that drew us together, the video of the filly, was somehow connected to the stallion. You were so dead set to get Speed Dancer back, I was afraid if you knew where he was, you'd insist on coming here."

"I would have! And I would have taken him home."

Now he reached out and touched her hair, his fingers gentle yet possessive. "From the very first, Deluchi had someone watching this place. One attempt to move the stallion and he would be dead, and so would you. I had to keep you as safe as possible. And I needed your help."

Searching his eyes, Dawn saw the truth. "When I discovered you'd lied to me, I couldn't stand it. You should have told me. You can't protect me by keeping things from me."

"Never again. Not even to protect you."

"Promise?" She placed her hands on each side of his face. The crow's-feet around his eyes were suddenly visible as he smiled.

"You'll know the horrible truth, without a moment's delay."

She leaned forward and he caught her in his arms, rising to his feet as he held her. "I love you," she whispered against his neck.

"Thank goodness. I was getting afraid I'd have to cancel the evening's surprise."

Dawn pressed her palms against his chest, pushing slightly away. "What are you talking about?"

"I've been keeping one other thing from you, something I have to tell you as soon as you agree to marry me."

"Luke O'Neil, what are you up to now?"

"Consent to marry me?"

Dawn walked around him, surveying the smug look on his face, the laughter in his eyes that he couldn't hide, no matter how he tried.

"Okay. I'll marry you. Now tell me."

A kiss was his response, a kiss that made Dawn forget all about the little mystery he'd tantalized her with. When he released her, he lifted the phone.

"She's agreed. Bring him up."

"What is it?" Dawn picked up the thread of excitement that swept through the house as Luke hustled her onto the porch.

In the shadows cast by the barn she heard the sound of hooves in gravel. In another moment she could distinguish Ramone leading Speed Dancer toward them.

"It's taken a long time, Dawn, but now he's finally yours." Luke held her against him as he spoke.

"Luke, if this is a trick..."

"No trick, no untruths. Ann and I worked out an arrangement. She felt you should have the horse."

"Oh, Luke!" Dawn kissed him quickly and then ran down the steps to Speed Dancer. He whinnied loudly, then buried his nose in her stomach.

"He loves you," Ramone teased her. "He's like Luke, only much better behaved."

"Ann knew this when she called, didn't she?" Dawn hugged Speed Dancer, then ran back up the steps to throw her arms around Luke.

"Am I going to get in trouble again?"

"Maybe not." She ran a finger across his lips. "Then again, if you're lucky, maybe you will."

"Ann helped me keep you here. I had to have a chance to explain. And there is one other thing I haven't told you."

"Another?" Dawn kissed his chin, his neck. "It had better be important to interrupt me now."

"Tomorrow you need to go into town and find that special hat."

"What hat?" He'd finally gotten her interest.

"The one to wear to the Derby on May 6. Private Stock's signed in to race, wearing the Dancing Water colors."

"You're kidding?"

"No, I'm through fooling around." He put both hands on her shoulders and pushed her lightly toward the door. "From this moment forward, everything I do, I'm doing with serious intent."

Harlequin Intrigue

COMING NEXT MONTH

#117 SECRETS OF TYRONE by Regan Forest
Haunting images inhabited Karen Barnett's dreams
all her life: shadows on a staircase, a hand without a
body, heartbroken sobs. Then, in her mother's
effects, she found a photo of the house in her
nightmares. It led her to Steve Hayes, mayor of
Tyrone, Nebraska, and a man she felt oddly attuned
to. Tyrone was the beginning of Karen's perilous
journey. Love was waiting for her there—but so was
creeping horror....

#118 CLOAK AND DAGGER by Jenna Ryan
Did the infamous Raven Man live only in memory?
Or was the death of Blair Connelly's aunt proof that
Adrian Brock had returned from the grave a century
later to complete the cycle of murders he'd
committed one haunting Halloween? Blair knew
writer Erick Corvett was intrigued by the legend, but
she could not accept the supernatural explanation.
That left her with only one chilling conclusion.
But could Blair and Erick unmask the killer before
they became the final two victims of the Raven
Man prophecy?

Your favorite stories with a brand-new look!!

HARLEQUIN
American Romance

Beginning next month, the four American Romance titles will feature a new, contemporary and sophisticated cover design. As always, each story will be a terrific romance with mature characters and a realistic plot that is uniquely North American in flavor and appeal.

Watch your bookshelves for a **bold** look!

ARNC-1

ANNOUNCING . . .

Harlequin Romance #3000

The Lost Moon Flower
by Bethany Campbell

Look for it this August
wherever Harlequins are sold

HR 3000-1

You'll flip . . . your pages won't!
Read paperbacks *hands-free* with

Book Mate · I

The perfect "mate" for all your romance paperbacks

Traveling • Vacationing • At Work • In Bed • Studying • Cooking • Eating

Perfect size for all standard paperbacks, this wonderful invention makes reading a pure pleasure! Ingenious design holds paperback books OPEN and FLAT so even wind can't ruffle pages—leaves your hands free to do other things. Reinforced, wipe-clean vinyl-covered holder flexes to let you turn pages without undoing the strap...supports paperbacks so well, they have the strength of hardcovers!

Pages turn WITHOUT opening the strap

SEE-THROUGH STRAP

Reinforced back stays flat

Built in bookmark

BOOK MARK

BACK COVER HOLDING STRIP

10 x 7¼ opened
Snaps closed for easy carrying, too

Available now. Send your name, address, and zip code, along with a check or money order for just $5.95 + 75¢ for postage & handling (for a total of $6.70) payable to Reader Service to:

Reader Service
Bookmate Offer
901 Fuhrmann Blvd.
P.O. Box 1396
Buffalo, N.Y. 14269-1396

Offer not available in Canada
*New York and Iowa residents add appropriate sales tax

BM-G

Coming in June...

Harlequin Presents...

PENNY JORDAN

a reason for being

We invite you to join us in celebrating Harlequin's 40th Anniversary with this very special book we selected to publish worldwide.

While you read this story, millions of women in 100 countries will be reading it, too.

A Reason for Being by Penny Jordan is being published in June in the Presents series in 19 languages around the world. Join women around the world in helping us to celebrate 40 years of romance.

Penny Jordan's *A Reason for Being* is Presents June title #1180. Look for it wherever paperbacks are sold.

PENNY-1